LOVE, LITERALLY

J. T. TIERNEY

CURTISS STREET
PRESS

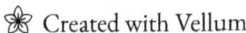 Created with Vellum

For Sue

1

Hallie

August, 2020
Brookline, Massachusetts

M y sofa has morphed into a giant sponge, now on the verge of developing its own ecosystem. The ceiling fan churns the thick heat and humidity with lethargic indifference. Wearing only loose gym shorts and a camisole—all the clothing I can stand—I've abandoned that clammy couch for the bare hardwood floor. I lie here, playing a sad game of 'connect the dots' with water stains on the ceiling. My breath hitches as I try with limited success to keep my sobs on lockdown. A tear slithers from the edge of my eye, mingling with the sweat sheen that's turned me into a human slip 'n slide.

I clench my eyes closed, but there's no shutting out the stifling realities of my 42-year-old life. The universe is dishing out lemons to me at mach speed. I've been laid off my set-design job because of COVID closures; my roommate of five years has moved out, leaving me solely responsible for the rent; and my boyfriend Nick has abandoned me. It's as if the world has conspired against me, stripping away every semblance of stability and security I once had.

Nick ... that asshole Nick ... vanished without any warning, like he'd entered the Witness Protection Program. Left nothing but a text message that glowed from my phone screen, mocking me. The text blathered on about how he couldn't afford his rent any longer after being laid off, so he was moving to Maryland to live at his mother's. Then he ghosted me. Not another word from him—nada, zilch.

Reading that message had shaken me to the core, its last two sentences a painful punctuation point: *My feelings about us haven't changed at all. I still love you, Hallie.* Yeah, Nick. When you love someone, you just up and leave them without warning, deny them the courtesy of an actual conversation. If that's love, it's some unknown, cruel kind that scorches everything in its wake.

Christ! I really can't take the mugginess in here. It's like an overzealous hug from a sweaty sumo wrestler. I grab a couple of crumpled tissues from the soggy pile next to me and sop at the heaviest rivulets trickling down my face and body. Morbid curiosity lures me into a quick sniff-check of my pits. Oh, good lord! Like a zoo during a heatwave!

My inner critic trolls me. *Nice, Hallie. Aren't you a well-put-together person! Really coping well here! Taking good care of your-*

self, girl! Maybe a shower this month would be a good idea, eh? I call this charming little self-disparager "Halloway." That's my middle name, the source of my nickname. Halloway's the authoritative, proper, stern me. She's the Gordon Ramsay of self-judgment. I hate her. You would, too. What does she expect me to do? Dance around this apartment in a gingham pinafore singing happy show tunes? 'Oh, what a beautiful morning / Oh, what a beautiful day, I've got a wonderful feeling / Everything's going my way'?

Shut up, Halloway. Don't you realize my life is shit? It's not just Nick. My financial situation's also a gaping sore. Sure, I got Massachusetts unemployment benefits after the theater laid us all off, but now those funds are about to expire. And the COVID stimulus money? A band-aid on a compound-fracture, not even enough to cover rent and groceries.

I release a sigh and curl up like a wounded fawn hiding in tall grass. I try to empty my mind, but my worries are hungry coyotes, patiently circling me, ready to pounce any second. Plus, it's hard to shut out Halloway, who's still doing her monologue, giving me a report card of straight F's—chronicling my every flaw and failure, flop and foul-up. The weight of her criticism presses on my chest, making it even harder to breathe in this sauna. I want to scream, *Halloway, you miserable c—*

Before I can finish hurling my favorite vulgarism at her, a shrill ring from my phone slices through the heavy air like a bull-horn in a monastery. With a groan worthy of a B-movie monster, I peel myself off the sweat-slicked floor and shuffle toward the sound, trying to locate the phone. "Come out, come out, wher-ever you are," I coax, then spy it buried in a graveyard of empty takeout containers on my kitchen table. I swipe away crumpled paper plates and soggy napkins until my fingers close around the device.

"Hey, Maria," I murmur into it, enjoying the cool of the metal and glass against my moist cheek. A couple styrofoam boxes lose their purchase on the table and topple to the floor. I bend to pick them up, knocking over still more in the process.

"Hallie? *Tudo bem?*" Maria's voice, with its Cape Verdean lilt, is like a cool breeze through my messy life. "What are you doing? Sounds like you're excavating King Tut's tomb!"

"More like exploring the ruins of Hallie's Once-Great Civilization."

"A promising mini-series, for sure! I'll alert the BBC. What's the drama, *amiga?*" There's a clatter on her end. Probably unloading the dishwasher. Multitasker that she is, she may be replacing the refrigerator motor at the same time. I wouldn't be surprised if she juggles chainsaws when making that exquisite cod soufflé of hers.

"Where to start ..." My gaze sweeps across the living room, landing on remnants of a work project halted mid-stream: scattered sketches, little pieces of foam board, an X-Acto blade, tubes of glue and paint. It looks like a craft store threw up in here. "Let's see: the theatre has laid us all off; Sandy moved out, went back to Indiana; and Nick ... he left me, *via* text. Then vanished in a puff of smoke."

"Oh, shit ... that's really tough. I'm so sorry, Hallie. You sound like you're at the end of your rope." Maria's the perfect audience. She's been my closest friend for over twenty years—ever since we met during our college years in Providence—long enough to know that sometimes I just need her to listen, without judgment or advice.

After I've laid out the details, like an oncologist explaining unhappy test results, I come to my peachy prognosis: "So, yeah ... with no income, and Sandy no longer contributing to the rent, I won't be able to stay in this apartment." I fight back the tears. Damn, I don't want to cry right now. "Feels like the universe is telling me it's time to pack it in. I'm thinking of going to live with my brother in Los Angeles. He has room in his house, and I know he'd welcome me, but ..."

"California's a whole different planet, Hallie. You sure you want to do that?"

I let out a hollow laugh. "Am I ever sure about anything? ... I don't know what else to do, Mar! And maybe it'd be good for me to go someplace where my past isn't part of the décor."

We chat for ages, eventually winding down like an old clock. She signs off with, "I've got your back, Hallie. *Sempre.*"

After disconnecting, I take a deep breath, the knot in my chest a little looser now. Talking with Maria is like chicken soup for my train-wreck soul, refueling me just enough to tackle the chaos around me. I mutter, "Alright, Hallie, let's make this place less 'crime scene,' more 'adult living space.'" I start by attacking the takeout containers as if they're evil minions. They're an easy foe, unlike the kitchen sink, which overflows with crusty dishes. A stubborn patch of dried spaghetti sauce stares at me like it's a Hatfield and I'm a McCoy. I stare back at it for a while, then realize my withering look alone won't be enough to vanquish it. I launch a vengeful attack with soapy hot water and a scouring pad. I fall into a therapeutic, Zen rhythm: wash, rinse, repeat. Each cleaned plate and bowl marks territory regained, an occasion for a tiny victory dance.

Again, the phone screeches, jerking me out of my cleaning trance. Suds splash all over as I grab for a dishtowel and then the phone. *Back for more, Maria?* I squint at the caller ID. It's her alright, her name flashing like a neon sign.

Maria's voice crackles with urgency. "Hey, Hallie. Listen, I couldn't just leave it at that. You shouldn't have to run away to

California. Not when you have people here who care about you."

"Maria, I—"

"Wait, hear me out." There's a rustling sound, like she's pacing. "I've just had a chat with Mike. We insist on adopting you. We've unanimously voted you onto our little island. Jolivia's leaving for the fall semester next week; her room will be empty, so you're moving in with us. And this isn't charity, okay? It's what friends do. Plus, you'll be doing me a favor, helping me stay sane and have some fun. Just think of it: Sunday *cachupa* feasts, mocking Mike's terrible Creole ... Priceless! What do you say?"

A smile cracks through my gloom, tugging at my lips. Leave it to Maria to bulldoze my pride with her no-nonsense generosity. I can practically see her in a superhero pose, eyes blazing, a red spandex bodysuit with 'Operation Save Hallie' across the chest. A force of nature in human form.

"Maria ... I'm speechless."

"That's okay. If you can still make guttural noises, try these: *wye, eee, ess*. Piece of cake."

My chuckle is brittle but real. "It's tempting, it really is. I just ... don't want to impose."

"Imposing is showing up unannounced and expecting five-star treatment," she retorts. "This is an invitation. Plus, if you're not here, who'll save me from my own *feijoada* disasters?"

"Can't argue there. Your *feijoada* is a culinary calamity," I tease, feeling a surge of warmth that's different from the room's sauna vibe. Maybe this could be my life raft, a chance to regroup without totally capsizing or uprooting my entire life. Now come the waterworks, my voice wobbling. "Thank you, Mar. I don't deserve this. You have no idea how much it means to me."

She bursts out laughing. "Oh, drop the melodrama, you

twatwaffle." I grin, knowing that when she throws any of my favorite insults back at me, it's her way of giving me a hug—and, in this instance, telling me everything's going to be alright. She adds, "That's exactly the kind of drama-queen thinking we're going to flush out of you, ASAP. Starting tonight at 6:30. I'm thinking wine therapy, intravenous style, *stat*. Be here or be sober."

2

Hallie

Navigating the rollercoaster of recent months has taught me you can't know what to expect in life. Apparently, unpredictability and change are the only constants. Even so, I certainly hadn't imagined that only a few weeks after leaving my apartment to live with Maria and Mike, I'd be decamping along with them to stay here on Cape Cod for a while. As I urge my ancient Subaru wagon up a long driveway that could double as a ski slope in the winter, I remind myself how this peculiar plot twist, worthy of a Hallmark movie, developed.

Maria's friend Lisa had come up with the plan. She wanted to escape the suffocating sameness of the pandemic by leaving Boston for this second home she and her husband own in Chatham. Lisa had invited Maria and Mike along, too. And because I was then living with M&M, I also got an invite—a fifth wheel, as it were. There's to be a sixth wheel here, too: Lisa and her husband have invited their friend Quinn. You wouldn't be the first to wonder if Wheel #6 and I are the targets of an attempted fix-up. Trusting that Maria would never knowingly go along with a stunt like that, I'm satisfied that, like me, Wheel #6 is just another Covid castaway looking to survive lockdown with a modicum of sanity.

I pull the car to a rest in a spacious parking area. When I step out, the ocean air, briny and thick, hits my senses like a slap from Poseidon himself. I hoist my suitcases and duffels out of the back, plunk them on the cobblestone surface, and gawk up at the huge, gray-shingled house. It's so massive I wouldn't be surprised if it has its own zip code.

Maria and Lisa appear on a second-floor balcony above the front door. Lisa mimics John Oliver, extending her arms and yelling, "Welcome, welcome, welcome!"

Maria chimes in, "We'll come down and help bring in your things."

They show me to the tasteful bedroom I'll be staying in. It screams 'casual opulence.' Lisa says, "We're going to have light appetizers and champagne on the back patio. In, say, 45 minutes? Come out when you get settled."

Settled? You bet I'll get settled. I'm already thinking of spending the rest of my life here—and that's before I check out the view from my window. On the horizon, beyond a broad swath of green, is the ocean, all sparkly and Instagram-ready. This place is nuts. I'm half expecting George Clooney to stroll out with a martini.

I unpack a few of my things, then take a quick shower, brush my teeth, blow-dry my hair, and put on my favorite sundress—yellow with tiny, multicolor flowers. I strap on leather sandals, grab a light-green cardigan in case it gets chilly, then head downstairs, ready to embrace this unexpected chapter.

As I step out the back door, I take in the stunning outdoor space. A stone patio that's straight out of *Luxury Home Magazine*—a gas firepit, small reflecting pool, teak chairs with plush cushions. But it's empty. No laughter, no clinking of glasses. No one here.

Thinking they must've decided to stay indoors, I'm about to head back in, when a soft mingling of voices beckons from beyond a manicured hedge. I round the side of the house to find an even larger patio, this one a redwood deck partially covered by a lattice canopy that casts an intricate pattern of light and shadow on the ground. I'm in some weird parallel universe where the patios have patios.

A familiar voice cuts through the chatter. "Hallie, over here!" Maria stands by a huge, pink hydrangea, her silhouette framed by the blush of a sunset sky that illuminates her rich brown skin and highlights the loose curls of her short chestnut hair. As if Maria needs the sun gods to make her beautiful!

When I'm within reach, she pulls me into a half embrace and whispers, "Isn't this incredible? When Lisa told us this place could easily accommodate all of us, for some reason I didn't picture anything this grand. I should have, knowing how *basofu* Lisa's house in Chestnut Hill is! Anyway, I wasn't mentally prepared for this! It's unreal."

"Good lord. That's for sure. It's right out of *The Great Gatsby*," I say. "I could definitely get used to this!" And it's true: I'm not the least bit sheepish about being out here in this luxurious setting for a while on the Campbells' dime. Maria, on the other hand, generally doesn't like being around this level of affluence. She and Mike are fairly well off themselves, but having grown up in a relatively poor family, she insists on giving a lot of their money to charities, avoids unnecessary consumption, and generally deplores those who don't. But the Campbells are her friends, and she cuts them some slack.

We stand shoulder to shoulder, taking in the scene. A tall man, about fifty with blondish hair, peels the foil and wire cage from the top of a champagne bottle. He reminds me of a peacock, but with a tail fan of platinum credit cards rather than feathers.

Nodding toward him, Maria says, "That's Paul, Lisa's husband. *Gustoso*, eh?"

I smile. "Yep, very easy on the eyes." The sudden lump in my throat and pinch below my navel tell me that with all this pandemic isolation, it's been too long since I've seen a hot guy in the flesh.

Amidst the talk and laughter, a loud pop echoes across the patio, followed by cheers. All eyes turn to watch bubbly champagne spill down the side of the bottle, cascade over Paul's hand and soak his sleeve.

"Well done, buddy, well done!" another man teases, his sarcasm dripping like the champagne. "You nailed it like a pro!"

Paul shoots him a playful smirk, then flips him off. "Stuff it, Quinn. You can open the next one if you think you can do better."

Amused by this exchange, I whisper to Maria, "My amazing powers of deduction tell me that other one's Wheel #6." Not a mind reader, she doesn't get the reference, so I try again. "Quinn." I glance at him again. Handsome, about the same age as the other guy.

"Right."

"His wife died several years ago?" When she nods, I whisper, "Also not hard on the eyes!" I quietly mimic a cat in heat. "Remind me what he does for work."

"He's a professor of some sort at Tufts. English department, I think." She appraises me closely and says, with a raised eyebrow and a laugh, "Maybe you should go take a cold shower before I unleash you in this group. But if you think you can behave yourself without a cool-down, let's go over and join them."

"Hey, nothing wrong with a little objectification!" I say.

Maria's smirk signals her surrender. "Okay, but I know how long it's been since you've gotten any. Behave yourself."

"Me? Misbehave? You wound me!"

We make our way over to the others, and I greet Maria's husband Mike with a peck on the cheek. He introduces me to Paul and Quinn, while Maria goes off to help Lisa prepare a platter of cheese, crackers, and crudités. Soon, Paul is in a conversation with Mike about pro football, and I'm immersed in one with Quinn, talking about his late wife. It's always good to get uncomfortable subjects out of the way early

"Yes, Alison died of pancreatic cancer," he reveals. His voice is smooth, like worn leather, tinged with a quiet sorrow. "She was diagnosed in the summer, and by the start of the school year, she was gone."

"I'm so sorry for your loss, Quinn. I can't even imagine how awful that must've been for you." And it's true: I really can't conceive how people cope with the pain of losing a child or a beloved spouse.

We stay on the topic of his wife until I begin to wonder if he's one of those guys who drone on about their gone spouse until you're ready for a nap. Whether it's divorce or death that took her away, their endless yapping about her makes you want to shove a pine cone in their mouth. Fortunately, my worries are for nought, because Quinn soon interjects, "I appreciate your lending a sympathetic ear, Hallie, but let's change the topic to something more engaging for you."

A smile spreads across my face. In my mind, I'm adding notes to the contact entry I've started on him in my mind: *Chivalrous, perceptive, master of his emotions.* What I say is, "Tell me about your name. 'Quinn' is quite distinctive."

"My full name is James Quinlan O'Neill. People started calling me 'Quinn' because there were too many Jameses and Jims around—my dad, my mother's brother, a cousin. 'Quinn' stuck.

"I go by my middle name, too." I curtsy with comic formality. "Nice to meet you, James Quinlan O'Neill. I'm Charlotte Halloway Bancroft."

He chuckles. "You didn't want to go by Charlotte, or Char, or Lottie?"

I shake my head and purse my lips. "Nor Shar or Charlie or, god forbid, Cherry."

"Well, 'Hallie' suits you."

As I sip the champagne, enjoying its effervescence on my tongue, I squint at Quinn, pretending to take his measure. "I won't know if 'Quinn' is a good fit for you until I know you better. But, it's definitely a good nickname. I like it." I pause, then ask if he's currently teaching remotely due to the pandemic.

"No, I'm lucky. This is a sabbatical year for me. I'm glad I'm not having to prepare for some dismal Zoom class." His eyes fix on mine briefly. "Better to be here on the Cape, with charming new acquaintances."

My flirtation detector sends me an alert. That's one fast pivot he just made! One minute, he's waxing mournful about the cancer that whisked his beloved wife off to the afterlife. The next, he's giving me the ol' razzle-dazzle. Typical. Men are such swine.

He moves us close to the table holding more bottles of cold

champagne. He shouts, "Hey, Paulie!" He nudges me with his elbow, then whispers, "Watch this." He opens another bottle of champagne like a pro. Not a sound, and no foam dares escape. "See how it's done, Campbell?" Quinn calls, his tone taunting, and his eyes sparkling with delight.

I can't help but laugh at this friendly one-upmanship. "Decorously done!" I say to Quinn in a whispered voice. Before I can stop myself, I add, "Quiet as the Queen's queefs!" Oh, lord. Did I really just say that to this guy I don't even know? How horrible! One of my problems is that my mouth has a bad habit of sprinting ahead of my brain; another is that I can't resist jokey sex references.

Quinn's hearty guffaw causes his hand to shake as he pours more bubbly into my champagne flute. Now he gives me a close appraisal, like he's reassessing a matter he thought he'd already settled. I feel myself blush. His eyes crinkle with amusement. "Lisa wasn't kidding when she said you'd be a fun addition to the group here." A stray wisp of hair chooses this moment to tickle my face, and I brush it aside, feeling oddly self-conscious.

Soon, we're drifting effortlessly from topic to topic, our banter a spirited dance that elicits cackles and belly laughs from each other. There's something heady and zesty about this connection. At one point, Quinn's howl of laughter reverberates through the air, drawing the attention of the others. I catch sight of Maria watching us, a knowing smile on her face. She whispers something in Mike's ear, making him look our way and grin. "Seems we're the evening's entertainment," I remark to Quinn, *sotto voce*, tilting my head toward our audience.

Lisa comes over to us, a glimmer of curiosity in her eyes as she takes us in. "What's all the fun over here?" she asks, playfully nudging Quinn with her elbow. "Am I missing out on some scandalous conversation?"

Quinn chuckles, his gaze never wavering from mine. "Oh, Hallie's just entertaining me with her one-woman comedy act."

I roll my eyes, then bow. "I'm merely a humble court jester, sir." A giggle bubbles up from my throat. "But I ditched the cap 'n bells for tonight's gig, and I have better fashion sense than most of my occupational brethren." I execute a twirl, the light fabric of my sundress rippling as I spin. "At least, I'm livelier than poor Yorick." I watch Quinn's eyes twinkle with delight, his expression a mix of amusement and admiration that sends a pleasant shiver down my spine.

Lisa laughs. "Well, you're doing a fantastic job." Nodding toward Quinn, she says, "I haven't seen this guy laugh so much in ages."

I glance at him, a playful glint in my eye. "So, I'm not a mere joker; I'm a miracle worker! Should I start invoicing?"

I watch Quinn's face go buoyant, and I can tell he's enjoying all this. With a clarity that takes me by surprise, I recognize the sensation blooming inside me: pure, unadulterated joy. This evening's turning into a reminder of this part of me—the bringer of laughs, the life of the party. And boy, does it feel good.

3

———————

Hallie

Eventually, Quinn and I realize we're the last holdouts on the patio. So, we shuffle into the kitchen, and I apologize to the group. "Sorry. We got lost in chat-land."

Lisa laughs and gives Quinn a side-hug. "Yeah, I blame Mr. Chatterbox here. He's like a talk radio that never shuts off."

"Hey! I call foul!" Quinn protests, faux offended.

Paul joins in the teasing, placing a hand on Quinn's shoulder. "Truth's a bitter pill, Quinn."

Ah, I think, with a flash of relief. Gentle ribbing is the currency of the realm among these folks! Good. I can do good-natured chaffing. Easy-peasy.

Lisa clocks the time and turns to Maria. "It's seven! I didn't realize it's so late. I guess we should get dinner underway."

Forty minutes later, we're all gathered again out on the

redwood deck. The temperature still hovers in the low 70s, and humidity thickens the salt air. Seagulls, the thugs of the bird world, float lazily overhead, squawking and squealing, eyeing our dinner. Paul and Mike tend the grill like barbecue pitmasters, readying to cook burgers and ribs. Maria has made a Cape Verdean dish called *jagcida* that features rice and beans, linguica, onions, garlic, paprika, and bay leaves. I've been lucky to have it at her table many times before. Smells like heaven, and, oh god, is it good! Everybody's now drinking beer, except Lisa, who's alone on Team Wine.

Once the meats are grilled, each of us finds a seat at a round table that accommodates eight. "Cheers!" Quinn raises his beer in salute. "Thank you, Lisa and Paul. What a wonderful venture this is going to be. I feel lucky to be here with you all."

Hearty cries of "hear, hear" erupt from the rest of us. Warmth spreads across my shoulders like a cashmere throw. It's been a long time since I've felt this carefree and content. What a welcome change all this is from my solo Netflix marathons.

"Know where that comes from? 'Hear, hear'?" Quinn asks. "It's an abbreviation of the phrase 'hear him, hear him,' which British Members of Parliament would shout in the late seventeenth century as a way to draw attention to what another was saying."

I facepalm and groan playfully. "Omigod, our first lecture from Professor Pointdexter! If there'll be a series of these, we should charge admission!" Oh, no! There goes my runaway mouth again. Damn. Halloway yells, *Rein it in, Hallie! Sometimes your humor's too snarky! Not everyone gets it!* I peak at Quinn through my fingers.

His eyebrows hover near his full, thick hairline. But when it hits him that I'm only teasing, he cracks a wide smile and says, "Anyone who doesn't appreciate learning about words and phrases is a simpleton. A dullard. A pea-brain. A pinhead."

I can't help but grin back at him. Little does he know, I'm a word nerd. Words are my playground, my secret garden. They're my joy, my passion. I could spend hours dissecting language and uncovering the hidden meanings behind words. A pinhead, eh? Quinn's playfulness ignites a small fire within me. We're going to get along just swell, he and I.

The flow of dinner chitchat is smooth as butter, sliding easily from one topic to another. Laughter fills the air. I keep feeling pulled toward Quinn, as if he's a magnetic field.

Mike and Maria have been asking him questions about his late wife. When he speaks about her, pain and vulnerability linger just beneath the surface, betraying his palpable desire to have again what he lost when she died. I picture stability, settled companionship, a home life that's a refuge. Who wouldn't want all that? Hell, I'd like it, too. Fat chance, in my case.

Maria, ever the conversational pivot, turns the topic. "So, Quinn, did you always want to be a professor?"

"Not until my junior year of college. I had a few professors who really inspired me, and I wanted to follow in their footsteps."

I love that answer. "That's wonderful," I say. "What's your field?"

"Nineteenth-century British literature. You know: Austen, Conrad, Hardy, the Brontës—"

My heart blooms, and I eagerly jump in, adding names to the list. "... Eliot, Carroll, Tennyson, the Brownings ..." Quinn's admiring gaze has me puffing up like a proud peacock. "How exciting that you get to spend your career studying and teaching all that! It's truly the greatest period of British writing!" I realize my cheeks are warm. I'm gushing.

"You know your stuff!" he says, with a gentle tone of appreciation that just slays me.

My grin now stretches wider than the Cheshire Cat's. "Most of my favorite books come from that period," I say, finding myself transported by thoughts of those who taught me about that literature—how I idolized them for the way they breathed life into the authors, parsed their writing, read their words aloud with sensitive insight.

While I'm lost in my reverie, the conversation again dips into silence until Maria tosses another question Quinn's way. "Do you have children?

"Two. Jack's 30, a news anchor in Cincinnati for the local NBC affiliate there. And Megan's 28, a lawyer in DC with the Natural Resources Defense Council."

Impressed, Mike says, "Interesting jobs! How did Jack end up as a news anchor?"

Quinn traces Jack's journey from journalism school at Northwestern to a station in North Carolina and then finally, through a lucky break, to his current job in Cincinnati. "He'd rather be a reporter than an anchor. But he's telegenic, so they want him in front of the camera. They pay him well for that, and he needs the money."

I see an opportunity, and a slight smile comes to my lips. "I can relate to that. I need dough, too. I'm thinking of getting a job at a bakery."

They all look at me, confused. Quinn's expression carries traces of sympathy and concern, as well. Damn. My weak joke missed its mark. Never good having to explain a pun, but I mime the motion of kneading bread dough. A couple of groans greet me in reply.

Mike, ever gallant and always the joker, winks at me from across the table, his eyes bright with mischief. He quips. "I dropped out of a Communism class in college because of lousy Marx." I burst into laughter, and the others join in with some chuckles. Ah, Mikey. What a joy! He's been making me laugh for twenty years.

When Mike and Maria get up to help themselves to seconds, I ask Paul and Lisa how they met. They exchange a look as they decide who'll start the story. Lisa says, "The others know all this, so apologies to them. We met in Northfield, Minnesota, at a college party. I was at St. Olaf, Paul was at Carleton. We went out for a while, but then lost touch."

Paul jumps in. "After college, both of us ended up in Boston. I was studying at Harvard, which is where Quinn and I met." Paul and Quinn exchange thumbs-ups. "And Lisa moved to Boston on the heels of her college roommate, who got into Northeastern's law school."

Now Lisa picks up again. They're tag-teaming this how-we-met tale with a finesse honed over years of joint telling. "I didn't know where else to go, what to do with my life." She rolls her eyes, mocking her own youthful indecision—it's a flash of self-deprecation that doesn't comport with her poised demeanor. "I got a job as a flunky in the Career Counseling Office at MIT ... and ended up in a long and unhappy relationship with a chemistry grad student there."

Her eyes pass the narrative baton to Paul, who carries the tale across the finish line. "I completed my degree and started working for an economic consulting firm. Through coincidences that aren't worth mentioning, we reconnected and have been together since."

I say, "Nice story!" I turn to Lisa and say, with a teasing tone, "Not to bring up a sore subject, Lisa, but do you know what they do when chemists die?" Everybody's now wise to my inclination to joke, so they fall silent, awaiting my punchline. I draw out a pause, then deliver my zinger with a dramatic flair, "They barium!" This time, the chuckles and groans are more appreciative. Lisa wads a sauce-stained napkin and playfully chucks it at me.

As the night falls and the stars start their twinkly show, we do the dirty-dishes shuffle and return to the patio with bowls of vanilla ice cream, jazzed up with raspberry sauce and sliced peaches. We settle under a sickle moon. Quinn savors his peach melba like he's a food critic pondering the award of a Michelin star. He's a bit older than I, silver-foxing at the temples, which is apparently my new definition of eye candy, because—jeepers creepers!—I find him very attractive.

I'm pulled from my eyeballing when Paul speaks up. "For some reason, the ice cream reminds me of a funny story about my parents. So, this—"

Quinn interrupts, shaking his head and offering a good-natured admonishment. "Paul, rule number one of audience management: never say your story is 'funny.' That's for them to decide."

Paul, not missing a beat, flips him off and plows on. "This was before they were married. My dad was in a hospital in New Haven because of a bad abdominal hernia. My mom was his nurse after the surgery. When it was time for him to be discharged, she slipped him her phone number because she liked him and was worried she might never see him again. Days passed, and he still hadn't called. Then, one day, home from work, she was sitting at her kitchen window and saw him go into a little ice-cream parlor right across the street from her place. She ran down there and pretended to bump into him by accident. The rest is history."

Maria claps and coos, all hearts and flowers, "Oh, that's a sweet how-they-met story."

Paul nods in agreement. "It is. And here's the kicker. When my mom had dementia late in life, she loved telling that story, over and over again. I mean, she'd tell it several times in an hour, if you let her. But by then, all her inhibitions were gone, and she'd finish the story each time with this lustful look in her eyes and say, 'You have to understand: I was especially motivated, because I'd already *seen the goods!*'"

We're all in stitches at this, but nobody's delight can possibly exceed my own. I love it when people make bawdy comments. I do it as often as I can because it's fun. So I'm mentally high-fiving the old lady's waggishness when I say, "Omigod, what a great line. Your mother must've been quite a character!"

"They both were," Paul says.

We all return to finishing our dessert. After a long silence, I say, "One thing that's interesting about that story is that it speaks to what appeals to us in another person: a charming personality, great sense of humor, ... intriguing intellect ..." Here, I quickly glance at Quinn. "... or maybe broad shoulders, toned thighs, supple breasts ... whatever turns you on! ... I don't want to speculate on Paul's dad's ... endowment, but we can agree that ... *some*thing ... appealed to his mom." Chuckles all around. I pause for effect and then continue. "What's more intriguing is the 'ick-factor.'"

"The what now?" Paul asks, scraping the edge of his spoon around the inside of his bowl.

"The ick-factor—the opposite of what entices us. It's what repels us, the things that send us running for the hills."

"I'm not following you, Hal." Mike says, running his hand through his thinning hair.

"Okay," I say, with a grin. "Let me ask you this, Mikey. Back when you were single and ready to mingle—before my pal Maria nailed your ass to the marital cross—what were your turnoffs, your deal-breakers?" I glance at the others, then back at Mike. "Let's say, there you are at Brown, and you're completely infatuated with a gorgeous girl you've been dating for a while. Everything seems perfect until you notice something about her that just makes your skin crawl. Wham! You have to break things off with her. That's the ick-factor!

"Maybe she has dry lips and constantly picks at them, making them bleed. Or you hear her swearing at her sweet grandparents, or she's rude to restaurant servers. Whatever it may be, you suddenly find yourself repulsed by that person. The attraction vanishes. Make sense? That's what I'm asking about. What is that turn-off, that ick-factor for you? What have been your deal breakers?"

"I get it," Mike says, his eyes now doing a little dance of delight. "I actually was head-over-heels for this girl my freshman year. It was going great. Then I found out she was seriously into astrology, tarot cards, fortune-tellers. I mean, really weird, stupid shit! That was it for me. Done. Over!"

"Exactly what I'm talking about!" I crow. Looking to the others, I say, "More?"

Lisa, with a sly grin, confesses, "I was once with a nice guy who started calling my nipples 'nip-nops.' Instant turn off for me! He had to go." Now we're all laughing.

Maria, with a tone of revulsion, says, "I dumped a guy because he'd given his penis a name. I couldn't deal with that." I see Lisa glance at Paul and I suddenly know a little secret about him.

Lisa asks, "What'd he call it?"

We all lean in, eager for the answer. "He called it 'Simba.'... just so ridiculous!" Our laughter grows louder. Maria slowly shakes her head, still in disbelief about it.

Mike comes up with another. "What about dirty finger nails

or freakishly long toe nails?" A chorus of groans and "eewwws" fills the air.

"That's an understandable, universal ick!" I say. "But what about the ones that are less rational, more unfathomable, down-right idiosyncratic?"

"Like what?" Quinn asks.

"For instance, I once had this nice thing going with a guy until I found out he liked big bowls of baked beans. I mean, who cares, right? So what? No big deal! But for some reason that totally killed it for me. I couldn't handle it! Made no sense, but I dumped him like live bait off a fishing boat. Over the side, baby!"

Quinn nods, clearly enjoying the absurdity of that. "I went out with a girl in high school, until I found out she liked bologna sandwiches for lunch. For no good reason, that repulsed me. I had to end it."

Impish, I wink at him. "Good thing it wasn't German sausage. That would've been wurst, eh?"

4

Quinn

I haven't even pried open my eyelids, yet Hallie is already in my thoughts. My mind has been flickering through last evening's faces—Paul, always looking as if he's just stepped out of a luxury-watch advertisement; Lisa, draped in the latest fashion and always the perfect host; Maria, with her Cape Verdean beauty and vibrant laugh; Mike, cracking jokes that got funnier two beers in. But it's Hallie who lingers in my thoughts, like the aftertaste of a favorite single-malt Scotch. Dark blonde hair falling in soft waves to just below her chin. Early forties, slender, about 5'8", striking blue eyes that sparkled last night in the glow from the patio candles. And that voice! Low and velvety. Reminds me of hot chocolate.

Part of me wonders what it would be like to have Hallie in my life, not just for quips across the dinner table in a festive atmosphere, like last night—but in the quiet, cereal-for-dinner moments. To share genuine laughs that bubble up from somewhere real; to match wits, all thrust and parry; to engage in deep conversations that create true, lasting connections.

But what am I doing imagining Hallie in my life? It's like imagining that at this point, I still have a good chance of becoming a Navy SEAL or an astronaut. A charm bomb like Hallie wouldn't have any interest in a sad old geezer like me. I know that. Yet I can't stop thinking how she wields words with a scholar's precision; can't stop her infectious laughter from replaying in my head like some ear-worm melody.

Now all that is competing with the aroma of fried bacon, which is doing the rumba somewhere in my bedroom. I finally force open an eyelid, half-hoping to see a tray hovering above me on a breakfast-bearing drone. I squint at the clock—7:10. I haven't slept this late in years. For a moment, I indulge in the fantasy that it's the ocean air that has kept me in sweet slumber so late.

Then reality, with its less romantic edges, reminds me of last night's liquid adventures. I had a warm-up with a couple Jamesons, then several flutes of champagne, followed by a few beers with the meal. My head bangs like a teenager's first drum set. But hey, at least I'm not nauseated. And at least I know the headache's source; so, I'm not worried I've caught COVID. I haven't had that much to drink since before Alison died. I lost interest in it—and most everything else. But last night ... last night was different, in lots of ways.

I get up, dragging my feet across the cool wooden floor, making a beeline for the bathroom. My reflection in the mirror is a mix of mad scientist and hungover raccoon. "Nice look, Romeo," I mutter, splashing water on my face in a feeble attempt to erase the effects of sleep and too many drinks.

Twenty minutes later, I look slightly less like a desert-island castaway. I'm comfortable in my usual summer attire of a t-shirt, shorts, and Sperry Topsiders. My kids say I haven't changed my sartorial choices—or my hair style—in twenty-five years. In truth, it's been longer than that.

I shuffle into the kitchen in search of some caffeinated salvation. Hallie commandeers my attention the second I enter the room. A dark-green silk kimono sheaths her frame, her long, lithe legs crossed under the counter—the alluring pose effortless, but striking.

She looks up from scrolling on her phone and gives me a smile that penetrates deep into my solar plexus. "Good morning, Quinn."

"Morning, Hallie," I croak, my voice apparently having decided to take a leave of absence. The house seems devoid of life save for us two. "Pretty quiet around here. Where is everyone?"

"Scattered to the four winds. Mike's already working, and Maria left a note saying she was going for a walk. But I don't know where Lisa and Paul are."

I gesture toward her plate. "Looks good. Smells even better … I'm surprised you're not having Cream of Wit for breakfast."

She laughs and wipes her lips with a napkin. "Ah, I like what you did there. So, am I to believe I said something amusing last night?"

Amusing? Lord. That's putting it mildly. "You could say that. You have a talent for turning words and phrases into something … unexpected, refreshing."

"That's kind of you to say. Well, I try. Life's too short for boring conversations, don't you think?" She lifts a strip of bacon to her mouth. It disappears in three quick bites. With a triangle of toast, she presses scrambled eggs onto her fork and brings it to her lips.

Oh, to be that fork, I think. What's going on? Now, I'm channeling Romeo and his desire to be the glove on Juliet's hand. I shake it off, throw her a playful smile. "So, what's your secret? Some kind of cleverness drug you're on?"

Her dimples pop. "You ferreted out my secret! Okay, I admit it: I've been taking four Fuck-it-alls a day since March." She pushes off from the counter, the silk of her kimono whispering against her skin. She gestures to the sparse remnants of her breakfast. "Hungry? I can whip you up some bacon and eggs, if you like."

Lordie, I'd love that. It would do wonders for this hangover. But how can I impose on her? I barely know her. "I'll stick with coffee for now, but thanks."

Hallie points to the far end of one counter, where a high-end Jura coffee machine reigns, its sleek lines and multiple buttons promising a complexity of brew that might clear my foggy head. "Good thing that thing was already set up," she says. "I wouldn't have known what to do with it. Fortunately, Lisa left a note that said, 'Place mug under spout and press icon for one cup or two.' I did, and—*mirabile dictu!*—it worked."

I laugh. "*Mirabile dictu?*"

"Latin. It basically means 'amazingly enough.'"

"I know." I turn my thumb toward my chest, which I playfully puff out like a proud penguin. "High-school Latin guy here. ... I don't think I've ever heard anyone actually use that phrase."

She teases, "I like to trot out my language chops occasionally for hard-to-impress guys like you—rock you back on your heels."

"Consider me impressed." A smile tugs at my lips. "But, hey, don't think I'm a pushover. Try this on for size: *Semper ubi sub ubi.*" I've thrown her every first-year Latin student's go-to joke, the oldest pun in dog-Latin.

She chuckles. "Always where under where."

"Yep," I say. "And, hey, it's good advice, don't you think? Basic hygiene is important."

"Can't argue with that," she says.

As the Jura spits and spurts rich dark liquid into a mug, the coffee's aroma fills the kitchen, mingling with the lingering savory scents of Hallie's breakfast. I say, "If I'd known there'd be a Latin scholar out here, I'd have brought along my Cicero or Vergil so I could bone up."

Her eyes twinkle. "You're already too late, my friend. I'll be on to Chinese or Japanese in a minute, and you'll be eating my dust."

"You don't speak—"

She releases a guffaw. "Course not. I'm teasing you." Her forthright, throaty laugh delights the hell out of me. Lord, how comfortable this is. It's like we've known each other for years.

Mug in hand, the coffee's warmth seeping into my palms, I open the French doors to the patio and scan down the broad swath of dew-glistened lawn, the ocean beyond, glittering in the light of the morning sun. "Amazing place."

"Certainly is." She joins me in the parallelogram of light that washes the space inside the door. "I assume you've been here before?"

"Several times. Paul and Lisa are generous in sharing their good fortune with their friends."

"I'll say."

We stand in silence for a moment, taking in the birdsong. Then Hallie starts humming the first few measures of "Oh, What a Beautiful Morning."

"I know that one!" I tease. "It's from *South Pacific*, right?"

Hallie regards me with good-natured disgust. "Good god, man. It's a good thing your field isn't American culture. You'd never have gotten tenure."

"Is it from *The Music Man*?"

She snorts. "You're a philistine!"

"*My Fair Lady*?" I grin.

"You gotta be kiddin' me."

I chuckle. "Yes, I'm teasing. I know it's from *Oklahoma*."

She gives me a friendly shove with her shoulder. "Do you always pretend to be culturally challenged, or is that something I bring out in you?"

"Only when I think it will provoke an interesting response. ... How about you? Are you a big fan of Broadway show tunes?"

Hallie grins. "A huge fan. I've loved Broadway musicals ever since I was a kid. I hope that doesn't offend your intellectual sensibilities."

"Not at all. But I'm an old man with a weak heart," I joke. "It's not good for me to be taken by surprise. I'm just asking so I know what to expect. Maybe you break into song or dance at the drop of a hat!"

As I'd hoped, she smiles at my reply. But, something seems to have taken her out of the moment, because her next comment is more somber. "Hasn't this year taught us we can't know what to expect? And that we should feel happy if we get beautiful mornings like this?"

"Are you? Feeling happy? Or just philosophical?"

"Of course, I'm happy!" Now she smiles again. "And why not? Look at this place. Amazing digs to be in while ridin' the COVID waves. Besides, 'Life is a mirror: if you frown at it, it frowns back; if you smile, it returns the greeting.'"

I feel my heart skip a beat. She's quoting Thackeray! Her intellect fascinates me. I get an involuntary contraction in my throat, my body reminding me how attracted I am to smart, quick women. I'm so nonplussed that all I can do is murmur, "Well said."

She grins. "Well quoted, perhaps."

I lean against the counter, watching Hallie move gracefully around the kitchen, the kimono highlighting the contours of her figure. There's an ease to her movements, like she was born to occupy this space. She pours the remains of her coffee into the sink and places the mug in the dishwasher.

She turns to face me, her eyes searching mine for a moment before she speaks. "Thackeray was right, don't you think? Life is what you make of it. We can't control what happens to us, but we can choose how we respond to it. In this moment, in this absolutely gorgeous place, I choose happiness."

Her words, simple yet profound, resonate deep within me. I've spent too much time wallowing in grief, allowing the weight of my sadness to consume me. Hallie's presence reminds me there's still beauty and joy to be found in this world.

A soft breeze rustles through the open doors, carrying the sweet scent of late-summer roses from the garden. Hallie tightens her kimono, revealing the elegant curve of her back. She brushes her fingers through her hair, summoning new, subtle shadings, as variable as her moods—sometimes vibrant, sometimes subdued. Her eyes fasten on mine and she smiles. "I'm going to take a walk. See if 'all the sounds of the earth are like music.' Care to join me?"

The invitation is tempting—an opportunity to peel back another layer of the puzzle that is Hallie, embrace the easy companionship she's offering, explore the area with her. But something holds me back. "Thanks. Would love to, but ... I should probably shower first. And check the news—see what the world's been up to while we've been out here playing hideaway."

"Ah, the siren call of responsibility," she replies with a gentle tease. "Well, if you change your mind, you know where to find me."

Back in my room twenty minutes later, thoughts of Hallie crowd out my effort to concentrate on the news. I register the sound of the shower running in the adjacent bathroom, noticing how the rhythmic patter of water droplets on tile matches the quickened beat of my heart.

5

Hallie

As the hot water cascades over me, I can't stop thinking about Quinn. He's lively, quick-witted, fast with word-play, entertaining. Could that tale he told at dinner last night about the nun and the priest at his elementary school have been true, or was it a joke? It doesn't matter. He was very funny! And although nobody would say he's movie-star handsome, he's undeniably attractive, and sports a charm-and-charisma combo that just knocks my socks off. I adore how he matches my teasing with his own. Just hits it right back to me, like we're playing badminton.

I step out of the shower into the steam-filled bathroom. Wrapping myself in a towel as fluffy as a cloud, I go into the bedroom. As I'm drying off, I look around this beautiful room and my mind wanders back about ten days ago, when the idea of this Cape Cod adventure popped up. In Boston, Lisa had invited Maria to join her for a walk. By then, I was living with Maria and Mike, so Maria invited me to tag along.

We had pulled up to Lisa's Chestnut Hill house, an absolutely incredible place—a huge old federal colonial on a beautifully landscaped lot of about an acre, surrounded by lush flower gardens and bordered by a stone wall. A dappled umbrella of maples and ash lent the property ample shade. A circular driveway had taken us to a brick-paved parking area by a four-car garage. When we got out of Maria's little Civic, I could see that beyond a long, grassy slope, the water of the Chestnut Hill Reservoir glittered in the afternoon sunlight.

Lisa had come out to greet us, dressed to the nines in designer fitness wear and diamond earrings that sparkled like tiny disco balls. She suggested that we do the walking path encircling the reservoir, so we set off in that direction. Lisa said, "It's nice to meet you finally, Hallie. Maria has told me about your job and your apartment. I'm so sorry. This must be a hard time for you."

That hardly began to capture the magnitude of my woes, but what could I say? I coughed up the standard I'm-doing-okay spiel, even though my life's report card was more of the "needs improvement" sort. "Thanks," I said. "It is hard, but Maria and Mike are helping me through it."

Lisa asked how Maria and I first met.

Maria said, "Ah, well, it's an involved story, but I'll give you the quick version. We were both in Providence for college. I was at Providence College, and Hallie was at the Rhode Island School of Design. We met through a cousin of mine who tried to hit on Hallie at a PawSox game. The two of them became friends and that's how I got to know her."

I added, "And I'm how Mike and Maria met. He was at

Brown, and his roommate had a twin sister at RISD who was a good friend of mine. She and I had a party that those guys came to. Maria was there, too, with her cousin." If Lisa cared to notice, she could have seen our eyes conveying mutual fondness aged by years of friendship. We'd been there for each other through parental deaths (both of mine; her father), and she single-handedly helped me get through a bad health problem in my mid-thirties. We both love books, bookstores, and show tunes. And although she won't admit it to you, she loves my vulgar sense of humor. I'm Sancho Panza to her Don Quixote.

Lisa and Maria started chatting about a mutual acquaintance, and I zoned out, thinking about the difference between Lisa's lavish lifestyle and Maria's frugal one. While Lisa obviously spends freely, Maria's always pinching pennies so hard they scream, which she doesn't have to do. She has money, but she'd rather give it to others who really need it than spend it on herself. Despite their apparent differences, she and Lisa have a real bond that's been forged over the eight years their daughters have been best friends. Those girls met in seventh grade and have been inseparable ever since. So, the parents have spent a lot of time together, come to know each other well, grown comfortable together, enjoy one another.

I'd listened as Lisa and Maria traded news about their girls. Both now juniors at Georgetown, they're living this semester with four others in Evergreen, Colorado. With campus closed down to most students because of the virus, and facing the prospect of spending more months doing courses online from their childhood bedrooms, they'd all decided to rent a house in a location that offered good hiking and other outdoor adventures. Pretty nifty setup, if you can swing it.

When we reached the walking path around the reservoir, our conversation paused as we adjusted to the new terrain and the presence of more people around. Then Lisa had said, "The girls are having such a good time living with others after being isolated and cooped up at home since March. Every time I talk with Maddie, I come away jealous of their living situation."

She did a little dance around a couple of geese that waddled into our way. "My envy has gotten me thinking how great it would be to break out of this boring, humdrum 2020 life, the way the girls have, by getting out of town. So—and here's why I wanted to talk with you today, Mar—my idea is that you and Mike come away with me and Paul."

This suggestion caught Maria up short, and she stopped walking, her face capturing her confusion. "You mean like get an AirBnB somewhere for a while? Oh, Lisa, I don't think we want to shell out for that right now."

Lisa said, "No, no. Let me explain—"

Just then, a pack of bronzed and buff Boston College boys doing laps around the reservoir thundered up behind us, interrupting our conversation. Four or five ran without tee shirts. Talk about a buffet of biceps and abs! Lordie, there are some fine-looking young men in this world! The three of us shifted aside to let them pass. I remember twisting toward Maria and Lisa and throwing them an eyebrow wiggle that said, *Hello, dessert!* Maria had snickered, then bumped me with her shoulder, saying, "Easy, Hallie. They're practically fetuses."

Lisa had laughed along with us, but then got right back to business. "You know that Paul and I have a second house in Chatham, on the Cape. We haven't been there since March because we let Paul's New York brother and his family use it. But they left when the kids' schools started back up last week. So, the house is now empty. We could go there. It's a huge place. Everybody would have their own space to spread out and do their own thing." *Just a casual mansion by the sea,* I thought. *No biggie.*

Lisa continued, "Look, I think all of us might benefit from a change of scenery. I know I would. New routines. Good company around. ... I know it's a strange idea at first glance. But wouldn't it be great to get away, be someplace different?"

Maria appeared to be considering it. "I don't know. I'm sure we'd have a good time. But I don't know what Mike would think of the idea."

"He's working from home now, right? He can do that from anywhere, right? So, why not from a new, different environment?"

"Gosh, Lisa, I just don't know," Maria said. "But it does sound great."

It was a perfect, early-autumn afternoon. A breeze had picked up, urging fast-moving clouds into a peek-a-boo game with the sun. The crowns of maples in the nearby woods were putting on a fashion show of reds and yellows. Honestly, it was like Mother Nature was trying too hard. Some tiny ducklings waddling near the shore stared at us as if they were judging our walking speed. We slowed and stared back at them, letting them know we weren't going to take any of their guff.

When we resumed our pace, Lisa returned to her topic. "You and Mike really should come, Maria. We'd bring Charlie, too, of course." She looked at me and explained, "Charlie's the big Great Pyrenees you saw in our yard." Turning back to Maria, she said, "And, Paul's inviting Quinn O'Neill, a friend we've known for years. Quinn's been a bit of a sad sack ever since his wife died a few years ago, but lurking underneath is a great sense of humor and a fun spirit. He's a kind, smart, sensitive soul."

I jumped in. "You should go, Maria. You and Mike would have fun. I could look after your house here in Newton."

Lisa said, "Well, actually, Hallie, I've just been thinking. You should come, too, if you'd like." The invitation seemed genuine, not like her hand had been forced by my presence. My heart leapt. Time in a big fancy house in Chatham? Count me in! Maria might have been hesitant, but I was already mentally packing my bags.

I said, "That's incredibly generous of you, Lisa. Honestly, I'm only now adjusting to the change from being alone in my apartment to being at Maria's house. But it sounds sublime. I love the Cape."

Maria asked, "When would we go?"

Lisa replied, "Soon, I'd say. We'd want to take as much advantage of the fall weather there as we could. In any case, we wouldn't all have to arrive on the same day. We could think of a particular date as a target for arrival, not a firm commitment."

"That's true," Maria said. She paused, then asked, "About how long would we go for?"

"At least, a few weeks. But, if it's working well for everyone, then who knows, maybe a few months! Of course, anybody could leave at any time for any reason. All I know is, I need to get out of here. And I'm so tired of being isolated; I want to have other people around me!"

After a long pause, Maria smiled and said, "As long as Mike agrees, it sounds like a plan!"

At this point, we were just about to leave the walking path to head back up toward Lisa's house, when the herd of college boys rumbled up behind us again. Once more, the three of us stepped aside to let them pass. Running from the other direction came three BC girls, identified by their tee-shirts and baseball caps. As soon as the boys passed them by, all three girls spun their heads around to gaze appreciatively at the receding display of masculine allure. A blonde with a thick ponytail, turning forward again, let out a huge breath and caterwauled. In mock agony, she yelled, "Oh, fuck! Give me some of that!"

Now, laughing at that last memory, my reverie ends. I finish toweling off from my shower and decide to put on a wee bit of makeup. I don't normally wear any. But today? Just a smidge. I'm feeling like a splash of color in a black-and-white movie, so why not! Clothes fly from suitcases to closet and dresser as I play fashion roulette, landing on skinny jeans and a pink linen shirt that screams "casual chic." Teeth and hair brushed, I'm ready to explore like a modern-day Magellan.

Off I go, wandering down Skyline Drive with a lost pigeon's sense of direction. The sun's working on my still-damp locks, and the scent of freshly mown grass lingers in the air. The road twists and turns among shrub oaks, small cottages, and grand mansions. The quaintness of the place settles around me like a well-worn shawl. As I continue on, the road widens into Old Queen Anne Road, marked by a weathered wooden sign. I turn left and continue until I reach Route 28, a bustling street filled with cars and people. Memories flood back to me from my last visit to this area some years ago, and I realize that a row of charming little shops I liked is just ahead.

I pass the post office on my left, follow the roundabout, and pause at various points along Main Street to window shop. The clothes at J. McLaughlin's whisper sweet nothings to my wallet, which screams back in terror. The Black Dog has better prices, but I really don't like logoed clothes, and this place has more of them than a Chevy in a Nascar race. Then, I gawk in the window of Chatham Jewelers, where diamonds are even more costly than my life choices. I hear Maria call my name. I turn and see her coming away from Chatham Clothing Bar holding a little plastic bag.

"What'd you get?"

She reaches into the bag and whips out an aquamarine baseball cap. On the bill is a navy-blue shark that's about to eat the word *Chatham*. "I forgot to bring a hat and figured I'd need one." She pulls the cap over her loose, short curls. "Feel like grabbing a cup of coffee?"

"Definitely. There's a café just back there that looks promising."

We pick up our hot drinks—a small coffee for Maria; and for me, a chai latte that doubles as a mustache maker. We find seating on the patio, shielded from the sun by a green awning.

"Did you sleep well?" I ask her, sipping my frothy disguise.

"Until about 4:00, when I'm guessing all that alcohol wore off. I drifted in and out until I finally got up around 5:00, drank a big glass of water, and plunked down on the comfy couch in our bedroom to read for a while. At about 6:00, I went down to find coffee." She smirks. "I thought I'd have to decipher the Da Vinci Code just to use that damn machine. Fortunately, I found instructions Lisa'd left."

I tease her. "You only had to push one button! It's not rocket science."

Maria's eyes light with amusement. "Yeah, but what if you accidentally push the wrong one? You could end up with twenty cups of coffee, or you might summon a butler or chauffeur by mistake!" She sips her coffee. "It's just so strange to me. ... I mean, I know there are people who live like this, but it still takes my breath away. The materialism is just so ..."

"Unnecessary?"

"To say the least! I was gonna say shameless. It touches a moral nerve in me."

I reach out and squeeze her hand. "I know it does." Nothing torments Maria like rich people flaunting their wealth. It's not that she and Mike aren't pretty well off themselves. It's that she just can't stomach unnecessary consumption, especially conspicuous consumption. People making a display of how much they have by spending frivolously or lavishly. And I get that. But for some reason it doesn't bother me the way it does her. I say, "So, how are you going to handle being here?"

"I honestly don't know. I guess I'll have to figure it out as I go along. ... Now, how about you?" She squeezes my hand in return. "It looks to me like you might enjoy yourself here! You and Quinn sure seemed to hit it off last night."

A smile plays on my lips, and I know I'm blushing. I'm an inveterate blusher. "Quinn's really charming. We had some fun conversation last night—and again this morning. He seems like a great guy. But let's not jump to any conclusions," I say, downplaying the interest I feel. But inside, my heart's doing little leaps like I'm a teenager at a boy-band concert.

Maria knows me too well to let me get away with this nonsense. She raises an eyebrow and snickers at me. "Oh, come on. I saw the way you two were flirting with each other last night. The sparks were practically laying tracks between your crotches!"

I laugh, my stomach fluttering in excitement at Maria's words. "Well, maybe there's something there," I admit. "But I don't want to get ahead of myself."

Maria nods. "I get it. You've had a lot of tumult in your life this year." She takes a sip and looks at me over the rim of her mug. "But don't let your nerves hold you back. Who knows? He may be the one!"

That thought is so electrifying that it causes my heart to do a double backflip and I fumble my cup, spilling a little river of foamy coffee toward Maria. She hurries inside to grab some napkins and is back in thirty seconds.

"Wow," I say with a grin, "You're as fast as a gunslinger's draw!"

Shock registers on her face as she hears me use an expression I learned from her own father. "What?"

I smile. "He was one of a kind, your dad."

"Oh, God. Right? He sure was." A warm smile overtakes her features, and after a long beat, she says, "None of us could figure out how this man, born and raised in Cape Verde, knew all these distinctly American references. He'd say my mom's touch was 'as gentle as a 4-H Club girl handling a baby chick.' How did he even know about the 4-H Club? He was such a character. Crazy guy. But he loved his adopted country dearly."

Listening to her, I get other memory flashes of Maria's dad, whom I absolutely adored. During our last two years in college, I went with Maria many times to visit her family in New Bedford and got to know them all well. And our bonds only grew deeper in the following years. I grin at her. "Remember the time your dad told Manuel his new girlfriend was 'as fat as a Texas hot dog'? You told me later that your brother didn't speak to him for weeks after that."

She laughs, "True. He didn't."

After we finish our coffee, we walk back through the beautiful streets of Chatham, our conversation all about the town's quaint charm and the wealth that permeates life here.

"We fit right in, don't you think?" Maria quips.

I burst into laughter. "Like the hand in O.J.'s glove."

6

Maria

When Hallie and I get back to the house, I roam the halls in search of Mike, finding him in the room set aside for his use as an office while we're here in Chatham. Surrounded by the trappings of his temporary sanctuary, he's as content as a cat in a sunbeam. The room is small but inviting, comfortably furnished with a desk and chair, a bookcase, and a recliner. I ask, "*Kuma, chérie*? Need anything?"

"Doing fine, thanks. And I'm all set. This is gonna work out great. The internet here is incredibly fast." Leaning back in his sleek, ergonomic desk chair, he waves his arm in a circle. "And this is a nice room to work in. I'm glad we didn't shoot down Lisa's idea to come here."

I lay a kiss on a patch of pale scalp that peeks through his retreating landscape of hair. I playfully tug at a few strands to tease him, then leave him to work. I, too, am glad we agreed to come—pleased that Mike likes his work space here, happy we're somewhere other than Newton for a while.

The day is much too lustrous to sit inside and read, which is what I'd probably be doing at home. I decide to go for another walk—a short one, just to explore the immediate neighborhood. As I meander, I find myself playing "Spot the Mansion." I can't help but think of Lisa and Paul and their life in this lap of luxury. They've got everything: this seaside getaway property, that stately home in Chestnut Hill, cars that probably cost more than my house. Don't get me wrong. I'm not pointing all this out because of envy. I don't want what they have. And while Mike and I aren't in their tax bracket, we're doing just fine—in far better shape financially than I ever imagined we'd be. Most of that, of course, is because of Mike's successful work the past twenty years as a software engineer for Fidelity Investments. But I'm no slacker. Before COVID forced layoffs, I worked two jobs —one full-time, as a program coordinator in Boston College's Study Abroad Office, and a part-time gig at Newtonville Books.

So, we're more than comfortable. But, between you and me, our affluence makes me uncomfortable. It embarrasses me. So, I can't let myself just enjoy what we have. I'm tight-fisted around the house. And I'm diligent about giving away a lot of our money to people who need it more, especially poor Cape Verdeans in Boston and New Bedford.

When Hallie asked me at the coffee shop earlier how I'll handle being here, surrounded by the Campbell's wealth, she was referring to my discomfort with conspicuous consumption, which is repugnant to me. I don't understand it. Look at the Campbells' houses. They're just ridiculous for three people. They'd be ridiculous for families of ten! And all the jewelry and designer wear that Lisa spends money on. Why? What's the point of it? I don't get it. I really don't.

Maybe it's unfair of me to judge them. Maybe they give away vast portions of their wealth every year to charitable causes. How would I know? But I'm guessing not. And it makes me uncomfortable to think that they sit on this big pot of gold when there are so many who struggle. I think of the Cape Verdean families I know in Dorchester and New Bedford, working their tails off just to keep the lights on. Even here on Cape Cod, not everyone's living the high life. There are plenty of families out here fighting hard to make ends meet. Now, walking back up the driveway and seeing the Campbells' enormous, gray-shingled house, I know that I can't let myself stay here without finding a way to help those on the Cape in need.

I spot Lisa, decked out in Fendi yoga pants, planting mums in two terra-cotta containers that stand like sentinels on the wide steps to the front door. She says, "I thought the entrance could use a splash of color. These should brighten things up."

Yep, I think, *amazing what dropping several hundred dollars on chrysanthemums can do for a porch.* I say, "Those are going to look gorgeous. Need any help?"

"No, thanks, I don't have much left to do here."

"You know, I was thinking it would be fun to do a Zoom call together with Maddie and Jolivia. You up for that?"

"Sure. Want to see if you can arrange it? I'll finish up here. Shouldn't take me more than twenty minutes or so."

An hour later, Lisa and I are cozily positioned on a blue-striped loveseat in this big sunroom at one end of the house, my laptop on a pillow supported by our abutting thighs. I click on the Zoom link Joli sent. Soon we're gazing at our daughters' smiling faces.

"Hi, you guys!" Joli's voice brims with excitement.

We smile and wave back. Lisa fusses with the angle of the screen. "Is that better? Can you see us okay?"

"It's perfect, Mom," Maddie says, her image flickering, then stabilizing. "So, you're all together at the Cape house?"

"Yep," Lisa replies. "It's great to be here."

"God, I love it there!" Maddie crows. Turning to Joli, she wiggles her brows and says in a bubbly tone, "Remember that February break when the four of us went there?"

Joli's expression changes abruptly—her eyes grow huge and the edges of her mouth curl down. She gives a slight, alarmed head shake. Clearly, there's something she doesn't want me to catch on to, but I decide not to pursue it. Instead, I ask, "How are things? Anything new?"

They fill us in on their studies, the autumn climate in Colorado, and their slowly involving cooking skills. Lisa asks what they're doing for entertainment.

Joli's eyes brighten. "We play lots of games. Last Saturday night, after dinner, we played "Never Have I Ever," and when it was Ashley's turn—"

Seeing confusion on Lisa's face, Maddie interrupts. "It's a drinking game, Mom. Players take turns asking other players about behaviors or actions. Like, you might say, 'Never have I ever hitchhiked.' Players who have hitchhiked respond by taking a drink. Those who haven't, don't."

Lisa says, "I see. Sounds like it could get out of hand pretty quickly."

"True, it can. But usually it's, you know, things like ... *shoplifted, been arrested, shot a gun, been caught cheating on a test* ... so you only get one or two taking a drink, if any.

Joli interrupts. "But Ashley and Sean were trying to be funny and get people drunk. So they started asking stuff like, *gone commando, sexted, watched porn, gotten yourself off* ... And everybody was taking drinks. Then—"

I've been laughing along as the girls describe the drinking game, but Lisa suddenly brings the call to a close. "You guys certainly have an interesting life!" she says, her words bursting out in a rapid, elevated pitch. "Glad you're having fun out there! Maria and I'd better sign off."

Maddie raises a brow in an expression that speaks more of familiar disappointment than surprise. "Well, okay, bye then."

"Great seeing you both." Joli sends a virtual kiss our way.

Lisa and I return the gesture and disconnect. As we head to the kitchen for some tea, I decide to delve into what just happened, asking Lisa why she ended the call so abruptly.

"You know, I guess I'm old-fashioned. All that sex talk in their drinking game ... it just made me uneasy." She gives me a side glance. "But it didn't seem to faze you."

I cock my head at her, trying to find the right words. "Well, I'm not delighted by it, but I figure they're college kids, testing the limits on what they find acceptable. Our generation might not've been so open about sexual matters, but I'm okay with them having their kind of fun, as long as they're safe and aren't driving after drinking."

Lisa nods, considering what I've said, then admits, "I guess I struggle around Maddie when it comes to sex. Like, if there's a sex scene in a movie we're watching, I sometimes have to leave the room. It just feels too awkward."

Not sure how to address Lisa's discomfort, I decide to speak only of my own experience. "Joli and I have always been open with each other. We've had frank discussions about sex and intimacy since she was in middle school. Joli tells me everything—sometimes more than I'd like." I chuckle. "I feel fortunate all that's been easy for us. It's probably because I had the same kind of openness with my own mom."

Lisa says, "That sounds really special. It's wonderful that you two have that bond."

I nod. "I'm lucky. And I'm happy to say we grew even closer in the months after Georgetown sent them all home."

Lisa's eyebrows crease together slightly and her eyes betray a twinge of envy. "That's not how it was with Maddie and me. We were like strangers sharing a house."

"Well, I'm not saying it was all sunshine and rainbows, but once Joli's online classes ended in May, we had more quality time together—like when she wanted me to teach her to cook traditional Cape Verdean dishes. We spent hours in the kitchen, laughing and talking. That brought us closer."

Lisa's expression is wistful. "Sounds wonderful. ... Maddie has mentioned how good a cook Joli is. "

"Ah, that's sweet to hear. Joli has a talent for cooking, and she enjoys it," I say, as we sip our tea. I tell Lisa about those long afternoons in the kitchen with Joli, how I'd told her stories I'd never shared with her before—about growing up in New Bedford, going to Masses held in Creole, working in cranberry bogs as a teenager, dancing the *coladeira* with my high-school boyfriend, making out with him in his car, teasing my brothers about their taste in girls.

Lisa is quiet for a long time. With a rueful smile she finally says, "God, I've never once had moments like that with Maddie. ... My house is more like a mausoleum, with Paul and Maddie emerging from their crypts only every now and then. I wonder what that says about me and my family."

Nothing good, I think. *Time to cut down on the trips to Saks in search of designer labels. Do something with your daughter.* But I give her arm a reassuring pat. "It says you're a family like any other, with your own challenges and dynamics. I'm no expert, but I think these things ebb and flow, especially with teenagers. Maybe you can find something you both enjoy—perhaps a little mother-daughter yoga. You'll figure it out."

7

Hallie

At Nauset Beach, Quinn and I easily find a parking spot on this quiet fall afternoon. Only two other cars in the lot. We grab our tote bags, then footslog over the low sand dunes until we find the Goldilocks spot on the beach—not too close to the water, not too far from it. Quinn unfurls our beach blanket with a flourish that would make a magician jealous. I watch it settle onto the sand like a sigh. Gazing up and down the endless shore, I say, "Want to take a walk before we eat?" I've never been to the Cape in the fall before; it's definitely the best time to visit.

As we stroll north, we leave footprints in the wet sand next to the ocean swash, our feet pricked by the grit. Quinn shares a memory from his grad-school days when he and Paul, accompanied by two female friends, drove to this very spot on an idyllic autumn afternoon. "We spent the afternoon playing Frisbee on the deserted beach. I still have a photo from that day—the wind flapping Jan's dark hair just I snapped the shutter."

I'm hit with a strange pang of nostalgia for an experience I wasn't even part of. I angle toward the right, each step taking me a bit farther into the foamy water. "You know, it's not as cold as I expected." I glance at Quinn. There's something about the ocean mist dusting his freckles, the distinguished touch of gray at his temples, and the casual strength of his stride: that urges me into playful mischief. I send a splash his way, teasing, "Come on, Frisbee boy. Get your feet wet!"

At first, he manages to avoid my splash, dodging like he's in the Matrix. But then he gives in and joins me, and we amble along in silence, the bubbly surf and backwash playing tag with our feet. Quinn folds his shirt sleeves higher, and suddenly I'm all about those forearms.

Swallowing back desire, I say, "I'm curious about your family, Quinn. You have siblings?"

He nods. "Two brothers—one older, one younger." He talks about their boyhood antics.

"Omigod," I say, "three boys born within five years! Your poor mother! What a hectic household that must've been!"

"It was wild," he admits, his tone tinged with sadness. "My brothers and I were a handful for her. We were savages, running roughshod over everyone and everything that got in our way. And our dad was an enabler, a kind of accomplice. ... I'll share some other wild stories with you sometime, if you're nice to me." He jostles me playfully with his shoulder.

"What was she like, your mom?"

That gentle smile of his makes an appearance. "She was a kind, quiet soul. She never finished college. And once my older brother arrived, she didn't work outside the home. She did all the cooking, laundry, cleaning, shopping, and managing for a family of five. My dad was busy with his work—he was an electrical engineer—and she handled everything else. His job gave him daily contact with people. She didn't have that, and I think the isolation was really difficult for her."

He's quiet for a moment. "She struggled with anxiety and depression much of her life. When she was 24, she and her mother were in a bad automobile accident on a highway in a snowstorm. Her mother was killed instantly, and my mom was badly injured."

"How horrible!" A wave of nausea washes over me; I'm uncertain if it's from hearing his story or from my own painful memories. But this is his time to talk, and I'm not about to hijack the conversation to tell my own tale.

"When I was in the sixth grade, she had what they used to call a 'nervous breakdown.' Basically, it was emotional exhaustion. She spent a few months in a psychiatric hospital where she eventually received electric-shock therapy." He kicks at the water. "Those barbaric doctors and their primitive machine took away much of her memory."

"That's awful," I say, feeling his anguish.

He nods. "She had another breakdown about six years later, when I was a senior in high school." He pauses for a long moment, breathes deeply and rakes his fingers through his hair. "But that time, she, uh ... she took her own life."

I stop walking and squeeze his forearm. "Omigod, Quinn. I am so sorry to hear that. How awful for you, and for your brothers and dad."

"It was very hard. Took me a long time to get over it." His eyes have lost all their brightness. "May still not be, if you want the truth."

How could he be? I can only imagine his grief—the feelings of confusion, anger, guilt, and profound sadness. The sense of abandonment, betrayal, insecurity. I gaze at him, somewhat in awe that he doesn't seem deeply cynical or depressed himself. Uncertain whether he wants to tell me more, I decide not to press. If he wants to say more, he will.

A silence descends on us as we shift to the firmer sand on our left, making it easier to walk. After a long while, I suggest, "Let's head back to the blanket. Those leftovers won't eat themselves."

We tuck into the remnants of the *frango assado* that Maria had cooked for dinner the previous evening, along with a couple of the empanadas she'd made for appetizers. When Maria had served them, she'd explained, "These are spicy. They're made with tuna, garlic, and chili. We call them *pastel com diabo dentro* —pastry with the devil inside." Mike and I already knew this dish well, but the others didn't, and they whooped and gasped when hit by a powerful burst of spicy heat.

Quinn and I wash our meal down with two Yuengling lagers that we'd unfortunately left sitting too long in the uninsulated tote. Holding the lukewarm green bottle, he says, "This is better cold."

"And that's better hot," I say, pointing to the *assado* residue. As the rhythmic murmur of the surf whispers in the background, we each pull novels from the tote bag—mine is Joyce's *Ulysses*, Quinn's is Ann Patchett's latest.

"*Ulysses*?" Quinn's eyebrows go up in surprise.

My dimples appear. "This is my third time through it. I just can't get enough of it. What's that Oscar Wilde line? Something about how if you can't enjoy reading a book multiple times, there's no point in reading it at all?"

"Yeah," he says, taking my book and flipping the pages, "but this one is especially challenging. It has, what, something like 30,000 unique words—most of them completely made up?"

"That's part of what makes it so great!" I say. The grin he gives me matches my own.

We settle on the blanket—I on my front, he on his back, our shoulders brushing in a silent hello. As I listen to the waves lap the shore, I try to concentrate on Joyce's complex narrative and convoluted sentences. But I really can't focus. I keep sneaking glances at Quinn, observing the way his thoughtful eyes trace the lines of his book, his brow furrowed in concentration. Every so often, he peers at me over the rim of his reading glasses and catches me in my not-so-sneaky surveillance. His face, softened when his smile appears, holds subtle marks of age and experience. I'm all in for it.

The September sunlight is still strutting its stuff, beaming down like it's trying to prove a point. I crave its warm embrace on my skin, but worry about making a bold move. Would Quinn think I'm being too forward or familiar if I strip down to my bikini top? Eh, he's seen more of the world than my back, I reckon. I sit up, whip off the shirt, and recline on my stomach, reaching behind me and unhooking my top. "Hope you don't mind. I have a personal vendetta against tan lines."

His response is concern about sunburn, because, of course, we can't all be reckless sunbathing anarchists

"I'm counting on you to be my personal sunburn siren. If I start sizzling, promise you'll save me." I close my eyes and release a long exhale of pleasure at the sunshine's kiss on my back.

"Seriously, shouldn't you put some sunscreen on? You'll get a burn. ... Do you want me to rub some on your back?"

My mind floods with conflicting thoughts. I hardly know him. Wouldn't that be a tad too intimate to have him touching me like that? Cross some boundary between casual acquaintances? On the other hand, he's probably right: it's wise to be precautious. A gentle ocean breeze tickles my bare skin, whispering, *Go for it. Wouldn't it feel good to have his hands on you?* Damn right. Life's too short to deny oneself simple pleasures. Plus, I'm a sucker for peer pressure from the wind. Meeting Quinn's eyes, I hand him the tube of sunscreen. "Would you mind?" I ask, my voice barely above a whisper.

Quinn blinks, apparently surprised that I've accepted his offer. I see in his eyes what I think is a mixture of desire and wariness. He takes the sunscreen. I hear the snap of the cap. I shift my body slightly, exposing the canvas of my back fully to him, awaiting his touch. He leans in closer. His breath warms my skin before his hands even make contact. Every nerve ending in my body comes alive with anticipation.

His touch is tentative at first, like a cat testing a sofa. But as his hands start to move in slow circles, something shifts. His touch becomes less about application and more about connection, each stroke feeling like a caress. I let out a moan that could probably be heard two beaches over, despite my best efforts to keep it under wraps, then I close my eyes again, surrendering to sensation, the tenderness of his touch. My body relaxes in waves. Dissolving under the gentle care of his hands, I let myself drift away.

Thirty or forty minutes later, I wake up to Quinn gently serenading me. "The West coast has the sunshine / And the girls all get so tanned ..." The warmth of the sun has seeped deep into my bones, leaving a languid heaviness that tethers me to the edge of sleep. Thanks to Quinn's crooning and the cool breeze off the ocean, consciousness begins to creep back in. With what feels like monumental effort, I stir, turning my head to him with a smile of utter contentment. "Mmmm. Hi there, beach boy. What's next, a rendition of 'Kokomo' or 'Surfer Girl'"?

Quinn chuckles, his eyes sparkling with amusement. "Well, I

could give either a shot if you'd like. Just don't blame me if your ears start to bleed."

I reach my fingers behind me, clasping my top with a dexterity honed from years of experience. Sitting up slowly, I pull my soft, worn tee-shirt over my tousled hair. I breathe in, savoring the salty sea air as it mingles with the faint scent of coconut sunscreen.

Quinn has been watching me. "For chrissake, I can barely touch my butt, much less reach that high on my back and manage something like what you just did." His tone betrays genuine amazement. "You're so flexible and nimble! How on earth do you bend your limbs like that? Have you done years of yoga?"

I chuckle at the compliment, but deflect it. "It's probably a lack of muscle that allows me to do that." Then, in what I hope is a comically seductive tone, I say, "In any case, flexibility has all kinds of perks, you know." I stretch my arms overhead and arch my back. When Quinn's eyebrows shoot up in amusement, I snort with delight, then say, "And, no. I don't do yoga! Life's too short to be bored like that, don't you think?"

He nods. "Alison tried to get me to do it a few times, and that was exactly my reaction! I don't know how Lisa can stand it. She's at it for at least an hour every day!"

"I know. She's a real yogaholic! I'd much rather spend my time with books, thank you very much."

"Books are definitely better. ... Speaking of which, I've been meaning to ask you something. How is it you're so familiar with Nineteenth Century British literature?"

I tuck a strand of hair behind my ear, a habit I have when I feel a surge of self-consciousness. Quinn's curiosity is like opening a Pandora's box of bookworm memories. "Brace yourself," I warn him with a giggle. "This story could stretch longer than *Ulysses!*"

I dive into my childhood, painting a picture of a house so full of books it was like living in a library that happened to have a kitchen. "I was the kid who spent hours nestled in a cozy nook by the window, lost in Austen's elegant debutante balls and Brontë's moors while the other kids were outside playing."

He nods, his smile encouraging me to continue.

"As I got older, I adored the genre novelists, too: Stevenson, Wells, Doyle. My mom and dad helped steer me to all that. In my later teens, Mom introduced me to the poets—Tennyson and the Brownings. And Dad, more of a joker than Mom, made sure I had the fun of reading Edward Lear's limericks."

Quinn's listening like I'm narrating the most riveting novel he's ever heard. His eyes sparkle with the understanding of someone who's walked in the same shoes. "What a lucky girl you were to have your parents lead you to such great literature."

"I know. ..." My mind plays snippets of conversations with Mom and Dad. "But I was also fortunate that RISD had a cooperative arrangement with Brown, so I was able to take British literature courses there." I pause, searching for the right words to continue my story. "For me, those courses at Brown were like finding the secret level in a video game. Just magical! I found the professors there simply amazing! ... You understand what that's like. You said your professors similarly inspired you! And I bet you're terrific in the classroom yourself! ... Do you like teaching?"

He considers. "You may know Cormac McCarthy's line: 'He may be dead; or he may be teaching English.' That's sort of the way I feel about it sometimes. ... Oh, I like it okay. But less than I once did. The college classroom has changed in the time I've been teaching. Most students come now for the 'college experience,' not for the education. So, you're lucky if you have two or three students in any given course who care about the subject and are motivated to work hard."

"Oh, that's no fun."

"No, it isn't. Worse yet, you no longer can teach a course like 'The 19th Century British Novel.' Now, the curriculum has to be concerned with identity, intersectionality, and moving the canon of literature away from 'white' and 'Eurocentric' foundational texts."

"I know it's politically incorrect to say this, but what a shame!"

"I agree, but there aren't too many people I can admit that to."

His gaze catches mine, and he holds onto it for a long, long beat. I feel a ping, a pleasant pinch somewhere below my navel. He says, "Finally—and I'll stop after this—I've grown tired of doing research and writing. There just aren't enough remaining important topics for my brand of scholar to analyze. So, most of the academic work coming out in my narrow field—including the stuff *I've* churned out—is inconsequential." His thoughts carry him away somewhere, and it's a while before he returns to me.

Eventually our conversation resumes, stretching over a couple more hours and meandering like a lazy river. I tell him about my love of words. How my mother spoke to us in several different languages, sparking in my brother and me an eagerness to learn them. How, as a girl, I rewrote children's books, trying to improve the wording, making them more vivid and intense, more to my liking. How, in my later teen years, I'd happily toiled away at translating a French young-adult rom-com.

"You mean you didn't just read it, you actually translated it —re-wrote it in English?"

I smile at the memory. "Yep. I loved finding just the right words to express what was happening."

He tells me about his marriage, about Alison, how they met. Then, eventually, saying he hopes he's not prying, he asks why I never married.

Now's certainly not the time to give a full answer to that, but I decide to share a bit. "I'm not anti-marriage on principle or anything. I've just never met the right person. I suppose it's simply that the kind of love that makes you want to marry has eluded me so far. Oh, I've had close relationships, sure, but nothing that's truly felt right. My friends have been playing matchmaker for ages, convinced they've found my perfect match. Yet, no matter how attractive, funny, or smart the person is, there's always something missing. Usually, it's the feeling that the person gets me, you know—like they truly understand what I'm about." I lock eyes with him. "I guess that's it. I have a self-defeating notion that my soulmate's out there—my personal unicorn who will understand me completely, get my brand of crazy. So, yeah, think of me as a unicorn hunter." I say, painting on a grin that's one part jest, two parts, "Did I really just say all that?"

Now feeling too exposed, I spring up. "Let's take another walk," I suggest, steering us in the direction of a colony of squabbling seagulls. They remind me of times my dad and I would laugh at similar noisy gull quarrels. So, I shift the topic to him—how, as a boy, my dad never developed a love for sports, but was thoroughly devoted to one outdoor activity: listening to birds.

"Bird watching?" Quinn asks.

I shake my head. "Not so much watching birds, as locating them with his hearing and listening to them. He was a professional musician—a cellist with the Philadelphia Symphony

Orchestra— and he had amazing auditory discrimination." I tell Quinn that when my dad was a kid, his friends teased him about his large ears. "They weren't freakishly large," I insist with a laugh. "In fact, on his head, they didn't look all that unusual. But they were big scoops—that's what he jokingly called them— and apparently they enabled him to take in sounds others might have to cup their ears to catch."

He playfully reaches over and lifts my hair away to inspect my ear. "You've got pretty big scoops yourself."

That gets a laugh from me, but I drive my index finger into his rib and snarl, "Hey! I'm no Dumbo! You're nasty!" Quinn recoils playfully, his laughter filling the air as he dodges another of my retaliatory jabs. A fresh layer of ease wraps around us, cozy as a shared blanket. I wonder if it was my brief moment of vulnerability—my 'soulmate' comment—that has brought us closer. Or maybe it was his spa-grade sunscreen pampering. Whatever the magic ingredient, we've cooked up a richer blend of comfort between us. We stroll side by side, letting the moments stretch lazily, lost in a silence that feels like a warm hug. But as the afternoon light begins to yawn and the ocean breeze gets a chill, we agree it's time to retreat to the warmth of the house.

Maria intercepts us on the porch. Studying us, she asks, "How was your afternoon?"

"We had fun!" I say, brushing sand from my legs. "The beach was beautiful. And your leftover *assado* was terrific." I throw her a Chef's kiss. "*Muchibus thankibus!*"

Maria looks to Quinn for explanation. He theatrically rolls his eyes. Teasing me, he says to Maria, "She thinks she's clever, quoting James Joyce's funny dog Latin. I refuse to give her the satisfaction of laughing."

"I know you're chuckling inside!" I say, pinching his cheek.

"I'm off to take a shower. I can't stand this coating of salt on my skin, the stiffness of my hair. Yuck. See you two later."

I catch Quinn's eye. We both know we're on the brink of something more than just beach buddies, and I can't help but feel a thrill of anticipation, mixed with a dash of 'What are we doing?' and a pinch of 'Is this going to work?' But hey, isn't that part of the adventure?

8

Quinn

The evening light oozes through the bay windows like the last gloopy drops of honey from a jar, giving the dinner table a warm, cozy aura. Plates brim with vivid salad greens and hefty squares of Lisa's Italian-sausage lasagna. The aroma's so thick you can almost taste the basil in the air. We clink glasses filled with a nice *Montelpuciano* I'd picked up, its deep ruby color promising notes of fruit and earth.

In his usual spot at the head of the table, Paul shows every sign of already having had a lively rendezvous with his Scotch companion. His glass is a little too eager to meet his lips, and the mean-spiritedness that usually trails his liquor adventures lurks in his eyes.

Our party of six is knee-deep in discussion about the latest entertainment buzz—what popular movies and TV shows have captured our attention, which books have managed to divert us. The conversation shifts to Ellen DeGeneres, who's recently made headlines for allegedly turning her production staff's emotions into her personal pin cushion.

Swirling his wine, Mike muses, "Ah, yes, the queen of kindness turns out to be not so kind after all."

Paul, in all his intoxicated glory, seizes control of the conversation. He blurts out, "Ellen, huh? She's a lesbian, right? She doesn't look like one! They're usually supermodels or biker chicks—or sofa spuds." He chuckles at his description and takes another swig of Scotch, oblivious to the cringe-worthiness of his comment. "All these people—the whole LGBTQ brigade— they're all so fucked up! Why are they all so sexually confused?" He scans our faces, as if seeking assistance in unraveling this queer mystery he's concocted.

His awful words hang in the air, and the clinking of cutlery on porcelain comes to a screeching halt. Lisa and I exchange knowing glances, accustomed to Paul's rude talent for steering conversations to uncomfortable topics. But the others aren't used to the gravitational pull of Paul's liquor-infused black holes, and their discomfort is evident. Maria's brow is deeply furrowed. Her eyes flick toward Hallie with concern. I wonder what boundary Paul has crossed this time—and why it feels like he's not just stepped over it, but trampled it underfoot.

Hallie lowers her fork and neatly tucks her hair into a low bun. She clears her throat and fixes Paul with a flinty stare. The air in the room shifts, charged with tension, like the moment before a cat pounces on a laser-pointer's dot. Her voice slices through the silence. "Is that really what you think, Paul? Or is that just the Scotch talking?" she says, each word edged with righteous indignation.

Whoa, what's happening here?

Paul squints at her, a sneer contorting his face. "Yep, that's what I think! They're as confused as a ... as a chameleon in a bag of Skittles." He roars with self-satisfaction.

Hallie leans forward, elbows on the table, her face growing crimson. "So, you think people should just fit comfortably into that little hetero orientation box you find acceptable?"

"What's wrong with that?" Paul asks with a smirk.

She says, "Sexuality isn't about fitting into a prescribed category, Paul. It's about being true to oneself and embracing the full spectrum of human experience."

Paul snorts and gives her a dismissive wave. "Ah, I don't need a lecture from you, Hallie. Whadda ya know about it, anyway?" I clench my fists beneath the table, nails carving crescents into my palms.

Hallie surveys the room, her gaze making pit stops at each of us, settling longest on me. "Actually, I'm bi," she declares, with a matter-of-factness that seems to suck oxygen from the room.

"You swing both ways, eh?" Paul says, elbowing the empty space beside him as if sharing a private joke with an invisible friend.

I yell, "Goddamnit, Paul, you're being incredibly rude. If you can't be decent, then leave the room. And don't let the fact that you own the place slow you down." Paul curls his lip, then sinks more heavily into his chair, as if withdrawing from the conversation.

Lisa jumps in. "Hallie, I'm so sorry ... Paul didn't mean to—"

Hallie pays no mind, either to me or Lisa. She stares at Paul with the heat of a thousand suns. When she speaks, her voice drips with disdain. "Yes, Paul, I swing both ways. And guess what? So do lots of other people—more than you can imagine."

Lisa makes another attempt. "Once again, Hallie, I'm so—"

Hallie cuts her off. "Please, Lisa. There's no need to apologize. It's fine. I'm not embarrassed or ashamed. I have no reason to be, however much Paul may think otherwise. In fact ..." She pauses, seeming to consider whether to say more, then continues, "As long as the topic's come up, I might as well tell the rest of you what Maria and Mike already know: until August, I'd lived for five years with my partner Sandy, a woman."

Paul hoots. "Oh, boy! Why aren't you back in Boston with her, in your little lesbian crib?"

The muscles in my jaw twitch as I slam my hand on the table. "Paul! For chrissake, stop it! What the hell is wrong with you?"

Hallie takes a sip of water, looks at Maria, then at me. "You really want to know, Paul?"

He nods.

I raise my hand to stop her. "Hallie, please. You don't owe anybody an explanation of your personal life."

Hallie glances again at Maria, who returns a look that I interpret as, 'Go ahead, if you want to.'

Hallie takes a deep breath. "She left me," Hallie says. "She found out I'd been seeing a man I'd met through work." She pauses several beats, then adds, "The guy, his name's Nick, he left me, too." Tears now shimmer in her eyes.

Maria extends her hand to comfort Hallie, who's clearly battling emotional rapids. Hallie clutches Maria's hand as if it's a lifeline. With her free hand, Maria delicately brushes away a tear sliding down Hallie's cheek.

Paul sits up straighter, presses his hands flat on the table, and stammers at Hallie. "Wow! You're kind of a fuck-up, aren't you? Sexually befuddled and a cheater!"

Enraged, I spring from my chair like a jack-in-the-box. "That's it, Paul! Leave the room. Now!" I demand, my growl low and unwavering.

He tries to fix me with a hostile glare but can't seem to make his eyes focus. He blinks a couple times, then smirks. He gets up from the table, swaying slightly and trying to find his balance. With an unsteady gait, he makes his way out of the room.

Speaking over one another, both Lisa and I launch into a frantic round of apologies.

But Hallie just sits there, a portrait of stoicism and resilience. She nods with an air of 'I've got this, folks.' She says, "Thank you, but no apology is necessary. He's just had too much to drink. I'm sure he didn't mean to be rude. And honestly, I always prefer to be open with my friends about my life, messy though it may be." She smiles. "There's not always an easy way to bring it up. Paul just unlocked a door I'd want to open at some point anyway. So, I should thank him for the favor."

A laugh escapes from me, dry and devoid of humor, as if I just witnessed someone thank a tornado for rearranging their living-room furniture.

"He didn't unlock the door ... he blew the hinges off it," Lisa murmurs, her eyes downcast. There's something disarming about seeing Lisa, the epitome of composure and quiet elegance, grappling with the raw, untidy edges of our conversation. It's like watching a swan try to rap.

Maria jumps into the fray. "You know, I've known Hallie for years, and she really does prefer to be open with people." Then, teasing her friend and obviously trying to lighten the mood, she adds with a mischievous grin, "I've seen her open up in ways that would make Dr. Ruth blush."

Hallie lets out a belly laugh, clearly grateful that Maria has thrown a comedic life preserver into the choppy waters of this conversation. Hallie stands to clear some dirty dishes from the table. The rest of us follow suit, and soon we're all in the kitchen. I station myself at the sink and begin rinsing off the plates and utensils the others bring to me. I catch snippets of their conversation as they chatter away.

Without Paul's toxic presence, the talk is now filled with playful banter and affectionate teasing. Showing her that, to them, it's no big deal, Lisa and Mike start joshing Hallie about her bisexuality. Mike says that, of course, he's known for years that Hallie's bi, and doesn't know why he's never talked with her about it before. He snaps at her playfully with a dishtowel and says, "Spill the beans. Who's your bi celebrity crush? Kristen Stewart or Halsey?"

"Oh, for chrissake," Maria protests. "Leave the poor woman alone."

Hallie, finding the humor in it, responds, "No, it's okay, I'm all good. And between those two, I'd choose Halsey." She hands me a stack of plates, her fingertips brushing mine briefly. It's a small touch, a flicker of connection amidst the evening's chaos, but it sparks something hopeful within me. They quickly establish she also prefers Evan Rachel Wood over Miley Cyrus.

"Okay. That's enough. Give it a rest, you guys," Maria says, again trying to protect her best friend.

Hallie again laughs off the protest. "No, no, no. I'm enjoying this. It gets my juices flowing."

Thinking this is an instance of Hallie's usual bawdy humor, we all look at her, aghast.

She howls in protest. "You pervs! My *cognitive* juices! It gets me thinking about what I like in a woman's outward appearance."

Maria decides to join in and pours herself some wine from a half-full bottle she's found. "Okay. How about ... Anna Paquin or Cynthia Nixon?"

Hallie adopts a thinking pose, tapping her index finger on her lips. "Let's see ... Cynthia Nixon!"

Maria says, "Really? I'm surprised."

Feigning offense, Hallie says, "Hey, I thought this was a safe, judgment-free zone!"

"Right. Sorry," Maria mutters,

Lisa says, "Angelina Joli or Drew Barrymore?"

In a heartbeat, Hallie delivers a thumbs-down. "Ugh. Neither. I pass"

I laugh at this and call out from across the room. "Aubrey Plaza or Amber Heard?"

With a sultry tone, Hallie responds, "Ooooh, now we're talkin'! But that's a really tough one. ... Mmmmm. Amberrrrr." Her reply elicits giggles from us all.

Maria thinks for a moment. "Sarah Paulson or Megyn Fox?"

Hallie replies instantly. "Oh, my god! Sarah Paulson! There's no contest. In fact, Sarah Paulson beats 'em all. And thanks very much for that, Maria! Now you really do have some of my other juices flowing. I'd better take myself off to my room for a few minutes!"

Ribald laughter fills the kitchen. When it subsides, Lisa turns to Hallie with a curious look. "Do women who know you're bi ever hit on you?"

I finish with the dishes and join the conversation, raising my eyebrows at Hallie, curious about her answer.

Hallie thinks for a moment, then smiles. "Yeah, it happens once in a while. Like this one time, a woman came on to me, claiming we knew each other from the Vegetarian Club."

Mike says, "What? The Vagitarium?"

Hallie swats him. "You swine. I said *vege*tarian, the Vegetarian Club." Now she winks at me. "But I knew she was wrong. I'd never met herbivore!"

I burst out laughing and playfully roll my eyes at her. "Maybe she was going incogmeato!"

9

Hallie

The morning sun peeks through my curtains like a nosy neighbor. Padding toward my bathroom, I spot a folded slip of paper skulking under my bedroom door. Half-asleep but fully intrigued, I snatch up the note and unfold it. The handwriting is neat, unfamiliar. My guess is that it's a note of remorse from Paul about his behavior last night, but the signature tells a different tale—it's from Quinn! My heart does a somersault as I dive into his words:

Hallie,
    Finding someone genuinely fascinating in this world is a rarity, like unearthing a treasure amidst the ordinary. That's

how I feel about having met you. Every time I learn something new about you, I find myself wanting to know ~~more~~ everything.

I hope this confession doesn't make you pack your bags and flee, because I thoroughly enjoy your company and our conversations. Would you be willing to spare some time today for us to talk further? Perhaps we could meet on the patio this morning at 10. If that time doesn't work for you, just let me know. Thanks.

Yours,

Quinn

Reading this, I'm buzzing like a squirrel on a cocaine rush. He finds me fascinating, likes spending time with me and talking with me, wants to know more about me! Well, isn't this a happy plot twist! My pulse races with what-ifs as I reread his note twice, finding intensity, vulnerability, and a dash of daring in his words.

A few minutes before 10, I make my way to the patio, my palms sweaty enough to germinate sprouts. Quinn's already there, sitting at a small table with a pitcher of lemonade and two tall glasses, looking like the charming protagonist of a rom-com.

We ease into conversation with small talk about how well we each slept, the weather, the punny jokes we'd thrown at each other last night. Lost in thoughts about that merriment, I realize I've completely zoned out and that Quinn has just asked a question: "... where does all that come from?"

I exaggerate a snapping-out-of-it expression. "Sorry, I was still pondering 'incogmeato.' What were you saying?"

Quinn gives me a half-laugh. "I was talking about the gift you have with words—your obvious love of wordplay, language. Last night's 'herbivore' is a good example. Where does all that come from?"

What a lovely thing to say, I think. I can't help but tease him. "Did you just compliment me?"

He grins. "Guilty as charged."

Answering his question is a breeze. "I have my parents to thank for it. They were word enthusiasts. Words and language were the most valued currencies in our family, our favorite pastime, our religion. We had shelves full of books about words, volumes on idioms and slang, compendia of aphorisms and maxims, dictionaries, thesauruses, crossword puzzles, word games—you name it. I grew up knowing how words and languages work in the way other girls knew how to do a hand-spring or head a soccer ball."

"So, I know about Latin, and you must be fluent in French. You mentioned translating from French to English when you were in your late teens. Are there other languages, as well?"

"Actually, yes." I feel a blush creeping up. How much should I reveal? Despite the bashfulness I always feel when I tell people this, I decide to share it with Quinn. "I'm also fluent in Spanish, conversant in Italian and Portuguese."

He's gobsmacked. "You've got to be kidding me!"

All I can do is grin. "Nope. Remember I told you my mom spoke to my brother and me in several languages when we were kids? I have her to thank for laying the foundations in French and Spanish. Then I studied those in high school and college. Teachers always said I had a natural facility."

The look he gives me is pure, unfiltered awe, a mix of admiration and surprise that sends a pleasant jolt through me. But I downplay the whole thing, "You know, it's really not as impressive as it seems. While there are differences among all those languages, the basic grammatical structures and syntax are similar. Plus, there's significant overlap in vocabulary among them due to their common Latin roots. Lots of words are either identical, have minor spelling differences, or are recognizable cognates. So, yeah, cool, I guess, but not Olympic-level impressive."

While Quinn shakes his head at this, I pause, trying to recall what he said that got me started down this path. It hits me, and I add, "But I do have a special place in my heart for Latin. It was in my Latin classes that I really came to appreciate the nuances of sentence structures, grammar, and the derivation of words."

"I get it. I feel the same way about Latin. My understanding of English grammar is better for having studied it. ... And, of course, there was Miss Carroll."

I arch an eyebrow.

"Marilyn Carroll. My Latin teacher for four straight years. Young, gorgeous, dream-worthy."

I laugh. "Ah, we get to the rub of it."

Now Quinn smiles sheepishly. "Well, there was plenty of rubbing, yes. My little magic lamp got frequent polishing during those years. My god, I coveted her. And in my dreams, I had her, kissing the full length of her lithe body, *a capite ad calcem.*"

I guffaw and applaud, liking what I hear about his sexual appetites. "Good for you! And, I must confess to a similar experience. Ingrid Johnson, my AP Latin teacher, was spectacularly beautiful. I think that was the year I realized I'm bi. There was more than a little rubbing on my part, too." I wink at him. "I released my genie so often I ended up having to walk like John Wayne."

Quinn roars with delight, then toasts me with his lemonade glass. "To inspirational teachers."

"Hear, hear."

Our chat meanders, much like it did on Nauset Beach a few days back, wandering once more into the territory of our childhoods and the families we came from. Quinn admits, "You know, after our beach day, I felt a bit embarrassed—and okay, a tad guilty—that I'd told you all about my family while hardly grazing the surface of yours—aside from your dad's legendary ears. So, tell me about your brother."

"Carter's my only sibling. He's the family golden child, five years older than I."

"Golden child? How so?"

"He took full advantage of my parents' best legacy. He's a linguist. A professor at UCLA. Specializes in pragmatics."

Quinn considers the term. "Pragmatics is all about how words can be interpreted differently based on the context, right?"

"Exactly. He's good at what he does and is highly respected in the field." Actually, he's the best. World renowned. But I resist the urge to boast that my brother is basically the Mozart of pragmatic linguistics.

"Very impressive. Do you get to see him often?"

"Not as much as I'd like. He's always swamped with work, plus there's the inconvenience of a continent between us. But he comes to Boston now and then for conferences and such. We always get together when he's in town. I adore him. He's better at wordplay than anyone I know." I shoot Quinn a playful smile. "Though, I guess I may have to reassess that opinion now that I know you."

Quinn throws me back a look of appreciation. His smile's warm enough to bake muffins. "Is he married? Kids?"

"Yeah, he and Shannon have been married for 20 years. They have a son and a daughter, both in their late teens. I love them to bits."

We sit in silence for a beat before Quinn changes the subject. "I told you about my mom. Would you tell me about yours?"

"Valerie? She was an incredible woman. Graduated summa

cum laude from Swarthmore, fluent in four languages, champion debater, tennis captain—she was smart, elegant, and kind. But not the world's most attentive mother. Not always tuned in to what was happening at home." Maybe someday I'll say more to him on that point, but certainly not today.

"Did she work outside the home?"

"She did. She spent 25 years at *Philadelphia* magazine, the last 17 as its editor-in-chief."

"Impressive! How'd your parents meet?"

"At a charity event for the Philadelphia Children's Hospital, where my dad's cello performance was part of the entertainment. A mutual friend introduced them. Apparently, the guy did it with hyperbolic flair, calling my dad a world-class cellist and Valerie the smartest woman in Philadelphia. Whenever my dad told that story, he'd get this sort-of puffed up, self-congratulatory look on his face, like 'Ain't I the cat that got the cream?!'"

"Well, I can see why. Your dad apparently did well for himself."

"They both did," I reply, pondering which one got the better end of the deal.

"So, how did they get together?"

"The mutual friend sensed some chemistry and made sure they had each other's contact information. Four days later, before my dad could muster the courage to call her, Valerie beat him to it and asked him out for dinner. They hit it off."

Quinn grins. "Valerie wasn't a shrinking violet."

"Nooooo, she wasn't."

After a long pause, Quinn asks in a softened tone, "How old was she when she died, Hallie?"

"Forty-six."

"That's way too young. What happened?"

"She—both of them, Mom and Dad—died in a horrific car

accident, a massive pile-up during a blinding rainstorm on their way from Philly to Pittsburgh."

Quinn grasps my hand.

"I got the call from the Pennsylvania state police when I was on stage at the Emerson, working out set details for *Porgy and Bess*. I simply couldn't process—couldn't believe!—what the cop was telling me." Quinn squeezes my hand, offering silent support as I struggle with tears and the weight of the memory. "It was the worst day of my life," I whisper, that pain as fresh as ever.

After a stretch of quiet, Quinn breaks the silence. "Losing your parents so young is heartbreaking. Yet, the legacy they've passed on to you is incredible, Hallie."

Feeling the mood's dipped a bit too low, I aim for a lighter tone, holding my fingers beneath my chin and batting my eyelashes dramatically like an old-time movie star. "Are we talking about these genes?"

Quinn chuckles. "Absolutely. Your looks, for starters. But there's so much more—your multilingual talents, your love for words and books, your stellar education. And your knack for connecting with people—I assume that comes from them, as well. It doesn't just happen."

Curious, not angling for more praise, I ask what he means.

"How you engage people, your genuine warmth, listening skills, and ability to put people at ease. And let's not forget your infectious humor. It's all pretty amazing."

Now, I'm floating, my ego puffed up like a parade-balloon character. I tuck back a stray hair. "That's all very kind of you, Quinn. In fact, I'm starting to think you have me confused with someone else." I pause to think what else I can tell him about my parents' influence on me. "One last thing I'd say about my parents is this: both of them believed that finding joy and fulfillment in one's work is essential to happiness and self-worth."

He considers this for a while. "That brings up something I'm curious about. Why didn't you go into some occupation involving words or language? Become a translator, say, or an editor?"

Oh, lord. He's hit a nerve, zeroed right in on the central question. How has he managed to do that? I feel heat rush to my face and my pulse quicken. "It's a valid question. And the answer's pretty straightforward: Carter and my mom had already staked out that turf, and I wanted to do something that differentiated myself from them." I leave out my fears of not measuring up to them.

Quinn mulls over my words. If he sees through me, he opts not to dig deeper. "You mentioned your work at the Emerson. I'm curious how you found your way into stage design."

I decide to give him the whole scoop, starting from scratch. "From a young age, I was all about drawing. I'd spend hours sketching, everything from individual objects to whole scenes. Then, around eighth grade, my mom's love for musical theater hit me. She'd blast Broadway tunes at home, much to my dad's classical-musician dismay. He called them fluff, but she was undeterred. That was her jam, and she was sticking to it! Before I knew it, I was hooked, too. So, I started drawing scenes for those musicals, immersing myself in the context and imagining the settings. It was pure fun." I smile, recalling how Quinn teased me that first morning on the Cape after I'd hummed a tune from *Oklahoma*.

"I bet it was."

"Then, as a teen, I volunteered at a summer stock theater, where I experienced musicals up close—ushering, spotlighting, managing props. And I was over the moon when I got to be in the chorus or would snag a small role. The musicals we did those summers—*The Sound of Music, Oklahoma, The Music Man,* and, my top pick, *My Fair Lady*—are still my favorites. When I wasn't busy with whatever tasks I'd been assigned, I'd draw alternate set designs. It was a terrific experience."

Quinn says, "I'm guessing you were into musicals in high school, too?"

Beaming, I nod, then take a leisurely sip of my lemonade. "Absolutely. But roles were more structured in high school, and I didn't have the chance to try as many different things. On the other hand, I definitely was the go-to person for set design, which paved my way to RISD and my career." I wrap up my tale with a cheeky "ta-da!"

He laughs and gives me a round of applause. "It must be terrifying for you right now, being out of work with no clue when the theater world might wake up from this COVID-induced coma."

I agree, with a wry smile. "Terrifying is putting it mildly. I've been lucky in my career, always managing to scrape by. My paycheck may never have had too many digits, but at least it was steady. Now, for the first time, I'm having a staring contest with economic hardship, playing a high-stakes game of financial chicken. Luckily, Maria and Mike have tossed me a much-needed lifeline."

Quinn offers a sympathetic nod. "What's your plan?"

Taking a deep breath, I confess. "I wish I could say I have a brilliant strategy, but I don't."

"Ever tried your hand at something other than stage design, something you could turn to in the interim?" Quinn asks.

"This isn't the sort of thing you have in mind, but I spent my teen years and college days in food service," I reveal, "and honestly, I wouldn't mind dipping my toes back into that world for a while. Whether it's restocking shelves or whatever, I'm game. Not picky—or too proud to do it. Plus, jobs in that sector are in demand now. Regardless, I'll have to slip into my metaphorical ruby slippers and plunge into the job market soon. When we're back in Boston, I'll figure things out."

He leans back in his chair, studying me with those compassionate eyes. Just as I'm about to ask him what's going on inside his head, he says, "If I remember the *Wizard of Oz* correctly, those ruby slippers are a metaphor for the untapped potential within each of us, the power to chart our own courses."

I nod in agreement.

"What I mean is, you're so talented that I'm sure you can accomplish anything you set your mind to, Hallie."

10

Hallie

C hatham's wrapped in a mist so thick, you'd think the fog is trying to hide the town from the rest of the world. I squint out the solarium windows, trying to make sense of the mouse-gray stew. The taillights on Maria's little Honda play a brief game of peek-a-boo before getting swallowed by the murk. Talk about commitment! She's off to her twice-a-week gig, helping out at a food pantry in Harwich.

In September, right after I turned Maria's house into a makeshift storage unit for my life. She roped me into a drive into Boston, where she was going to donate to the food pantry at the Greater Boston Catholic Charities' HQ in Dorchester.

"How long have you been doing this?" I'd asked her as we merged onto Soldiers Field Road.

"Donating to the food pantry, you mean? Oh, for years. But I started going more frequently when the lockdown hit people so hard."

I glanced at the three hefty boxes of groceries in her back seat. "Do you always bring this much?"

"Sometimes more. I've been gradually increasing the amount. The demand is enormous, and this is a simple way to do a little good."

To our left, the Charles River sparkled in the early afternoon light. Normally, at this time of year, college crew teams would be out in full force, fours and eights skimming the water. However, this year, the coronavirus had forced the cancellation of the Head of the Charles Regatta, leaving only a handful of collegiate crews and a smattering of singles on the river. On our right, the Harvard practice fields that typically host multiple intramural soccer games are empty. Commenting on all that, Maria said, "It feels like we've stumbled into another dimension, doesn't it?"

"Yeah," I agreed. "I haven't been around this way since students were sent home in March. And it's definitely not like this in Brookline! BU and BC are open for the fall semester, so my neighborhood is now as bustling as ever with college kids. But this is like stepping into a 'Twilight Zone' episode."

We continued in silence for a mile or two. Maria exited Storrow Drive near Kenmore and headed over to Mass Ave., where she turned right. Traffic, as always, was heavy in the area near Berklee College, but soon we passed the Christian Science mother church on the left and Symphony Hall on the right. When we stopped for a red light at Tremont Street, we observed a line of people waiting outside the door to the PLS Check-Cashing Store. She said, "I hate to see the poor getting fucked by those usurious assholes at PLS!" The driver behind us laid on the horn, prompting Maria to jerk her Honda forward and make a right turn.

As we traveled further down Tremont Street, the economic struggles of the area's residents became increasingly evident. Property values seemed to drop with every quarter mile. Maria maneuvered through Egleston Square on Roxbury Street, along Seaver Street near the Franklin Park Zoo, and finally onto Columbia Road. Half a mile later, we reached the GBCC pantry, and Maria pulled the car into the parking lot on the right. Unbuckling my seat belt, I said, "Good lord, that has to be the most convoluted route anyone has ever taken from West Newton to Dorchester! Why on earth did you go that way?"

Maria stuck her tongue out at me. "Well, for one thing, I absolutely adore that stretch along the river. It's so picturesque. And the rest of the route serves as a reminder to me of all the less fortunate people in this city who rely on food pantries like this one."

Each of us donned a face mask, grabbed a substantial box of food items, and ascended the ramp to the door at the corner of the three-story brick building. We had barely set foot inside when a short, stout man with a lively mustache greeted us, "Hey, Maria! Good to see you. Need a hand?"

"No, thanks, José. There's just one more box."

"Save it for when you're leaving. I'll go out with you to get it."

"José, this is my friend Hallie Bancroft. Hallie, meet José Gomes. He and I practically grew up together in New Bedford." José and I exchanged a friendly elbow bump, chuckling at the awkward new social etiquette. Maria then turned to me. "José is the reason I know about this place. He's the fairy godfather of the Cape Verdean community in Boston. Runs the best food pantry in Dorchester."

"Thank you. You're kind." He circled her shoulders with his arm and pulled her close, saying to me, "Maria was the smartest girl at New Bedford High School, by far. The most gorgeous, too. Everybody wanted to be her boyfriend."

Maria laughed. "Okay, okay, enough."

"It's true!" José's eyes twinkled.

Trying to deflect the praise, Maria changed the subject, asking José for updates on mutual friends. After about ten minutes, José clapped his hands and declared, "Alright, I'd better get back to work. Let me follow you out to your car." He hoisted the remaining box out of the back seat and rested it on the car's hood while Maria and I hopped in and fastened our seatbelts. Maria lowered her window and handed José a thick white envelope.

José beamed at Maria. "*Obrigadu*, my lovely friend." He squeezed her arm with affection.

"Don't mention it. *Nta amabo.*"

José's eyes sparkled with appreciation. "You, too."

When he'd turned to go back inside, I playfully nudged Maria with my elbow. "I'd say José is smitten with you."

"He's the sweetest man, and he does mountains of good." Maria backed the car out of its parking space, and made a left onto Columbia Road. "Shall we take a more direct route home? Would that make you happier?" Maria teased, lightly poking fun at my route criticism.

"Thank god."

After winding our way through Franklin Park, past the south end of the Arnold Arboretum, and onto the VFW Parkway, then Hammond Pond Parkway—all lush, verdant, and tranquil—I remarked, "I see what you mean about the route making a difference. ... How often do you go in there?

"To the pantry?"

I nodded.

"Every week. Sometimes twice. Mike and I are so fortunate, and there are so many in desperate need."

"You're a true saint, Maria Barros. Do you know that?"

And now, this morning, Maria's still at it—helping out in Harwich, while I sit here in my jammies, surfing the web, sipping my coffee, reading Joyce. Ashamed of my lack of charitableness, I do something that soothes me when I'm feeling down on myself: I start a pen-and-ink drawing.

In this case, it's to be a drawing for my brother of the Campbell's house here in Chatham. Sure, I could snap a photo of the house and text it to him. But there's nothing personal in that—and no satisfaction for me. So, working from memory, because exactness isn't important, I use a pencil to do a light sketch, getting the proportions and perspective right. Then, using a fine-tipped pen, I outline the major structural elements—roofline, walls, windows, and doors; add some ornamental aspects like shutters and pediments. I add shadows with cross-hatching and stippling, elevating my creation to a level of sophistication that Carter won't appreciate but that's important to me. When I finish, I look it over, pleased with what I've done, but sprinkle a bit more shading here and there for extra oomph.

Next, I pivot to the more serious business of penning a letter to snail-mail along with the drawing. Sure, I've sent Carter some brief emails in the past few weeks, giving him the Cliff notes of my life's recent plot twists—the whole Cape Cod saga, the lowdown on the digs here, and the utter joy of changing sceneries and being around new people. But when it comes to reaching inside for my innermost thoughts, nothing beats the old-school charm of applying ink to paper.

My favorite writing pen is a slender, black masterpiece—a

seamless fusion of form and function—that feels as though it was crafted specifically for my hand. It's more than a writing instrument. It's an extension of me, a faithful ally that helps me sort through brain clutter, find my best words, and strip my feelings down to their birthday suits.

I dive into the writing, trying to convey the emotional turmoil of my prolonged unemployment. I tell Carter that it's like having a colossal chunk of my life abruptly amputated. I also pour out my soul about Nick's sudden vanishing act, the pain of his abandonment still throbbing like a freshly stubbed toe. My feelings gush out, every stroke of the pen acting like a pressure-valve release for emotions that have been roiling on the back burner. In the quiet of the Campbells' sunroom, this writing turns into my own personal therapy session.

But I don't want this letter to be a total downer, so I make sure to sprinkle in some gratitude for the sunshine in my life—Maria, Mike, and the Campbells, heroes without capes, every one of them. I try to tell Carter something about Quinn, too, but boy, trying to capture my feelings for him is like trying to catch smoke with my bare hands—a neat trick that I struggle to perform even with the aid of my trusty pen. Each word feels inadequate, too flimsy to represent what Quinn has begun to mean to me. It's as if my own emotions are a language I don't yet understand, a playscript too complex to transcribe.

Sure, I could sketch Quinn's smile, describe his intellect, recount his wordplay. Or I could detail how he makes me feel—how, just yesterday, for example, his early-morning note had thrilled me, his compassion warmed me, his compliments made me feel seen, his belief in me made me stand a little taller. How the whole conversation left me feeling like I'd been touched by sunlight after a long stretch of gray days.

But how do I even begin to explain all that to Carter? And is it premature to try? After all, other than Quinn's sweet note and his kind words, I have no real indication he wants a more serious relationship with me. I hope he does. But for all I know, I'm on this train all by myself, and it's the express to Just-Friendsville.

11

Quinn

My knuckles hover in mid-air as I muster the courage to knock. Taking a deep breath, I rap lightly. My stroke is so timid it's like there's a scared mouse at the door. Hallie's cheerful "come in" greets me, and I enter to see her ensconced in an oversized chair, *Ulysses* spread open on her lap. A strip of morning sunlight bestows its blessing upon her long legs which stretch onto an ottoman. The air carries hints of vanilla and gardenia from her perfume.

"Hey, Quinn!" she says, throwing me a radiant smile.

"I hope I'm not bugging you. I'm actually about to take Charlie for a walk at the Monomoy Wildlife Refuge, and I thought you might fancy joining us."

Hallie scrunches her face, clearly weighing the prospect of leaving this coziness against the promise of fresh air. "I'm all good. But hey, there's room right here for Charlie if he'd rather stay here." She pats a vacant spot next to her. "I might even make space for you, Quinn."

What made me think she'd want to go for a walk? Just because she seemed to have a good time at the beach the other day? Obviously, I'm not playing with a full deck here. "Okay, well, if not today, perhaps another time. Enjoy your peace and quiet. Charlie and I will brave the wild outdoors by ourselves." Oh, lord. Now I'm just heaping lameness on lameness. Why don't I just take out an ad that reads, "If you see this man, please put him out of his misery."

I embark on a mission to locate the dog's harness and leash, which have a habit of playing hide-and-seek. After a search worthy of the Coast Guard, I finally locate the gear and call for Charlie. It's then that Hallie emerges, fully dressed and ready for an autumn trek. She grins. "I figured if Charlie wouldn't come to me, I'd come to Charlie. How could I resist such a splendid dog?"

I play along. "Well, maybe I should just let you two gallivant without me. I wouldn't want to come between you and your best friend."

"No, no, you must come!" She sweeps a stray lock of hair from my forehead. "You have a charmingly shaggy allure, and you'll fit right in. Those who see us will say, 'Look at that kind lady taking those two mongrels for a walk.'"

I chuckle. "Mongrel, eh? I'll have you know I'm a purebred ... something. Not entirely sure what, but something distinguished."

"I'm sure you are, champ. But let's not keep Charlie waiting. He's the best in show, after all." We step out to crisp autumn air. I fix the harness around Charlie's massive shoulders. He bounds ahead, leash trailing behind his wagging tail.

Halfway down the driveway, I propose an alternate plan. "You know what? I just got a better idea. Let's go to Morris Island. There's a terrific trail there that showcases the different habitats of the Cape's shoreline. And it's connected to the mainland, so we can drive there in about ten minutes. Easier to get to than Monomoy."

"Very well, good sir. Hie us to this so-called Morris Island. It intrigueth me."

There's no competition for the available spaces in the parking lot on Wikis Way. We locate the trailhead at the southeastern edge of the parking area. Withered wildflowers and gangly grasses engulf us on each side. Rabbits, chipmunks, and squirrels scamper about, driving poor Charlie into a frenzy that I struggle to contain. Birds abound, too—goldfinches, chickadees, finches, a cardinal, and a bluejay. I say, "Your dad would've loved this."

A warm smile fills Hallie's eyes. "That's true, he would've! ... You're a good listener, Quinn—a rare trait in a male. Color me impressed."

"Most of the time, I listen about as well as a know-it-all teenager. I only pay attention when something genuinely piques my interest." With a wink, I add, "I listen avidly to everything you say."

Hallie halts in her tracks, turning to me with a sly smile. "Oh, really? Why's that?"

"Because you're endlessly fascinating. And because I like you." I admit, tired of holding that inside.

Her smile is like the sun coming out. "I like you, too, Quinn."

"Well, that's good to hear," I say, trying to maintain a casual tone, even though this unfamiliar moment of emotional clarity has my heart racing. She lets me take her hand, and we continue on a trail that winds from scrubby pines to grassy dunes. Charlie settles into a rhythm, no longer pulling at the leash with every new scent. Soon, we come to a breathtaking ocean view: South Beach Island straight ahead, North and South Monomoy Islands in the distance to the right, a vast expanse of water stretching away after that. "This is spectacular," Hallie says. "I'm so glad you brought us here."

"Glad you decided to come along," I reply, feeling like a jackpot winner.

Hallie points to some straight, twiggy shoots coming out of the ground in bundles, dotted with dark blue-purple berries. "Know what that is?" she asks. I shake my head. "Arrow wood. Indigenous people used the shoots to make arrows and hunting bows."

"How do you know that?" I ask with unreserved admiration.

She grins. "Mysterious are my ways." She pauses a long beat. "My dad, of course."

Charlie splashes in tide pools that cut wet paths through the sand. His tail wagging furiously, he chases the tidal swash in and out, lowering his front and barking when the rushing water approaches him. We warn each other away from patches of poison ivy amidst the beach grass. Hallie draws my attention to various kinds of gulls—laughing, herring, and great black-backed—then points out willets in the taller grasses. "My dad loved listening to them. They say their name in flight."

Floored by the scope of her knowledge, I say, "You're a walking, talking Audubon Guide!"

"Not really. It's just that I spent a lot of time with my dad, and he was really an excellent teacher."

We pick up the trail again, coming to a patch of trees and woody plants that thrive here despite the wind and sandy soil.

"Oh, we're lucky to be here in the fall," Hallie says. "Look at all the berries!" Large blueberries hang heavily on their branches, and tiny grayish-blue ones, hardly bigger than sesame seeds, cling to the juniper trees.

"And smell that?" she asks, calling my attention to an earthy scent of damp soil and decaying leaves, mixed with something salty and primal. "That's pitch pine." She points to distinctive three-needle bunches on a cluster of gnarled, stubby trees.

We see a red flash overhead. As if I'm a kindergartner on a field trip, I'm just about to say, *Look at that purdy bird!* when Hallie squeals, "There's a red crossbill finch!" *Yes, precisely what I was just thinking.*

Amidst a quilt of fallen needles, a large flat stone lays between two patches of junipers, short blades of grass forming a little goatee around its perimeter. Hallie picks up a sturdy stick, pries it under the slab, and flips the rock over. Wondering what she's up to, I ask, "What're you looking for?"

"Nothing. I just decided this rock had lain like that too long; it needed to be flipped. If I'd left it alone, the poor thing might've stayed as it was for another century. How sad for it!"

I laugh, delighting in the wackiness of that response. We bend low, scrutinizing tiny creatures the flipped rock has exposed—pillbugs, woodlice, worms, and a spider. They scurry about as if trying to hide from the sudden, bright light that has descended on them, like a spotlight slanting down from a flying saucer.

Hallie giggles. Invoking Lewis Carroll's "Jabberwocky" verse, she says, "They're gyring, all slithy and mimsy!"

Her enthusiasm enchants me. "You're a very peculiar person, Hallie Bancroft."

She pops up from her crouch and gives me a quick kiss on the cheek. "It's true. I'm a bit quirky; I've got some looney tunes in my soul. But I'm totally on board with Jane Eyre's contention that it's better to be happy than dignified."

Grinning at that, I pull Hallie to me and kiss her back, intending it to be sweet. But in two beats it becomes intense on my part, almost desperate. *Good lord, what must she think of me?* But my worry evaporates when she slides her tongue against mine and her hands travel to my hips, pullling me against her. Oh, god! My breath quickens ...

Just then, Charlie launches at some bird-filled bushes, sending avian squadrons into flight—ten, fifteen birds at a time. He barks like a maniacal dervish and yanks me far away from Hallie. All I can do is look back at her and hope my eyes say, *Sorry. Maybe another time. SOON!* When Charlie finally stops his mad pursuit, his wagging tail and unapologetic eyes seem to ask, "Did I do good?"

"Traitor," I mutter to him.

Hallie catches up with us, laughing and shaking her head in sheer disbelief. "That's one way to break the sexual tension!" She takes the leash, and soon we come to a spectacular salt marsh, the ground covered at this time of year with brilliant sea flowers in varying, vivid shades of violet and heliotrope. "My god, that's lovely," I say, taking her hand and savoring the view.

Farther along we reach the Morris Island flats, stippled with various migratory birds hunting for food in the shallow water and mudflats. American Oystercatchers probe the sandy and stony areas for lunch. Hallie calls my attention to a tern diving into the water. "Probably going after sandlances," she guesses.

I can identify an Oystercatcher—and a tern, if pressed. But who on earth knows terns go after something called sandlances? Unable to help myself, I burst into laughter. "Omigod, you have a lot of nerve!"

"What?" Wary, Hallie grins at me.

"You, of all people, had the audacity our first night in Chatham to call me 'Professor Pointdexter' when I merely noted the derivation of 'hear, hear.'"

"Did I?"

"You did! Yet here you are, a walking, talking Bloomsbury—part English professor, part ornithologist, part plantswoman, and maybe even part ichthyologist."

She gives me a playful shove. "No, I'm not."

"Oh, but you are! Prepare yourself, miss, for I shall now commence with the name calling!" I grab her, tickling until she squirms away. "Let's see ... how about Bonnie Bluestocking? Harriet Highbrow?"

Hallie's shaking with laughter. "Oh, we're playing that game, are we? Okay. You're ... Alliterative Albert. ... Factoid Phil."

Now I'm chortling, too. "You're Barbie Brainbox! Pattie Polymath! ... Lola Logophile!"

"You're Bennie Booksmart! Dexter Didact!"

"Didact? ... Oh, now you've done it. ... You're ... I've got it! Clara Clever Clogs!"

"Clever Clogs?"

"Take that, you! It's almost as scathing as 'Dexter Didact!'" Adopting a pompous tone, I declaim, "It's a Britishism, meaning an intellectual who's ostentatiously and irritatingly knowledgeable."

"Is that what I am?" she asks, fluttering her eyelashes provocatively like a Hollywood ingenue.

"I wouldn't have said so until today. But I see that a thorough reexamination of you is in order."

"Sounds fun. Should we do it clothed or unclothed?"

"What?" I'm unsure I heard her correctly.

"Will I be taking my clothes off for this ... 'thorough reexamination' ... or will I be leaving them on?" she asks with a puckish grin.

I lunge at her, but she eludes me. Omigod, I can barely stand how much fun she is. "I see I'll have to adjust my list of names for you." I ponder for a moment before announcing: "Your pick: Cody Coquette or ... Mindy Minx."

She coyly saunters back to me, swaying her shoulders, "Oooooh. That's a tough one! I think I'll go with Mindy."

"Mindy Minx, it is!"

Laughing like idiots, we collapse into each other's arms, a moment of pure joy. We're just about to kiss. But once again, Charlie—that goddamn dog!—barks and yanks me clean away from Hallie. He pulls me down the trail, where the loop now has taken us almost back to the parking lot.

When we reach my little SUV, I cast a wary eye at Charlie's muddy paws and sand-coated legs. I reluctantly coax him to hop onto the back seat. "It's alright, Charlie. Not your fault. Coming to a beach was my idea, not yours."

Climbing into the passenger seat, Hallie says, "I admire a man who takes responsibility."

"That's me. Responsible Randy."

Her impish grin reappears. "You're randy? Well, we should take care of that." She playfully runs a finger all the way up my thigh. Then down. Up and down. Oh, god.

I laugh, grab her wrist to stop her torture, then tickle her until she squeals.

12

Hallie

At dinner the evening of our walk at Morris Island, Quinn proposed a trip to Nantucket. "It'll be fabulous!," he said to the group. "We can catch the fast ferry and spend the entire day there." Mike and Paul, tied up with work, couldn't join us, but Maria, Lisa, and I agreed to go, swept up by the spirit of adventure and Quinn's infectious enthusiasm. Now, a few days later, the Grey Lady IV eases from its berth in Hyannis Harbor, gliding effortlessly on water smooth as a shark's fin. Thick fog obscures any visual indication of motion. "Are we even moving?" I ask, glancing at Quinn who sits to my left, with Lisa and Maria chatting in the row behind us.

"I think so, but it's hard to tell in this pea soup," Quinn says.

Surveying the crowded indoor deck, I say, "Feels like a New York subway during rush hour. And look, some people aren't even wearing masks! What's the point of a policy if they're not going to enforce it?" My face heats with anger. "So frustrating! Maybe I shouldn't have suggested this later ferry. I bet the 6:10 wouldn't have been this jam-packed."

"It's okay. We'll go outside to the upper deck when the fog lifts a bit," Quinn says. "We can take our masks off out there."

I sigh in relief. "Thanks, Quinn. I haven't been in an indoor space with so many other people in a long time, and it's kind of freaking me out." I take a deep, cleansing breath, willing myself to calm down. "I'll be fine once we get some fresh air."

We chatter aimlessly as the ferry slices through the fog, the thick mist dulling the noise from the engines. Quinn throws a curveball into a conversational lull. "Do you hear anything from Nick? That's his name, right?"

This shocks me like a bolt from the blue—not just that he remembers Nick by name, but that he would poke at this tender spot. He's got to know it's a sore subject. "No. Nothing."

"How long were you two ... "

"Twenty months," I say, swamped by a wave of embarrassment. "Look, I want you to know I'm ashamed I cheated on Sandy with him. My only defense—no, I shouldn't say that. I realize there's no defense. It was wrong of me."

Quinn raises his palms. "Absolutely no judgment from me." He's quiet for a moment. "What attracted you to him?"

Once again, I'm taken aback by the question. I hesitate to answer, unsure if I want to delve into it. But I like Quinn too much to shut him down; his earnestness deserves an honest answer. So I reply, "We had this shared 'I-get-you' vibe because we're both set designers and worked in the same theater world." I pause. "Plus, he was fun, handsome ... and 180 degrees different from Sandy."

"I can understand all that," he nods. "Do you still have feelings for him?" His tone is a mix of curiosity and dread, as if he's bracing for impact, but can't back off.

I meet his gaze and opt for naked honesty. "I'm not sure. It's not that I still think we can be something; that ship's sailed. But feelings ... they hang around longer than you want." We sink into a thoughtful silence. "So why did you ask about him?"

"I ... um, curiosity, I guess."

I nudge him for more. "Curiosity? About what?"

"I guess about ... who you were when you were with him."

His answer catches me off guard. What does he mean? Is he wondering if I'm likely to cheat again? Is he somehow measuring himself against Nick?

Before I can even think how to respond, Quinn continues, "I'm sorry, Hallie. I don't mean to discomfort you with my questions. It's just that I'm getting ..." He pauses, trying to find the right words. "I'm liking this ... us." His gaze meets mine. "I guess I'm curious about your romantic past in part because it's so ... recent."

"I understand," I manage, though part of me wishes he'd just let the past be past.

He must somehow catch on to that, because he backs off with a smile. "Listen, let's move off of Nick. We'll change the subject, alright?"

A sigh of relief escapes me. "Great. What should we talk about?"

Then, with a glint in his eye, he says, "Let's talk about Sandy. Do you hear anything from her?"

"Quinn!" I squeal in protest. "Please! Can we not?"

He seizes my hand, trying to calm me. "Bear with me, Hallie. Your love life has been ... a bit more complicated than mine, and I want to have some sense of what I'm up against."

His explanations for all these questions about Nick and

Sandy—with signals that he sees an "us" in the making—shift something in me. So he, too, thinks there's something real here for us to explore. That disarms me. I roll my eyes and playfully slap his arm. "Trust me, it's not that thrilling."

"Maybe it just seems that way because I've never met a *femme fatale* before—"

I chuckle and swat him again. "Watch it, buster."

We let the silence sit for a moment. Then, feeling it's only fair, I open up about Sandy, too. "To answer your question: No, Sandy and I haven't talked. And I doubt we will."

"Is that tough?"

Sandy's absence from my life feels surprisingly okay, even though we lived together for five years. I really don't miss her. "No. It's been a long time since I felt anything for Sandy."

"And where is she now?"

"She moved home to Indiana—something she'd been thinking of doing for quite a while, actually. That was one of the things that loosened our bond—her desire to move there to take care of her dad. But like me, she had a job that was hard to give up. So, she stayed on in our apartment even after she found out about Nick."

"What's wrong with her dad?"

"He's struggled with advanced prostate cancer and also is now in the fourth of Parkinson's. He's confined to a wheel chair and needs lots of assistance. Sandy's mom had been there for him, but she died of COVID in late June. Sandy left for Indiana soon after that."

Quinn nods. "I feel for her. And for her dad. Sounds like a rough road ahead ..." His voice trails off. Then, in a hushed tone, he stuns me: "I had prostate cancer six years ago. Dealing with it is no picnic."

My heart stalls. Prostate cancer! The words spin in my head, stirring an emotional storm. "Oh, Quinn, that's tough to hear." His expression is stoic. But I know all too well how people can mask their deepest struggles with a veneer of strength and resilience. I link my arm through his, offering comfort.

As the ferry leaves Lewis Bay, its horn cuts through the silence, signaling our passage around Point Gammon into the open waters of Nantucket Sound. Quinn suggests we head outside. When we reach the upper deck, we remove our masks and brace against the wind and chill.

I hold onto him. "Would you share more about it with me?" I add, "Only if you're up for it. No pressure, if it's too personal."

He exhales. "I don't mind." Then he begins to unspool a long story that is, at least in the way he tells it, alternately harrowing and funny.

"I thought prostate cancer was an old man's problem!" He admits to being embarrassed at how little he knew about it, especially given his own father's struggle with the disease. "I knew it's treatable, when caught early, so I wasn't afraid I'd die from it. Still, it's cancer, and nobody wants to get that diagnosis." His biggest worry, he told me with a bashful smile, was that treatments like surgery or radiation might mess with his sexual function or have him shopping for adult diapers—or both.

"How awful! What horrid prospects, Quinn. I can't even imagine." My mouth is so dry all the water in Nantucket sound couldn't rehydrate me.

He recounts a story about visiting his oncologist with Alison in tow. The nurse asked him to rate his sexual function then, at 48 years old, versus when he was 21, rated on a scale from 1 to 100. "I confidently gave myself an 85, but Alison, her eyes glued to the floor, softly suggested a more earthbound number: 'Um, no. More like ... mid-60s ... or lower.'"

Quinn's laughter at the memory is infectious; I can't help

but laugh, too. "That's only because you were a super stud at 21, right?"

"Exactly!" He zips his jacket up further. "Turns out, my doomsday Googling had produced an outdated prognosis. Surgeons had gotten more savvy about sparing the nerves that count, and there was now a somewhat better chance of keeping the flag flying, so to speak." He meets my eyes again. "Too much information?"

Is it? No man has ever spoken to me about such intimate matters before. I'm finding it both riveting and overwhelming. "No, it's okay. Keep going."

"So, I decided to have the surgery. Unfortunately, about a week later, my doctor delivered the disappointing news that the surgery hadn't successfully removed all the cancer. In order to eliminate any remaining rogue cells, I'd have to undergo radiation therapy five days a week for seven weeks. But first, I'd need a powerful hormone drug to starve the cancer of its food, testosterone. The doctor listed the side effects of the hormone therapy like he was reading off a menu of bodily curses: mood swings, muscle loss, hot flashes, belly fat, man boobs, joint pain, and shrinking testicles. Oh, and as a bonus, my sex drive would disappear! All enticing prospects, right?"

"Oh, how hard for you!" A lump has formed in my throat as I've listened to his ordeal. I caress his hand with my thumb, trying to convey a silent message that I care and want to comfort him.

He breaks the silence, sharing more about the aftermath. "Sure enough, I lost my libido. And the hot flashes were intense and unpredictable, each of them like being trapped in a sauna. But the mood swings were the worst part. Minor irritants—say, a din from nearby leaf-blowers—would produce utter fits of fury. Tears would come over the smallest things, such as a broken shoelace, spilled laundry detergent—or, most memorably—when a singer I liked on a TV talent contest flubbed her performance." He chuckles and shakes his head. "And then, after the weeks of intense radiation treatment, I could only wait and hope for the best."

He says this just as Lisa and Maria join us on the upper deck, their appearance changing the vibe instantly. "We're pulling into Nantucket," Lisa says. "Weren't you two chilly out here? You look like you've been blown to Nova Scotia and back."

Quinn shrugs and glances at me. "I'm alright," he says softly, sounding drained by our conversation. I'm sure it's been exhausting for him, and it's left me with lots of unanswered questions about the results of his treatments and his current health. As we make our way to the disembarkment ramp, my concerns thrum in my head against a melange of sounds—excited voices, seagull cries, the drone of ship engines, the clattering of luggage being wheeled across the deck. Stepping onto the concrete dock, I welcome its solidity, a stark contrast to my uncertainties about whether Quinn's truly alright.

13

Hallie

As the ferry dock recedes behind us, we approach the Corner Table Cafe, a small coffee shop with outdoor seating spilling onto the sidewalk, I catch myself watching Quinn. He's perked up, his stride more confident, his smile brighter. He turns to the three of us. "Coffee?" he asks, already reaching for the door handle.

"Definitely," I reply, my stomach growling at the thought of a sweet treat and hot drink. The interior of the cafe is cozy and inviting, with chalkboard menus hanging on exposed brick walls and strings of fairy lights adding a whimsical touch. When we've got our coffees and pastries in hand, we cross the street to a small park and settle on wooden benches, sipping our drinks and nibbling on flaky croissants filled with chocolate.

"Why did you two go outside to the upper deck?" Maria asks me, her voice tinged with something like irritation.

"Oh, I didn't like how many people inside weren't wearing masks. It wasn't really that chilly out there, once we got used to it." Looking around at the lovely, quaint, Colonial-style buildings in various colors lining the streets, flower boxes adorning the windowsills, I ask, "So, what are we gonna do?"

Maria says, "Good question. This is a rich person's fantasyland, like Williamsburg, or Woodstock, Vermont. Anything here for normal folks?"

There's an acerbic tone to Maria's voice that sets off a tiny alarm in me. I disregard it and turn to Quinn. "What's your suggestion? Have a plan?"

He says, "I thought we'd spend the first part of our day here in town, looking in the shops and galleries. The Whaling Museum would be interesting, but I read that because of COVID you can't just show up. You have to reserve a time to visit and buy the tickets online." He pulls out his iPhone. "If you'd like to go there, I'll see if I can get us tickets for later this morning. Okay?" When we all nod in assent, he says, "Good. Feel free to wander. I'll find you."

Lisa says to Maria and me, "Good idea. Let's walk a bit, take in the Nantucket ambience."

A dark look crosses Maria's face. She says, "Ambience! Don't you mean 'quaintness overload?' It's like a crop duster sprayed this whole place with cloying pretentiousness."

Lisa stiffens at this, but says, "I'm sorry it's ... not to your taste, Maria, but I hope you can find things to enjoy about it."

Maria sniffs. "All I see are fancy boutiques selling overpriced trinkets to wealthy people."

I've apparently missed something. I don't understand what's

turned Maria venomous. She continues to hiss. "Maybe I should pop into one and buy some precious preppy clothes to protect myself from being wrestled to the ground by the local cops."

Lisa jolts, as if Maria's thorny remark pricked her skin. Her bewilderment slices through the air. "What in the world are you talking about? Why do you say that about the police?"

Whatever sparked Maria's earlier barbed comments now bursts into flames upon Lisa's reply. Maria holds Lisa's gaze with an unyielding stare. "Are you kidding, Lisa? Have you not been paying attention at all to what's been happening in this country —Black lives being extinguished at the hands of cops? Can you really be this obtuse?" She takes a deep breath, as if trying to steady herself.

"Of course, I'm aware of all that," Lisa says. "But you're not doing anything wrong!"

"Omigod!" Maria's thunderous gasp caroms against the clapboarded building next to us. "You are clueless! You think all these Black people around the country who've been killed by cops were doing something wrong? You think Breonna Taylor was doing something wrong when those Louisville cops smashed into her apartment and shot her dead? You're unbelievable!"

Lisa looks stunned at Maria's admonishment.

This whole thing is going nowhere but further downhill, so I step in, hoping to defuse the situation. In as calm a tone as I can muster, I say, "Hey, you guys. C'mon. Let's walk." I gently rest one hand on Maria's shoulder, giving it a reassuring squeeze, and with my other, lightly tug on Lisa's arm, encouraging her to move ahead, leave this moment behind. Maria's eyes glisten with unshed angry tears, while Lisa's face is etched with confusion and turmoil.

I make stabs at light-hearted conversation to reduce the

tension, but my efforts are making little headway when Quinn suddenly catches up with us, like a *deus ex machina* arriving to deliver surcease. His disheveled hair and slight windedness suggest he's been hurrying to find us. "Hey, glad I found you guys," he says, his eyes darting between Maria and Lisa as he senses the residual tension in the air. "I got tickets for 11:45. We can have a late lunch after." He comically polishes his knuckles on his shirt, ready to accept accolades for his successful efforts.

Neither Lisa nor Maria even looks in his direction, much less thanks him. But I smile and say, "Terrific. Well done!" Responding to his questioning eyes, I lean close to him and whisper, "I'll tell you later. Just go with the flow."

Maria abruptly asks, "Is there a book store around here?"

When it's obvious that Quinn and I will be of no help on this, Lisa sullenly points toward an old two-story brick building on the next corner. "Mitchell's is just up there." Maria nods and heads away on the cobblestones.

I call out, "Wait, Mar, let me come with you!" To Quinn and Lisa, I say, "Let's meet there in 45 minutes."

Catching up to Maria, I link my arm with hers, finding an easy and familiar rhythm in our stride. We enter the bookstore, and the tension eases on Maria's features almost immediately, as if this sanctuary has a rule prohibiting stress and agitation. It's no wonder to me that she sought refuge here. Bookstores are where she and I always seek peace amidst chaos.

She wanders down an aisle, scanning the shelves, running her fingertips over the spines of various titles. I trail behind her, giving her space, but staying close enough to offer support. I know she's not ready to discuss her argument with Lisa just yet. She needs this moment of calm to soften the sharp edges of her recent anger.

After browsing for a while, she stops at a shelf labeled

"Social Justice," her gaze fixed on a particular book that seems to call out to her. With a delicate fingertip, she plucks it from its place. As I look over her shoulder, she holds up *Stamped from the Beginning* by Ibram X. Kendi. She flips it over, scans the back cover, and reads aloud: "An eye-opening journey through the history of racist ideas in America." She looks at me and says, with a wry tone, "Do you suppose it's too late for me to present Lisa with a hostess gift?"

I chuckle, sensing that it's now safe to speak. "Don't be ridiculous. You know Lisa's not racist. ... I hope you don't mind, but I can't help but ask: What happened back there? You got so frustrated and angry with her. And so fast!"

She lets out a huge sigh. "Well, it wasn't so fast. It had been percolating almost from the moment we sat down on the ferry in Hyannis. Our conversation was so infuriating! She wanted only to talk about the various shops she likes on Nantucket and things she remembers buying here. I'd try to change the topic, but she kept returning to that crap."

Well, that explains a lot. Lisa's stumble about the police may have been the spark that lit the firestorm back there, but the thick, brittle clump of kindling was really Maria's disapproval of Lisa's conspicuous consumption. Knowing how that must have driven Maria crazy, I squeeze her shoulder in a feeble show of solidarity.

Almost as if the squeeze presses another thought into her head, she says, "And then her shitty remark about the cops! It's just ... she doesn't get it! Like, at all!" Maria shakes her head in disbelief. "She lives in such a bubble, oblivious to what's happening in the world outside."

"Look, you know I'm on your side here. But do you think it's possible you over-reacted about her police comment because you were already angry about all her buy-buy-buy babble? I mean, her remark was definitely … insensitive, but it didn't deserve that level of outrage."

Now Maria's look is sheepish. "Yeah, maybe …" She pauses a long time, then looks up at me. "I don't know if you've noticed, but I sometimes can be more than a little self-righteous."

I laugh and give her a side hug. When we've paid for our books, we decide to take a walk around the block before meeting Lisa and Quinn. I say, "You asked why Quinn and I went out to the upper deck. As I said, it was partly the mask problem; it was also that we were having a delicate conversation. He was telling me about his diagnosis of prostate cancer six years ago and how it was treated. He was just getting to the aftereffects when you guys showed up."

Her eyes meet mine with genuine concern. "Oh, poor Quinn. He's too young for that! I'm sorry we interrupted before he could tell you more."

"That's alright. I'm sure he'll share more another time if he wants to."

We sync up with Lisa and Quinn at our rendezvous point. Maria gives Lisa a sheepish smile, pulls her into a hug, and says, "Sorry about that, kiddo. Didn't mean to fly off the handle like that."

The relief on Lisa's face is palpable. She says, "And I'm sorry about my doltish comment about the police." Then, playful, she adds, "And just so you know, I think you'd look great in some pink and lime-green clothes. Let's keep our eyes peeled for some."

"Ooooh. Good idea," Maria says.

We meander northward on Centre Street, our pace slowing as we're lured by the charm of cozy boutiques flaunting their vibrant window dressings. Quinn stops us in front of Ladybird Lingerie, its window a stage for mannequins clad in the kind of delicate, pricey, lace-trimmed intimates that prompt a double-take, at least from some men. Wearing an expression that's a mix of bafflement and curiosity, he turns to us. "Seriously, who shells out for this stuff?"

Lisa laughs and covers her face in embarrassment. "Oh, God. It probably says something awful about me, but I do!" Just out of her line of sight, Maria's face scrunches up in silent commentary, while I find myself pressing my lips together to hide my amusement.

We veer right at the stately Jared Coffin House, charting a course down Broad St. until the Whaling Museum looms into view. Quinn, ever mindful of the time, checks his watch: "Perfect timing: 11:43," he declares, as if we deserve a trophy for this achievement.

Inside, our group disperses like seeds in the wind—Lisa and Maria venture solo, while Quinn and I pair up, drawn to a room where the story of whale ecology unfolds through touch and tech. As we explore the interactive exhibit, I find myself quietly humming the melody of "Blow High, Blow Low" from *Carousel,* a spontaneous soundtrack to our museum meanderings. After a bit, Quinn tilts his head against mine and softly sings several lines of the song. My laughter bubbles over, and soon we're duetting on the closing line—"For many an' many a long, long day!" Our performance peaks with an incongruous flourish of jazz hands before we collapse into a hug. This hug, though, feels different from our earlier embraces. There's an extra layer of tenderness and affection to the connection—softer, more charged, as if we're both waking up to the fact that there's something real and growing between us.

Drifting next into a gallery devoted to the tragic loss of the whaler Essex in the Pacific in the early 1800 my brain scrambles to recall the title of that exceptional book I'd read on the subject.

It had won a Pulitzer, or perhaps a National Book Award. My mental search is cut short by Quinn's enthusiastic, "Ooooh, did you read *In the Heart of the Sea*?" Our smiles lock on, and we do a deep dive on the book, weaving it into our observations of the exhibit, our conversation a lively dance of thoughts and insights.

Eventually, we wander into sanctum of the Scrimshaw Gallery, advertised as a treasure trove of the world's most significant scrimshaw collection. Together, Quinn and I admire the artistry carved into each piece of smooth ivory—decorative vases, practical tools, and delicate jewelry, every item telling a unique story of its own, skillfully etched by sailors into the bones of their ocean brethren.

Maria rushes up to us, her voice bubbling with excitement. "Hallie! Quinn! Come! You have to see this!" She leads us to a nearby room where there's a large exhibit about Cape Verdean heritage on Nantucket. My long association with Maria's family has endowed me with a solid base of knowledge about Cape Verdean culture and history, so this exhibit sucks me in fast.

Back in the 1800s, Nantucket's whaling ships had a routine layover at the Cape Verdean islands of Brava and Fogo, where they'd pick up local men to bolster their crews. These recruits, prized for their prowess as harpooners, helmsmen, and all-round seafarers, joined the ranks for grueling voyages in pursuit of whales—a job as perilous as it was poorly compensated. As the age of whaling waned, many of these men settled into Nantucket life, turning their hands to shellfishing, gardening, carpentry, caretaking, and culinary arts.

We pivot to find Maria mesmerized by an exhibit showcasing a Cape Verdean family altar. A poignant snapshot of spirituality, the display is a mosaic of personal history and faith: faded photographs of departed loved ones, hand-crafted prayer cards, and fragile religious symbols. Maria is visibly moved, her face and voice full of wonder when she says, "This is like stepping into my grandmother's living room. She had a home altar just like this one, every piece a story, a little puzzle piece. I used to spend hours just looking, trying to piece together my own story from hers."

Finally, Quinn lets out a gush of breath and says, "I don't mean to be rude, but I've gotta eat. I'm famished. Do you suppose there's a stash of communion wafers around here somewhere?" Maria laughs and consults her watch. "It's almost 1:30! Yeah, let's get lunch." Quinn guides me by the arm, and the three of us round up Lisa, who's spellbound by the scrimshaw exhibit. We stroll to the Easy Street Cantina, just a five-minute walk. We snag a table on their patio, under a cheerful yellow umbrella, ready for a bite.

Fifty minutes later, lunch done and masks on, we squeeze into a taxi. It's off to Sconset at the far eastern edge of the island. The cab reeks of cigarettes, and the driver, fingers stained from nicotine, offers unsolicited advice for our day. "Don't miss Sconset Bluff Walk," he advises. "It feels like trespassing at first, walking through billionaires' backyards, but it's a public way. The views of rich peoples' gardens and of the ocean are amazing. The end of the walk will lead you to the main road where you can continue on to the Sankaty Head Lighthouse. Well worth doing."

The cabbie was right: the Bluff Walk enchants us. Quinn says, "This reminds me of the Marginal Way walk in Ogunquit. Have you all ever done that?" Lisa says she has, and she agrees with the comparison, but insists this is better. The two of them dive into a chat about Ogunquit as we hit the beach, kicking off our shoes. Maria dashes toward the waves, leaping and laughing. Quinn follows close behind her, splashing her with water as she shrieks and tries to run away.

As Lisa and I stroll along farther from the surf, we observe them from a distance. Suddenly, she surprises me with a personal remark. "You and Quinn have an amazing chemistry, Hallie. You really bring out the best, most vibrant side of each other."

I catch her eye and can't help but feel a little vulnerable. Here's this woman, whom I've only known for a short time, observing something between Quinn and me that I'm only now fully acknowledging myself. "You're right," I admit softly. "We get each other, understand what makes the other tick."

She says, "Yeah, I see that. I'm curious. What do you think makes him tick?"

I glance in Quinn's direction and see Maria running from him. "On one level, it's words and literature. But, on a deeper and more important level, poor Quinn is a wounded soul. He's faced such heartbreaking losses of important women in his life—his mother's suicide, Alison's death ... I think he yearns for a settled homelife, but is probably reluctant to pursue a new relationship, fearing another heartbreak."

Lisa says, "I think that's spot on. I know he really wants the comfort of a loving partner. The question is, will he let himself have that?" Quinn's now chasing Maria back toward us, so our *tête-à-tête* is about to end. Lisa gives me a half-hug and says, "He deserves happiness, Hallie. So do you."

Back in Sconset Center a half hour later, we spot our cabbie, chilling by his taxi near the post office, puffing away. He's already been to town and back. We snag him for the rest of the afternoon and, following his suggestions, dive into full-on tourist mode.

First stop: Altar Rock. It's the island's highest point, offering a stunning 360-degree view of Nantucket. Next up: Bartlett's Farm. It's a fall-fest there—tables piled with bundles of carrots, crates of shiny zucchini, cucumbers and peppers, trays of tomatoes and beets, corn in husks. Giggling kids clamber over an antique red tractor.

While Maria and Lisa are wandering through all the produce, I buy a cup of fresh peach ice cream for Quinn and me to share. "We'll share a spoon, too," I say. I lock eyes with him, then slowly draw the cream-filled spoon into my mouth. I prep a spoonful for him and say, "Your turn." I do a slow-motion lip lick, then send the spoon on a direct flight to his mouth. I watch his face as the flavor explosion hits him.

Now I up my flirt game, fill the spoon again and ever-so slowly lick around its edge, moaning as I do so, then close my mouth around all of it, like I'm in a soft-porn version of a dessert commercial.

I refill the spoon and aim it toward Quinn's eager mouth. "Eyes closed this time, please." His eyes shut and his mouth open like a fish, he's anticipating another taste of heaven. But I start scarfing down the ice cream like it's the last meal on a deserted island. He opens his eyes and a "you've got to be kidding me" expression overtakes his face. I giggle and say, "The best way to disable a male competitor is to invite Eros to join the party. Distract 'em with Cupid's arrow."

"Cheater! No fair using feminine wiles to get more ice cream!"

"I didn't, sweet cheeks. I used male weakness." I give him the last two spoonfuls as Maria returns to us, having picked up pumpkin bread for tomorrow's breakfast, and Lisa's right behind her, having snagged a couple dozen elegant beeswax tapers, now wrapped in white tissue with an orange ribbon.

A hop, skip, and a jump later, we're at Cisco Brewers, where we park ourselves on some scratchy hay bales, basking in the sun, drinks in hand—hot Cisco Ciders for Maria and me, a Pumple Drumkin iced ale for Quinn, and bottled water for Lisa.

Finally, at our cabbie's suggestion, we cap off the afternoon at Madaket Beach. From this westernmost point on the island, we watch the sun dip, spraying the clouds with orange and red hues and spilling bits of the same onto the whitecaps below.

14

Quinn

Around 7:45, a bit wobbly and giddy after a boozy, rich meal on the outdoor patio at American Seasons, we zigzag our way down Centre Street to Broad and then to Steamboat Wharf. Masks on, we board the ferry back to Hyannis like a band of merry pirates. Before the ship can even wiggle out of its moorings, Lisa and Maria are already snoozing, their heads lolling back in an ungraceful ballet. Hallie and I, perched a couple rows ahead, are still riding the vinous wave from dinner, our spirits high from the sheer joy we get from being together. We dive into easy conversation.

After a while, Hallie leans in, her voice soft and gentle. "I feel like we didn't get a chance to finish our talk from this morning. Want to pick it up again? If so, I'm all ears."

To be honest, I'm on the fence about sharing more.

Discussing my treatment is one thing, but wading into the murky waters of its aftermath is quite another. It's not as if I haven't spoken about it before. Some people I know seem weirdly intrigued and won't leave the topic alone. There's this guy in the History department who always gets his face right up close to mine and whispers, 'How *are* you?' What he's really asking is, 'So, is the machinery still in working order?' His curiosity borders on the macabre, a morbid fascination with my personal hydraulics. But he's not typical. Most guys would rather walk the plank than discuss it. They wouldn't want to talk about it if they were in my shoes, and they assume I don't either.

I've never discussed this with a woman, except Alison, of course. When I started regaining some sexual function, I was always anxious about what Alison thought of the new me. Her assurances felt like double-edged swords—claiming she harbored no expectations and that the changes were of no consequence to her. I didn't know what to make of that, and her comments raised a lot of questions in my already muddled head. I ended up seeing a psychologist who specializes in counseling cancer patients. She helped me rethink my ideas of what intimacy is, what it means to have a physical connection with someone.

Admitting all this to myself is hard enough, voicing it feels like scaling Everest. Yet there's this urge to let Hallie in on this chapter of my life. It's not just about unburdening myself to her; it's about showing trust. And maybe it will bring us still closer, make it easier for her to talk if she has anything she wants to share with me.

"Sure. Why not?" I muster, cloaking my trepidation with a veil of nonchalance. "Now, where did I leave off?"

"You were in the thick of your radiation treatments,

wrestling with mood dragons, waiting to see if you'd get an 'all clear' signal from the doctor."

"Ah, yes. Right," I exhale. "The tests eventually showed no cancer, but, of course, that doesn't mean 'cured.' Regular checks every few months are my new normal. Still, it was a huge relief."

"Not easy living under that sword of Damocles."

"No, but I don't dwell on it much." I pause a long beat, then acknowledge the elephant seated between us. "The question you haven't asked is whether I'm incontinent or impotent."

"We don't have to go there, if you don't want to. It's none of my business."

Maybe she's just being polite and really doesn't want to discuss this. But she asked for the remainder of the story, so I decide to dive in. "No, I'll tell you. There's no one I'd feel more at ease sharing this with."

She holds my hand, covering it with her other. "That's sweet of you. I appreciate that you trust me."

"Okay. So, on the topic of incontinence—I'm guessing you'd have noticed if that was an issue."

She nudges me playfully with her shoulder. "Maybe. And what about the other ... um, concern?"

Her lighthearted demeanor helps ease the tension. "Well, as for that, I guess one could say the ... uh, equipment works okay."

"Okay?"

"Yeah. Things don't work as well as they did when I was 21, but then again, what does at my age?" She chuckles, sharing in the humor of the human condition. "And it's a lot better than it was the first couple years after the surgery, when I waited— somewhat impatiently, I must tell you—for the swaggering, jubilant return of Mr. Something Percent." Hallie bursts out laughing. I give her a sad, puppy-dog look. "Oh, it was awful. Even with the help of 'the little blue pill,' my progress was slow, lackluster ... droopy. Like a cut string."

Her whole upper body now shakes with laughter. "Forgive me," she says, wiping her eyes. "I know it's not funny, but you must admit you're telling this in a very humorous way."

I nod. "That's true. And I'm glad you're laughing." I catch her gaze and hold it. "Let's see what you think of this." I lower the volume of my voice a couple notches, so I'm now speaking barely above a whisper. "My first climax after the whole ordeal was a pretty stark reminder I wasn't the same man I'd been before the treatment."

She clears her throat. Concern permeates her tone when she asks, "Why? What do you mean? It wasn't very good? Painful?"

Oh, god, why did I let myself go down this path. How to say it? "The sensation was ... well, almost as good, but ... nothing came out! It was dry as a tumbleweed. I hadn't realized: no prostate, no semen! My doctors never actually said anything to me about that. So, I was shocked that first time. I didn't understand what was happening—or what wasn't happening." I scrunch my eyes and wiggle my fingers in her face, "I'm a Phantom-cummer!"

Hallie's laughter fills the ferry's sitting area, piercing the relative silence and drawing the attention of some of the other passengers. Her amusement is infectious, and I can't help but laugh with her. As her giggles subside, she wipes tears from her eyes, letting out a deep sigh. "You really are a funny man, Quinn."

"Why, thank you. I aim to entertain. ... Like Puck, I hope nothing you heard made you too uncomfortable."

Her eyes reward me with a warm smile of recognition. "Ah, I wish that had merely been a midsummer night's dream for you, Quinn. Unfortunately, it was all too real. And really tough. I'm sorry you had to go through all that." She fidgets for a while with her jacket's zipper-pull like it's a puzzle she can't solve. I watch her mood turn; her smile slips away, leaving seriousness in its wake. Her gaze lifts to mine, heavy with intent and resolve. "Guess it's my turn."

I nod, waiting, wondering at what's to come.

She inhales deeply, as if bracing for a cold dive. "Well, like you, I also had a difficult situation with my reproductive system. ... I'll cut straight to the heart of it: in my mid-thirties, I had a hysterectomy."

Finding the right words feels like navigating a minefield, but saying nothing doesn't feel like the right course. How hard for you, Hallie. Do you want to talk about it?"

She appears to waver. "Well, I don't know ..." Then, with a self-deprecating knock on her forehead, she laughs at herself. "What am I saying? I guess I do! I'm the one who brought it up!"

The damn mask prevents her from seeing my smile, but my eyes offer her a bridge to cross, and she takes it. "It's actually pretty straightforward. I battled with severe, painful periods for years. Then, in my early 30s, it escalated. Bleeding between periods, unbearable pain. Turned out to be endometriosis. You know what that is?"

I nod. "The condition where the uterine lining grows outside the uterus?"

"Exactly. My doctor first chose a conservative treatment involving a hormone therapy, progestin—that had delightful side effects: weight gain, depression, acne, body hair ... So, when you told me what you went through, I could relate."

"Oh, no. I'm sorry."

She gives me a reassuring smile. "It was no fun, as you know, but I came through it alright. Anyway, my doc didn't want to leave me on those meds long because doing so leads to bone-density loss and increased risk of fractures. But some next step was necessary, and there weren't too many options. Surgery's not usually a desirable one, because it's so consequential. But because I had no interest in having children, my doc and I opted for it. So, when I was 36, they removed my uterus and ovaries."

"That's monumental, especially so young."

She acknowledges that, then flips to a lighter tone, bringing her mouth to my ear and whispering. "And just so you know, sex is still something I enjoy. If anything, it's better since the surgery."

The unabashed candor of her revelation hits me with a jolt, though an admittedly pleasant one. But the surprise of it causes my face to jerk up to hers.

Explaining her disclosure, she says, "I hoped you'd care. ... Do you?" Her question hangs in the air, charged with hope and desire.

"Of course, I care. In fact, maybe we could—"

Just as I'm about to elaborate, Maria materializes out of the ether with god-awful timing. "Hey there. We're almost at port. Wanted to make sure you two hadn't fallen into a deep slumber."

"Oh, we're wide awake!" Hallie responds with a chuckle. Maria's gaze bounces between us, as if she's satisfying herself on the veracity of Hallie's claim. "Okay, good."

The drive back to Chatham is quiet, with Lisa and Maria surrendering to sleep once more. Meanwhile, Hallie and I, having navigated our personal revelations with pluck and mutual empathy, bask in the warmth of our deepened connection.

Once home, our little group disperses toward slumber's call. Maria and Lisa disappear into their rooms down one hallway, while Hallie and I linger in our shared corridor. Pausing outside her bedroom, I capture the moment. "Today was incredible, Hallie. I had a great time. And thanks for opening up about your past troubles. I'm relieved to hear you're not in pain anymore."

She leans on her door, her smile a soft light in the darkened hallway. "That's sweet of you. And I should be the one thanking you. Opening up about what you've been through, sharing something so personal. ... That's huge. It's a big part of you. And I care about all of you, deeply. Every part of you." Her touch is gentle on my cheek.

I smile at the innuendo, intended or not, and try to match her. "Thank you. It means a lot to me that you care ... about the, uh, whole package, so to speak."

She laughs. "Well, I'm here for all of it, Quinn. The ups, the droopy downs, and everything in between."

I laugh, too, stammering and stuttering as I struggle with how to ask her to come to my room. "You know, I've been wondering—"

She presses her index finger to my lips, shushing me. "May I ask you something?"

"Sure. Anything."

Hallie takes one of my hands in hers. "Would you like to come in? See what number we can get Mr. Something Percent up to?"

She sees the answer in my eyes, so turns and opens the door. We tumble in.

15

Quinn

As we finish cleaning up the last of the dishes from our evening meal, I announce I'll be watching the final election debate airing later this evening. By unspoken agreement, the six of us largely have avoided discussing politics. So, my mention of the Biden-Trump debate causes some faces to tighten. They all nod half-heartedly as if agreeing to join me, but within the next thirty minutes, Paul and Lisa disappear into their bedroom with books in hand, and Mike claims he has urgent work that needs his attention.

So, at 9:00 PM, it's just Maria, Hallie, and me, plunking ourselves in front of the huge TV that looms over the living room like an incubus. Hallie and I claim opposite territories on the couch, while Maria settles into a pillowy armchair. The debate kicks off. Initially, at least, it's a surprisingly less chaotic affair than its predecessor. Trump's advisors seem to have convinced him to curtail his interruptions, paving the way for something that vaguely resembles an actual debate.

But as Trump doubles down on his ridiculous claims that the coronavirus is "under control"—the U.S. "rounding the corner" on it—Maria stands and jeers, "Yeah, you call it, 'rounding the corner'; the rest of us call it 'going in circles.' You motherfucker! We're making as much forward progress as ... horses on a Coney Island carousel!" She turns to me and Hallie. "Sorry, I can't take any more of this. I'm going up to read before my head explodes."

I suggest to Hallie that if she and I are to brave the remainder of this spectacle we'll require the fortifying effects of more wine. Turns out, a lot more is necessary. So, by the time the debate has ended, we're decidedly less burdened. With a flick of the remote, I turn off the TV, then pivot toward Hallie, stretching my stripe-socked feet her way. She mirrors my position, her feet gently brushing against my legs in a silent dialogue. "What shall we talk about?" I ask.

Her reply comes with a playful, naughty edge. "Who said anything about wanting to talk?"

I lob the tease back at her. "What do you suggest doing instead?"

She answers with a suggestive eyebrow wiggle.

"Hey, you don't want to discover the corrupting effects of alcohol on my already compromised ... capabilities. I doubt you'd find Mr. ... 30 percent sufficiently pleasing."

She giggles. "Just so you know: I'd find Mr. 10 percent pleasing. Besides, you showed me the other night that you have, um, *other* skills." She jabs me playfully. "Mr. Something Percent better watch out! He could well find himself out of a job!"

"You're a very funny person!" I chuckle, nudging her in

return. Then, with a more earnest tone, I ask, "Why do you think that is?"

"Hmmm. I guess I've never really dissected it." She pauses. After a few beats of reflection, she says, "Perhaps it's genetic? Both my parents were funny, quick-witted. So, there's that. Plus, I learned at an early age that wit and humor are the ultimate social lubricants; they go a long way in making friends. I have a bit of a knack for it, so I milk it."

"Bit of a knack! That's an understatement. I've never known anyone who makes me laugh as much as you do."

"Well, thanks. You're nice to say that, Quinn. The downside, I suppose, is that I sometimes use humor as a shield, a way of keeping people at arm's length or deflecting attention from serious subjects."

I sip my wine and consider this. "I understand. ... I often use it to avoid conflict." I pause, considering my aversion to discord. "I suppose it's a character flaw," I admit. Hallie starts to object, but I hurry on. "Not that there's anything great about conflict. But it's an unavoidable part of life. People have different interests and preferences, so we're bound to rub each other the wrong way at times. Dodging conflict doesn't really solve anything, but confrontations have never been my cup of tea."

Hallie cocks an eyebrow, ready to challenge my self-critique. "Okay, but isn't it going too far to call an aversion to conflict a character flaw?"

"No, I don't think so. ... It makes it hard for me to confront issues head-on or speak up about things that might ruffle others' feathers. I'd rather retreat or act as though all's well. And that's no good."

Her gaze is steady, thoughtful. "Remember how you didn't back down from Paul that night he made those cringey comments about lesbians? You didn't hesitate to put him in his place. You shut him down faster than a ninja on cocaine. You dove right into conflict that evening. You didn't hesitate to confront him. You were like a superhero for social justice." She pauses a few beats, then adds, "Speaking of Paul ... I don't think he likes me very much."

"Why do you say that?"

"Just various interactions I've had with him. His general affect with me."

I consider this. "Paul's intimidated by super-smart, witty women. They're kryptonite to him."

"'Super-smart and witty' eh?"

"Did I say that?" I grin, the picture of innocence.

"You did."

"Don't think so."

"Did."

"Didn't."

She grabs my socked foot and stabs her thumb into my sole.

"Ouch!"

"Admit it."

"No."

"Admit it or suffer." She digs harder.

"Alright, alright! Uncle!"

We sit for a moment, beaming at each other. She starts to gently stroke my sole with her thumb. I say, "Amazing what a different effect the same little digit can have when used properly." When she starts more fully massaging my foot, I moan.

"Did Alison give you foot massages?"

"No, not a part of our repertoire. In fact, I don't think I've ever received a foot massage before. It's nice. Thank you. ... Come to think of it, though, I did give Alison a few foot massages near the end of her life."

She fixes me with an empathetic gaze. "I've thought a

number of times how hard her last few months must've been for you."

"The last few weeks were especially excruciating. I felt powerless. And she withdrew ... lost in her religious fantasy, which was always hard for me to deal with."

"I'm not sure what you mean by fantasy."

"Oh, I'm just being nasty by referring to her faith as religious fantasy. To me, that's all faith is. Yet, for her, it was as real as the air we breathe. That difference in our view was always a source of tension between us. She was immersed in her Catholic beliefs, convinced that her suffering, offered up in prayer, could elevate her soul, earn her a 'higher place in heaven.' And her cancer gave her plenty of suffering for her greedy god. So, yeah, in her final weeks, she just shrank into some inner world and became unreachable. It may have helped her, but it magnified my pain a hundredfold."

"That sounds so hard, Quinn. I can't imagine."

"Yeah, it was. ... Anyway, I suppose I should be happy for her that she had her faith to comfort her at the end."

A long pause. She asks, "Were you raised in a religious tradition?"

"I was raised Catholic, too—something I'm always a bit uncomfortable admitting because I think the Catholic church is so despicable."

"What turned you away?"

"Growing up. Acquiring rationality. The Church's silly dogmas and orthodoxy no longer made any sense to me. The notion of an angry, spiteful, all-knowing god, eager to smite earthlings for their naughty thoughts and bad acts? Such nonsense. ... Or selling people the idea that if they went to Mass and received communion on the first Friday of the month for nine consecutive months, they'd basically get all their sins wiped off the slate and escape hell? Stuff like that was so ridiculous. Just a way of increasing church attendance and collection-plate takings. In fact, I gradually realized the whole enterprise is a money-making operation. It all struck me as immoral and insane. So, I walked away and never looked back. Been an atheist ever since. Sorry, is this a subject I should steer clear of?"

After a long pause, Hallie says, "No, that's basically me, too."

"Not a believer?"

"No. But in my case, it's less from having rejected bizarre religious dogmas than from never having marinated in them in the first place." She pauses. "My parents were half-hearted Unitarian Universalists."

"Half-hearted?"

"They didn't believe in organized religion—or a god—but worried about how to encourage in Carter and me a greater concern with the quality of the human spirit than with the material or physical, a respect for the web of existence and the search for truth. So, they occasionally took us to a church that had those moral values. Carter and I liked the youth group and appreciated that the UUs didn't try to ram the notion of a divine spirit down our throats."

I nod with respect for all that, then tease her. "You mean you don't believe there's a 'Supreme Being' out there that's going to scorch your sorry ass for screwing around with both sexes and not going to church every week? What are you, un-American?"

She laughs, then turns serious. "To me, it's sad that so many people choke back the ridiculousness of dogma in order to embrace the one thing they find comforting in religion—the idea of life after death."

I nod again. "Another thing I don't get."

"Neither do I. The notion of an afterlife—heaven, hell,

purgatory, ghosts haunting houses. Whatever. It's all idiotic. When you die, you're dead. End of story. And I'm okay with that. Frankly, I don't remember the black eternity before I was born as being so bad, so why should I be afraid of the dark eternity after I die?"

"Exactly my feeling!" I stretch toward her with a high five.

"And I always laugh when I see a single-panel comic that features a long check-in line at the pearly gates of heaven. It seems to me one point of heaven should be that you don't have to stand around in any fucking lines!"

"You're on a roll! I agree. And heaven itself isn't something I hanker for. After I leave this vale of tears, I look forward to a long rest. By myself! I don't want to spend eternity playing bocce with my dead uncles or pickleball with my nephews, no matter how nice the courts are in heaven. Anything would get pretty boring if you do it for eternity."

She bats her eyelids. "Even making love with me?"

"Well, now you're raising a difficult example." I smile, then adopt a determined expression. "But, yes, I'm sorry to tell you that I think if we do it for eternity, we'll both eventually find it boring. So what's the point of aspiring to some heaven? Eternity is just too damn long to do even the best things!"

"Okay. I grant you: making love with you might get tiresome after a thousand billion years, but I'm not bored yet!" She giggles and throws back the rest of her wine, then grabs my glass and downs its remaining ounce, too. *"Ad fundum."* Bottoms up. She pounces on me, pressing me into the deep couch cushions with every inch of her body.

16

Hallie

Quinn's busy writing letters of recommendation for a few students, so I head with my book to the sitting room at the other end of the second-floor corridor. As I pass Maria and Mike's bedroom, his voice, ringing with disbelief and frustration, pierces through the closed door.

" ... It's almost $25,000, Maria! What the hell did you do with it? Where did it go? No, don't turn away from me! Answer me! Now!"

I pause, rooted to the spot. Eavesdropping isn't in my nature, but concern for my friends overrides my guilt and better judgment. Maria's reply, broken by sobs, barely reaches my ears. "It was for José ... to help them."

"Who's José? Who's 'them'?" Mike demands.

A sound down the hall jolts me from my dishonorable

spying. I hurry away from the door, the argument fading into a hush as I distance myself. Dropping onto the sitting room's sofa, I toss *Ulysses* aside, uninterested in it for now. A storm outside sends windswept rain hard against the window, mirroring the churn of my thoughts. I groan, absolutely hating the thought of Mike and Maria in distress.

Sinking deeper into the cushions, I'm besieged by a memory —vivid, insistent. It's early September, and I'm with Maria, driving to the Dorchester food pantry. My mind sharpens the image, drawing connections. Could Maria have been funneling family funds to that guy she introduced me to—who she said is the linchpin of the Cape Verdean community? But why in secret?

My reverie shatters, as Maria, disheveled and tear-streaked, appears in the doorway. "I ... I didn't know anyone was in here," she stammers.

I draw her into the room, closing the French doors behind her, then wrap her in an embrace, feeling her tremble. Once her tears subside, we sit. "Talk to me, Maria."

"Oh, Hallie, I've screwed up!" She gradually spills the story. She's been regularly withdrawing money—at least once a week, usually in $500 increments—from an account she holds jointly with Mike. This has been going on since April. Right before we all came to the Cape, she withdrew $5,000. She guesses it all totals over $20,000. "Naturally, Mike's furious."

I wait for her breathing to slow and ask, as gently as I can, "What did you need the money for?"

"It wasn't for me. I took it to give to others."

"What do you mean? To whom?"

She sighs, wipes her nose with a tissue. "Remember when you and I went into Dorchester? You met José at the food pantry?"

"Yeah, I remember."

"I gave it to him. Nobody knows Boston's Cape Verdean community better than José. He knows who's sick, who's suffering in other ways. ... He knows where the greatest need is." She dabs again at her eyes and nose, then draws a deep breath before continuing. "After the pandemic started, I asked José what else I could do in addition to bringing groceries to the pantry. He looked me in the eye and said, 'People need money, Maria. They need cash.' So, I started making withdrawals and giving the cash to José. I knew he would get it to people who most needed it."

A flash of that thick white envelope passing from Maria to José sears my mind.

Another long pause. "I didn't intend to keep doing it, didn't mean for it to spiral out of control. I thought, initially, I'd give a few thousand dollars. But then I ... I just kept going."

"Why didn't you tell Mike?" I whisper, feeling hypocritical to be asking this in light of all the times I've withheld information from my own partners.

"By then I'd given many thousands and I was too embarrassed and too scared to tell him. I was in too deep."

"Did you think he wouldn't find out?"

"I thought he might not. I handle the finances, and he almost never checks the accounts. I'd swear he couldn't tell you the balance at any given time in that account—plus or minus $30,000 or so."

He wouldn't notice a $30,000 difference? I stop myself from saying how nice it'd be to have that kind of money, and remind myself that this is Maria's crisis, not mine. "How *did* Mike find out?"

"An ATM glitch led him to check the account online. And he saw all the withdrawals I'd made."

"Oh, Maria ..." I sigh, the weight of her predicament now pressing on us both.

"I know. I know!" she sobs, her body shaking with each word. "And the worst part is that he says he would've agreed to give the money, if I'd just asked." Silence engulfs the room, save for the rain's relentless drumming. Maria dabs her eyes. "I'm sorry to burden you with this ... I feel so foolish."

"Don't." Then, thinking of all the secrets I've kept and the times I've strained the trust of those close to me I say, "We all make mistakes. At least your mistake involved helping others."

She offers a watery smile, a semblance of gratitude. "Thanks, Hal." We sit quietly for a long moment. Then, she stands. "I should try talking to Mike again." Pausing at the door, she turns back. "Thanks for listening."

"It's what we do for each other, Maria. Friends, *sempre*."

17

Hallie

Quinn and I are hitting Provincetown today. He's never been there. The last few days, I've been all, "Oh, we've gotta go! You have to see it. It's the Las Vegas of the LGBTQ world!" As a courtesy, I tried to rope in Lisa and Maria, too. But Lisa opted out, claiming P-town isn't her "cup of tea" —more like not her cup of fabulous, I guess. And Maria? She begged off, probably thinking Quinn and I would want some "us" time. Bingo!

So, now we're in Quinn's car, cruising on Route 6 through Eastham, Wellfleet, and Truro—towns with names that sound like they've been lifted straight from a storybook. I steal occasional glances in his direction, pondering my feelings for him. In so many ways, he's not my type—if there is any "type" of male that best suits me. A college professor who probably hasn't changed his wardrobe or hairstyle since the Carter Administration? Nah. He's retro-chic without the chic. But there's so much about him that I find absolutely irresistible—his intelligence, his wit, his word wizardry. The way he listens to me. How I feel when I'm with him. And oh yes, the ways he makes love to me.

We finally reach P-town, and it's like stepping into a rainbow-colored wonderland. We wander down Commercial Street, taking in the kaleidoscope of shops, galleries, restaurants, and cruising bars. Quinn's not really conversant with all the varieties of gay men or lesbians we're seeing. He's wide-eyed, trying to keep up as I point out different tribe members—bulls, twinks, chubs, gym bunnies; stone butches, diesel dykes, soft bitches, lipstick lesbians, high femmes. His face is a picture of fascination mixed with a dash of 'what world am I in?'

"It's even wilder and more crowded in the summer," I tell him as we watch a group of men walk by, their shirtless torsos covered with glitter. "But this is a good time to visit, too. Gays love Halloween, so this is a town that takes Halloween seriously." We spot a haunted house touting "lesbian-feminist ghouls" and another, featuring monsters that include "demented women's studies professors" and "polyamorous vampiric sex-positive grannies." A sign outside of the "Blood House" a little farther down the street claims it's so scary a few customers have actually pissed their pants. The management now promises a free tee-shirt to any customer scared pee-less.

Quinn grins and says, "That's what I want to wear: a tee-shirt that says 'I pissed my pants at Blood House.' Good lord. What a world!"

Farther down, an elderly couple sits on a bench in front of a line of shops. Both of them smile and nod at everyone whose glance they manage to catch. I can't resist—I bust out a sponta-neous jig for them, ending with a dramatic "ta-da." They laugh, and the old man touches the brim of his hat to show his appreci-ation. Quinn gives me that 'you're-crazy-but adorable' look.

Lunch at a harbor-view restaurant gives us a front-row seat to Provincetown's charm. We're at an outdoor table on a deck overlooking the busy little port. Quinn orders a bottle of sauvi-gnon blanc, which we start on as we wait for the arrival of our orders—a blackened fish sandwich for me, fish and chips for Quinn.

He leans back in his chair, sweeps his gaze across the bustling harbor. "It's easy to see why artists are drawn to P-town. There's something about the light here, the way it plays on the water and the buildings ... it's like it's designed to inspire."

"It's true. I've heard that said about the light here. It sure is a magnet for creatives." Responding to that inspiration, I reach into my purse and whip out a pencil and a fine-tipped pen. I flip the paper placemat over, and on its blank white back begin to draw the harbor scene in front of us.

I start by laying down a light sketch of the basic composition—the horizon line, major elements like boats, docks, and build-ings, and a few foreground and background details. Then, pressing harder, I outline the elements with clean, sharp lines. Quinn watches me, his eyes filled with some mix of awe and admiration that delights me. I create texture and shading, rendering the ripples on the water, the architectural features of the buildings, and details of the boats, such as masts, ropes, and hulls. When I've done enough, I sign it with a flourish.

Just then, a tiny chihuahua in the lap of a brawny, tattooed biker-type on the other side of the deck erupts in a barking frenzy. On the placemat, I write "yip-yip" in an unmoored cartoon-speech bubble above my drawing, and 'toot-toot' in another—the latter, a nod to a whale-watching vessel now noisily leaving port. "I'm better at capturing scenes than sounds," I joke.

The muscular bull with the little dog walks by our table on his way out of the restaurant. He has one arm holding the chihuahua, the other wrapped around a tiny, pink-haired young man wearing robin-egg-blue satin hotpants. "That was fun, wasn't it, sweetie?" the big bull asks.

Once they've passed, Quinn and I look at each other and break into laughter. "Which of them was he talking to, the dog or the boy?" I whisper.

"The reply from either would've sounded about the same: 'Yip-yip.'"

I can't help but laugh still harder. "I don't know which I feel sorrier for."

Later, when the check arrives, I start to pull out some cash, but Quinn presses his hand on mine to stop me. "Please, no. This is on me. My pleasure."

"This not paying for things is charming, but—"

"But nothing. You can repay me with a little song and dance sometime. Or, better yet," he says, taking my now-finished placemat drawing, "you can let me have this." He holds the drawing up to the actual view, and smiles. "You're incredibly talented, Hallie. You could do this to earn some money until your theatre work starts up again."

"Yip-yip. Toot-toot," I reply, squirming away from a conversation I don't feel like having. He can't know that it's something I've been thinking about more and more lately—the possibility that I might do something other than stage design. I suppose I could make sketches and three-dimensional models for sale. But something with language—perhaps translating or editing—is a more powerful lure.

We retrieve Quinn's car and drive out to Race Point Beach, its wide swath of sand stretching far off into the distance around the point. I'd suggested Race Point rather than Herring Cove Beach, where the water would be calmer. "If it were summer, and we were going to swim, Herring Cove would be better. But this late in the season, we're not going in the water anyway, so we might as well enjoy the rougher surf. And I actually think the landscape is more picturesque here."

We lay down a blanket and ditch our shoes. "It'd take us about half an hour to walk down to the Race Point Lighthouse," I say. "Wanna do it?" Quinn's game, so off we go, chatting and flirting like we're in a cheesy rom-com. Soon, we spot three people about fifty yards ahead—a man and two women—huddled above a big dark object on the sand. "Ahoy! Beach mystery ahead!" I say to Quinn. Turns out, it's a sea turtle. "Ohhh, it's a Kemp's ridley!" I say.

The shorter woman nods to me. "Sad. It's probably cold-stunned. The water temperature is now about 55 degrees. Sometimes, the turtles can't escape the cooling waters to migrate south because they get caught here in the hook of the Cape. If they get cold enough, they stop feeding and swimming. And then, if there are strong winds, like today, they get blown ashore."

Quinn asks, "What are you trying to do with it?"

"When a cold-stunned sea turtle washes ashore, it often appears dead but is still alive. So, we were just carefully checking this one out. Unfortunately, this little guy has died." Then, gesturing toward her companions, she says, "The three of us are volunteers for Mass Audubon's Wildlife Sanctuary. In the last three days, we've rescued seven of these on the Lower Cape's bayside beaches."

"What do you mean? You take them somewhere away from here?" I ask.

"Yeah, if they're still alive, we take them to a care center in Quincy or Buzzards Bay where they get rehabilitated and eventually released. Last year, volunteers saved about 300 turtles that got stranded on the Lower Cape's bayside beaches. Some years, it's over a thousand."

"Wow, I had no idea!" Quinn says. "I thought sea turtles were bigger than this."

I say, "Kemp's ridleys are the smallest of all sea turtles." Quinn gives me an inquiring glance, wondering at my knowledge of turtle trivia. "My dad taught me about them," I say. Turning to the volunteers, I ask, "Do you need a hand here?"

"That's okay. We've got it."

"Okay," I say. "Thank you for your good work." We walk silently for a while. Eventually, I let out a groan, releasing the emotion that's been building in me. "Life is so fragile. I always find it sobering when I see an animal that's died. I once saw a deer that had tried to jump over a spiked, wrought-iron fence. It was hanging there, dead, half-way over, impaled on the spikes. I almost threw up."

Quinn squeezes my hand. "You're a gentle soul."

"Thank you." I squeeze his in return. "But, no, I'm just a ... well, I don't know what I am!" I say with a laugh. "Frankly, sometimes I think I'm overly sensitive. Lately, I have a hard time with moments like these. I don't know. Maybe it's an effect of living through this pandemic. It feels like we're surfeited by reminders of our vulnerability and the delicate balance of life."

He nods. "We tend to go about our lives without thinking

about death. But nature has its way of reminding us of reality, doesn't it?" Then Quinn surprises me. He turns me fully toward him, lifts my chin, and says, "I've learned we should make the most of the time we have, with people who matter to us." His eyes gleam with meaning. "It's why I want to spend time with you, Hallie."

A warmth spread through me, pushing out the chill that's seeped in. "And I with you." I raise onto my toes and quickly kiss him. "I'm so happy we've met."

He wraps his arms around me and holds me close. I feel myself loosen with—what is that?—contentment, anticipation, hope. I reach behind his neck and pull his mouth to mine. Our lips slide against each other's for a while, then our tongues explore. The kiss turns more urgent, our breaths quickening and deepening. When he presses his mouth on my neck and scrapes his teeth down to my collarbone, I shudder and moan. He hardens against me, and—dear god!—I want to rip his clothes off. "I want to do unspeakable things to you," I whisper in his ear. I bite his lobe, then add a long exhale of warm breath. He moans. I playfully rub my pelvis against his. When he moans again, I spin away from him.

"Oh, god, no! Don't you dare move away! Hallie, come back here!"

I squirm, evading his efforts to grab me. "I know, I know! Believe me, I know. I want you, too. But if we keep that up, all hell's gonna break loose right here, and I do NOT like sand in my crevices!" He's chasing me in circles, and in the soft sand we get winded quickly. He stops pursuing me and stands whimpering, comically hangdog—his shoulders deflated, his hands hanging low at his sides. The look of desperation in his eyes makes me laugh. I say, "I promise that tonight I'll make you glad we waited."

"Really? Dead promise? Pinky swear?" He holds out his

little finger, waiting for me to hook it in agreement. When I get close enough, he lunges at me. I shriek and barely manage to elude him. Eventually, we stop behaving like middle-schoolers and resume our trek. Reaching the grounds of the lighthouse, we circumnavigate the tower a couple times. I take photos from multiple angles. Quinn says, "Maybe someday you could draw that for me?"

I kiss his cheek. "Maybe. If you play your cards right."

As we head back, the wind stiffens, and the surf grows heavy. I comment that I should've worn something heavier. Quinn takes off his jacket and helps me into it. "Thank you," I say. "That's much better. Let me know if you get too chilly."

We walk along in silence. The wildness of the beach mimics the turmoil that's growing within me as I try to decide whether now would be a good time to tell him. I hadn't intended to bring it up today, but I'm feeling close to him right now, and this seems as good a time as any. I swallow back my reluctance and say, "Quinn, there's something I've been waiting to tell you. About my past. Would that be okay?"

Quinn's brow furrows. "Of course. You can tell me anything."

"I've never told a man this about myself. We'll see how it goes." We resume our pace, and I take a long pause before continuing. "When I was eight years old, I was sexually abused by an older cousin—repeatedly, over the course of a summer. He had come to stay with my family for a couple months."

Quinn's face fills with concern and what looks like pain. He clearly wants to say something, but stays quiet, waiting for me to decide how much I want to tell him.

"Before all this happened, I had adored him. His name was Alex. He was seventeen. In my eyes, he was so smart, so handsome and funny. Carter was away for two months at summer camp. So, my parents had asked Alex to stay with us to take care of me when they were working. A couple weeks after he arrived, my parents went away overnight." My breath comes harder now.

Quinn squeezes my hand. "You can tell me anything you want. Or nothing at all. Whatever you feel comfortable saying."

I nod, gathering the strength to resume. "He ... came to my room soon after I went to bed their first night away, and he ... oh, I just can't tell you the details, not now. Anyway, that's when it started. He ... said it was a game ... a 'body game' ... our own secret game."

Quinn hugs me tight. "Oh, Hallie."

"A game. What did I know? I was eight! Not even a hundred months old! When I'd tell him he was hurting me, he'd shush me, tell me I was okay. He said there was nothing bad about our game but that my parents might not like that we were playing it. My mom had a temper. He knew I wouldn't want to anger her. So I went along with him. And I stayed quiet about it. This went on for weeks—whenever we were home alone, which was often. I did what he told me to do. And I let him do whatever he wanted to do to me."

"Oh, Jesus, Hallie, I'm so sorry."

And with that, the dam inside me bursts. I sink to my knees on the sand—sobbing, releasing long, shuddering howls of agony. Quinn drops to his knees, too, and again holds me close. We stay like that for a long time.

Gradually, we get to our feet, and I continue. "Eventually, I got to the point where I couldn't stand his game any longer. I hated everything about it. I tacked a sign on my door saying, 'KEEP OUT!! This means YOU, Alex!!' "I told my mother I wanted her to send Alex home. She was angry about that and wanted to know why. But I couldn't bring myself to tell her the real reasons—what he'd done, what I'd done. I couldn't. I just couldn't! And I never did."

Quinn stops walking and searches my face. "I ... I don't know what to ..."

I press my finger to his lips. "It's okay. You don't have to say anything. There's really nothing to be said. It's enough that you've let me tell you about it—that you've listened."

Quinn nods, a softness in his eyes that makes my heart ache. He pulls me close and enfolds me in his embrace. "I'm so sorry, Hallie. I had no idea you'd been through something so horrible." When I finally pull away from the hug, his gaze lingers on me and he holds both my hands. "You're strong," he whispers, his voice hoarse with emotion. "But you don't have to carry this burden alone anymore. You have me now."

My thoughts spin and collide. I feel exposed, yet empowered. As we find our way back to our blanket and shoes, I decide to take a further chance and tell Quinn about the effects of the trauma on my relationships, hoping it may give him a better understanding of me. "Quinn, there's one more thing I should say about all this ..." I pause a moment, gathering my thoughts. "I think part of why I've never been able to stay in a long-term relationship—why I always engineer a break-up—is because of what happened to me that summer. It left me feeling somehow tainted, unworthy of love."

I stop and take his hands in mine, squeezing them. "It's text-book psychology, isn't it? If that happened to me, then I must be worthless! I can't convince myself that anyone would really want to be with me. And if they appear to want that, then there must be something inauthentic about it—or something wrong with them. So, the couple times I've gotten really serious with some-one, I've ended up pushing them away."

Quinn's eyes soften with understanding. Then he cups my

face in his hands and gazes at me with an intensity that makes my heart flutter. I blush, feeling self-conscious under his ardent stare, a mix of adoration and admiration that's exhilarating, almost overwhelming. He rests his forehead against mine, our breaths mingling in the space between us. The words come from him on a long exhale, his voice barely above a whisper. "I'm not going to let you push me away, Hallie. You can try, but I'm not going anywhere. Being with you feels like home."

18

Maria

For our dinner, I'd whipped up a savory *buzio*, a slow-cooked stew brimming with mussels. Three bottles of *Pouilly-Fumé* are now just decorative empties on the counter; a fourth dwindling fast on the dining table. We've been indulging in the stew and sipping wine for what feels like hours now. Paul and Mike aren't here. They've zipped back to Boston for a couple days. Paul needed to grab some documents from his home office. When Mike caught wind of Paul's plan to go, he jumped on the Boston bandwagon, claiming he needed some work stuff, too. But between you and me, I think he's just avoiding me—he's still fuming and can't stand being in my presence.

With those two out of the equation, there's definitely a

different vibe at the dinner table. For starters, Lisa's wine intake seems to ramp up when Paul's not in her orbit. Also, when Paul's around, we typically avoid touchy subjects because he's human dynamite, his fuse easily lit. But tonight, the four of us have been deep-diving into all things political, the conversation now alighting on Amy Coney Barrett's recent elevation to the Supreme Court and what that means for hot-button issues like abortion rights and the fate of Obamacare.

Lisa's a bit tipsy, navigating her thoughts like a driver on a foggy road. "I'm no expert on how the Court works, but the whole ... *Roe* v. *Wade* thing being in jeopardy with Barrett's rise ... it's just scary to think about," she mumbles, eyeing the wine bottle as if it's silently begging her to have another glass. She gives in to its plea.

Hallie chimes in, echoing Lisa's concern. "I really feel for all the women who would be harmed if they overturn it."

Lisa's voice is unsteady. "At the clinic where I volunteer, I see them ... women of all ages. It's in their eyes—getting an abortion isn't a walk in the park. It's a heavy choice." She pauses, appearing to gather her thoughts. Just as Quinn opens his mouth to speak, Lisa continues, her words gaining momentum. "For many of them, having a child just seems ... impossible. Their life circumstances don't allow it. They come in to us, feeling ... cornered." She punctuates her point with a flourish of her wine glass, sending a mini tidal wave of wine sloshing over the table and onto Hallie.

As Hallie dabs at her wine-soaked clothes, and I tackle the spill on the table, Quinn says, "I've never shared this, but Alison had an abortion a year before we got married."

Lisa's eyes widen. "Really? I never knew that!"

"Yeah, it was awful. The pregnancy hit us like a ton of bricks. We were ultra-cautious—she always used a diaphragm, I always used a condom. We thought we were being more than careful enough. But life throws curveballs. She missed a period, and the pregnancy test tossed a big, nasty wrench into our lives."

Lisa lets out a sympathetic grunt, slapping the table. "Ooohhh, that sucks!"

"We were both swamped with grad school, flat broke, not even living together. The problem seemed insurmountable. It was a heart-wrenching decision, a really tough call. After wrestling with it, we felt we had no other choice."

As Hallie and Lisa murmur empathetic words, I stay quiet, the conversation tugging at my own conflicted feelings. Abortion is a topic I usually steer clear of, my views shaped by my Catholic background. I see abortion as an option only in dire situations like rape and incest, or to save the mother's life. These beliefs often set me apart in discussions, especially outside my Cape Verdean community. I've learned that voicing my stance usually leads to disapproval and fierce arguments. Tonight, I'm not in the mood for either.

Lisa, still showing empathy to Quinn, says to him, "And you were, what—in your mid-twenties? Just think about these high school girls, barely seventeen or eighteen, grappling with such a decision! How are they supposed to handle a baby? They've got their whole lives ahead of them. It's heart-breaking."

Quinn nods solemnly, "Absolutely."

After a moment of heavy silence, Lisa locks eyes with me. "Like your Jolivia!" she blurts, her fingers clumsily closing around her wine glass. "Just think if she had ... if she'd gone through with the pregnancy!"

A thick silence descends. I feel like I've been smacked in the head, stars spinning in cartoon fashion. Confused, I glance at Hallie, seeking some kind of explanation. What is Lisa implying?

Is she just hypothesizing about Jolivia being in a similar situation?

But Lisa doesn't stop. "I mean, I wasn't there to counsel her, so I can't say what she was thinking—"

"Hold on, Lisa! What are you getting at?" Panic grips me. I exchange a bewildered look with Hallie. I move quickly to Lisa's side, kneeling and gripping her forearm. "Lisa, what are you saying? Did Jolivia ... did she have an abortion at the Brookline clinic?"

Lisa looks at me, shock registered on her face. "Well, yeah. But you knew that, right?" She squints, dismissing the topic with a hand wave.

"I knew nothing about this. When did this happen?"

Lisa thinks. "Their senior year. Late May, I think."

"You're saying Jolivia went to the clinic for ... an abortion?"

Lisa straightens up, the gravity of her revelation now hitting her like a jolt of adrenaline. "Yes, I assumed you knew."

"I had no idea." Why would she think that?

Lisa tries to be more composed. "You told me you and Joli are open with each other about sex and intimacy, about your bodies ... You said she doesn't hide anything from you. I just assumed ..."

I take a deep breath to steady myself against these twin shocks—news of the abortion, yes, but, even worse, the realization that my bond with Joli isn't as close as I'd thought. She was having sex her senior year, and didn't tell me. "Well, I didn't know."

Lisa turns to Hallie and Quinn, seeming to plead for support, but not getting it.

I press on. "You say you weren't there. So, how do you know she ..."

Now noticeably more alert, she explains. "I volunteer at the clinic on Mondays and Thursdays. Jolivia came on a Tuesday. She was counseled by staff, then had to wait 24 hours before she could come back for the procedure. So, I wasn't there either of the days she came in. But that Thursday I was processing paperwork from the previous day, and I saw Jolivia's name on a set of forms."

A groan escapes me. Hallie moves over and hugs me from behind. "Keep going," I urge Lisa.

"I wondered if it might be someone else. But the address matched."

"Did you ever talk to Maddie or Jolivia about it?"

"No, that would breach confidentiality."

I snap, "But haven't you violated her privacy here tonight?"

When Lisa tears up, Quinn intervenes. "Maria, Lisa didn't mean any harm. She was trying to show empathy."

Lisa manages a wan smile for Quinn before her thin body starts to tremble, her sobs loud and guttural—each one, punctuated by a sharp intake of breath and followed by a shaky exhale.

As Quinn and Hallie help Lisa away to her bedroom, I'm left alone, my mind racing. This revelation about Joli has hit me like a thunderbolt. Why hadn't she confided in me? A deep sigh escapes me as I clamp my eyes shut, trying to process it all.

When Quinn and Hallie return, we silently clear the remnants of our meal, careful to avoid stepping on any more landmines. Hallie extinguishes the candles, and smoke curls toward the ceiling like dark whispers. Quinn busies himself with making coffee. Soon, we gather in the living room, Hallie and I on the plush sofa, Quinn in an armchair nearby.

I sink into the cushions, overwhelmed by emotion. "Oh, God. This is just awful."

Hallie's arm is warm and comforting as it gently drapes around me. "I'm sorry, sweetie."

"Why didn't she turn to me?" I cry in bewilderment.

"She probably was scared, unsure of how to approach you," Hallie suggests gently.

Each of us is lost in thought. Eventually, Quinn speaks up, "This might not directly relate, but it's worth mentioning: Alison was close to her mom, but couldn't talk with her about the abortion—even at the age of 23, five years older than Jolivia was. Maybe these things are just too sensitive, too personal to share."

I nod, unconvinced, then ask, "What should I do? Should I talk to Joli about it?"

After a moment of contemplation, Hallie replies, "Honestly, I don't see how you can't. It'll drive you crazy if you sit on it. And it's possible she's distressed by her decision to keep it from you. It might be a relief to her to know the truth is out, to be able to talk about it."

"Perhaps," I murmur.

Later, in the solitude of my bedroom, sleep eludes me. Despite the wine's dulling effect, my mind races with unanswered questions. Why didn't Joli tell me she was having sex? She promised me she would. Was Marcus the father? He was her serious boyfriend all of senior year. I remember being so disappointed when they'd broken up that summer. Had he accompanied her to the abortion clinic? Had he helped pay for the procedure? My thoughts whirl with uncertainties.

When I was in my sophomore year of college, I was involved with a boy named Jerome. We'd been cautious, never going all the way—I'd been firm about that. But we did pretty much everything else. And then my period was alarmingly late. Panic set in. How could I be pregnant? Had semen seeped into me or entered on his fingers? I remember the fear, the relentless anxiety. Eventually, my period arrived, its onset probably delayed by my stress and anxiety. At that moment, I didn't care about the reasons, I just was relieved not to be pregnant. I knew the challenges faced by many of my cousins and friends who had babies at that early age. And I didn't want that for myself. My education was too important to me.

Now, all I can think about is how crazed and desperate Joli must've felt! I try to recall any signs of distress during those late months of her senior year—was she unusually emotional, withdrawn, angry? Nothing stands out. She and Marcus had attended the prom. Was that before or after the abortion? What emotions were they grappling with? I resolve to talk to Joli in the morning. I'll never make sense of all this without doing that. When the churning of my thoughts finally slows, a fitful sleep claims me.

The next morning, I decide against a FaceTime call, not wanting to force Joli to deal with the issue on the fly. I opt for a more considerate approach: I write her an email, letting her know how I found out, reassuring her of my love and support, and expressing my desire to talk. This way, she'll have time to prepare herself emotionally for our conversation.

So, after I have breakfast and enough coffee to face the task, I compose the email and ask her to contact me via Zoom or Face-Time when she's ready.

Two hours later, Joli calls me on the phone, her voice thick with tears. "Hi, *Manman*."

"Oh, *chérie*, I'm so sorry you had to go through all that alone. I love you endlessly, no matter what. I'm here for you, always. I can't imagine what you've been through."

Joli tries to talk, but all she can do is cry.

"Why didn't you feel you could come to me?" I ask her.

"I don't know ... I didn't want to disappoint you. I ... I was afraid of losing your respect. If I'd had a ..."

She can't bring herself to say 'baby.'

"... My whole life would've changed ... I was in such a panic. It didn't feel like I had any other option."

"And you were afraid I'd try to talk you out of getting an abortion?"

"... Yeah."

"You didn't even tell me you and Marcus were intimate."

"I know. I'm sorry."

"It's my fault I didn't make our relationship comfortable enough for you to come to me. I'm sorry about that." I wonder if asking how the pregnancy occurred will seem like I'm blaming her. But I decide to broach it. "How do you think it happened?"

A long pause. "Over the weekend of February break, I lied and told you I was staying at Maddie's house in Chestnut Hill. But Marcus and I went with Maddie and Tyler to where you are now—the Campbells' house in Chatham. That was the first time we had sex. Both of us had too much to drink, and we didn't take precautions. We did every time after that, but not then."

I stifle a groan. We talk for another half hour. Gently as I can, I probe how Joli had reached the decision; how they'd paid for the procedure; how she'd felt afterwards, both emotionally and physically; how she feels about all of it now.

Eventually, Joli asks, "Is Daddy upset?"

"He doesn't know about it, Jo. He and Maddie's dad are in Boston for a couple days, so he wasn't at dinner last night when this came out."

"Can we not tell him?" Joli begs through her tears.

"I don't know, chérie. Seems like a bad idea to keep it from him. Secrets can be corrosive. And people get angry if they find out they've been left in the dark about something important. Let me think about it."

"*Manman*? ... I'm mad at Maddie's mom for telling you all this. Isn't that an ethical violation? Isn't there some privacy law against that?"

"Yes, there is. But, *chérie*, as I explained this morning in my email, Lisa thought I already knew. I don't think we should blame her. It just happened."

"Well, I'm still angry."

After our call, I take a long walk to clear my head. Returning home, I find Hallie and Lisa in the kitchen. They're aware I had intended to talk to Joli this morning. They ask how it went. I share the gist of our conversation, including Joli's struggles that summer, when she'd felt guilty, ashamed, empty, depressed. I disclose my feelings of failure, my guilt over not having been more attuned to Joli's travails.

Lisa's cellphone rings with the tone of an incoming Face-Time call, and she answers it. "Hi, Maddie!"

"Mom!! Joli just told me what you did!" Maddie shouts. Her anger pours through the little speaker on Lisa's phone and echoes around the kitchen. "How could you do that to her? You're horrible!" Lisa shoots a look of alarm at me and Hallie, then leaves the room to continue the call with more privacy.

Hallie says to me, "Oooof. That's not gonna be easy!"

She and I sit quietly, each lost in our own thoughts. Occasional words and phrases waft in from the living room. "... I thought Maria knew! ... didn't tell anyone ... she said what? ... wait, what 'affair'? ... that's outrageous! ... where? ... no, no, NO!"

Hallie and I exchange grimaces. "Uh, oh ..."

Lisa eventually returns, visibly shaken. "Well, Jolivia is very angry with me. So provoked, in fact, that after telling Maddie what I'd done to her, she got even with me by telling Maddie I was having an affair!"

I cry, "Omigod, no! She didn't!"

"Yep. She even had evidence that she laid out to Maddie in exquisite detail."

I blink rapidly, trying to process what I'm hearing. "I don't understand! How could Joli possibly have evidence about you having an affair?"

"Apparently, she saw me in Harvard Square one day, in a restaurant, having an intimate lunch with a man. She saw me leaning across the table to him, touching his hand, looking soulfully at him."

"Oh, Lisa ..." It pains me to know that Joli has done this. Joli's the one who screwed up here, and instead of owning it, she's taken her anger out on the inadvertent whistleblower.

"She hung around to watch us laughing and touching, then followed us over to the Charles Hotel, where she saw us go to the elevators and embrace warmly while waiting for the lift up to a room."

My palm shoots to my face, covering my mouth. "She said all this to Maddie?! *Oh nha maeeeee!* I'm so sorry, Lisa!"

"Maddie was pretty furious with me. She'd learned this morning not only that I'd spilled Joli's secret, but that I'd been sneaking around, having an affair."

Hallie steps back from me and Lisa, probably trying to give us space for this awkward talk.

A grin slowly appears on Lisa's face. "The only problem with the story is ... that was my brother Joli saw me with. I remember that day clearly. He was in town for a conference. And Joli certainly got all the details right: the restaurant, the hand-touching at the table; the hug at the lobby's elevator bank. I asked Maddie if Joli had described the man to her. She had. And when I said, 'That's your uncle Ian whom Joli saw me with,' Maddie was quiet as a moth for a long beat and then started laughing."

Now the three of us also burst out laughing in relief, reveling in the absurdity of the situation. Finally composing herself, Lisa adds, with a wry smile, "But Maddie's still pretty pissed with me for 'telling on' Joli, so I'm not completely off the hook."

19

Hallie

It's Halloween afternoon, and we're uncertain what to expect this evening. The Campbells have never been in Chatham over Halloween, so Lisa has no idea how many kids we'll get. The houses out here are spread pretty far apart, and there don't seem to be many children in the neighborhood. So, it's reasonable to assume there won't be many trick-or-treaters. But Maria and I don't want to be taken by surprise, like squirrels caught off-guard by a sudden snowstorm. Playing it safe, we hit the grocery store for several bags of candy bars.

When we return to the house, we find Lisa already having started to rig up our solution for safely distanced treat-giving—a long, DIY candy chute from the second-floor balcony down to the driveway. If any little monsters show up, we'll drop a couple candy bars down the chute to them.

We'd spent the previous afternoon carving four pumpkins. When we finished, we empaneled ourselves as judges for our own 'Great Pumpkin' contest. Quinn took first place. His theme was Zoom calls—he'd cut tiny jack-o'lantern faces into a 2x2 grid. Below, in big letters, the word ZOOM. He claims it's the embodiment of our collective pandemic dread. It's fabulous.

I went full-artist mode, using my skill with an X-acto blade to carve a likeness of Donald Trump—so accurate it was repugnant. I was proud of it. But I got robbed: the others unfairly subtracted points from my score for what they deemed predictability. Maria explained, "Trump pumpkins have been everywhere since 2016. Anybody with a shred of talent does them." I pointed out that mine was the only entry of the sort here. The logic of that passed over them. And they seemed unwilling to give me appropriate credit for my masterful shading and nuanced gradations. Robbed, I tell you.

Maria's jack o'lantern took her a long time to complete. She's not terribly artistic, and she struggled to map out the design. It's a clenched fist, hovering above the letters 'BLM'—more of a political statement than a Halloween decoration. She won second place.

Lisa played it safe with a classic design—a face with triangular eyes. But she added a trendy twist: beneath the eyes, she'd fastened a blue surgical face mask, held back at the "ears" by straight pins. Creative, sure, but I couldn't help thinking, *A masked jack o'lantern in 2020? Wow. Groundbreaking!* And they say mine is predictable! Sheesh!

This afternoon we've been decorating the front porch. It's looking like Martha Stewart-meets-*Ghostbusters* out here—pumpkins, tall corn stalks, multiple hay bales, all artfully arranged around our jerry-built candy chute. Lisa's motto is: if it's worth doing, it's worth overdoing with the help of a high-limit credit card.

We're taking stock of our handiwork when my cellphone erupts into life, shattering the moment. I pluck it from the pocket of my jeans and release an involuntary gasp when I see who's calling. "Omigod! Nick!" Flustered, I glance at the others. I see Quinn's devastated look, like I just canceled Christmas, but instead of reassuring him, I blurt out, "I really should take this," and dash off to my room, my head spinning. It's been months without a word from Nick. I've come to believe I'd never hear from him again. Why on earth is he calling now?

He starts out by wishing me a "happy anniversary." It was exactly two years ago that Nick and I came together. Halloween night, 2018. We'd joined a group of theater friends at a big party in Boston's South End, where the drinks were flowing and the costumes were questionable. Later, we went to Nick's apartment where, I swear to god, we made magic happen—like, fireworks-and-symphony magic. Damn good, for sex with a male. Just saying. Now, here he is on the phone with his "happy anniversary." As I object to this utter inanity, he talks over me, saying how much he's missed me. "My life has felt so empty without you."

I'm sure he thinks that sentiment will melt my heart; instead, it hardens it. "Really?! Well ... why haven't you been in touch? Did you fall in a black hole? It's been four months, Nick, and nothing—not an email, not a text, not a phone call! Nothing! So, if your life has felt so fucking empty, you could've tried to fill it by being in touch with me."

He doesn't say anything for a long moment. "I've needed a long time to think about what I want in life. And I've decided you are what I want, Hal. This period of separation has made that clear to me." I'm quietly groaning about the absurdity of all this when he throws me for an even bigger loop: "I want ... to be with you, always. We should ... think about getting married."

His words literally take my breath away. I'm forty-two years old, and this is the first time anyone has ever mentioned marriage to me. Okay, it's not a formal proposal, but it's equally preposterous. "Are you out of your fucking mind, Nick? After leaving me without a word and neglecting me for months, you expect me to welcome you back into my arms? You expect me to consider marrying you? Are you fucking crazy?"

Silence on his end.

"Nick, you can't mess with another person's life this way!" I yell into the phone. "I'm not your plaything." I grab the nearest object—a box of Kleenex—and hurl it across the room.

"I know that! Look, I'm sorry I hurt you. I apologize. I'm not proud of how I behaved. Please forgive me. I slipped into survival mode."

Yeah, well, I've now slipped into eye-roll mode. I let the connection hang silent for a long time.

"I ... I don't know what to say, Hallie."

A snort of disgust escapes from me. "You 'don't know what to say'! Well, I don't know what to say either. You know how I feel—felt—about you. But it'll take me a while to think about this. To process what you've said."

"I ... I was hoping you might agree to come here for Thanksgiving. I'll pay for your plane."

I truly can't believe what I'm hearing. "Omigod, you really are delusional! I am not getting on an airplane during this pandemic, and I am not coming to see you, Nick!"

"Well ... then I'll fly up there. Or drive up. I want to see you."

"You don't even know where I am! Where do you think I'm living right now?"

"I know you're on Cape Cod with Maria and Mike. I spoke with Grant; he told me. ... Look, Hallie. I understand that you're not feeling good about us at the moment. But we can fix this. We can work through it. Figure it out."

"Sure, Nick, and I'll win 'Dancing with the Stars.' Maybe we could have figured things out if you had stayed in touch all these months. But you didn't. You ruined it. I'm inclined to tell you to shove it, go fuck yourself."

"But you'll think about it?"

"About what? Thanksgiving? Getting back together? Your marriage fantasy?"

"All of it."

A long pause. "Don't get your hopes up. And don't expect to hear from me soon." I disconnect, throw the phone on the bed, then gape at it for a long time with utter disbelief, like the damned thing just tried to convince me that the earth is flat. Fury overtakes me. I grab a pillow and beat the phone with it, over and over—really go full-ninja on it—until I'm so winded I collapse on the bed.

I lie there, my mind spinning in circles, trying to make sense of this Nick madness. It feels like the world's playing a cruel joke on me, forcing me to confront the unresolved feelings I have for him. Why is he suddenly contacting me, selling castles in the air? Is he bored? Lonely? Does he genuinely want us to try again, to rebuild what we've lost? How could we pick up where we left off after everything that's happened? That would be like trying to unscramble an egg.

There's a tiny, ridiculous part of me—the part that still believes in fairy tales and happy endings—that whispers, *Maybe this could still work.* After all, I'd loved the guy. He's funny, charming, a wizard around a theater stage ... and in the bedroom. Our lazy Sundays were like living in a rom-com, complete with tangled sheets, brunch, and bad jokes. But let's face it, believing in fairy tales means also believing in witches and dragons—in unhappy endings.

Plus, there's Quinn to consider. He understands me, truly gets me—all of me—on a level that Nick never did or could. And it scares me to think of what I'd lose if I were to give in to nostalgia and go back to the familiarity of Nick. Quinn's the complete package—some moments, warm and comfortable like your favorite old sweater; other moments, exhilarating and invigorating, like a shot of adrenaline. He challenges me mentally. With him, every conversation feels like a dance of intellect and wit.

My phone buzzes with an incoming text. I feel around for the device, like I'm playing blind man's buff. Finally seizing it, I see the message is from Nick—a plea for consideration, for a second chance: *I know you're hesitant and I understand that. But don't say no yet. We owe it to ourselves to at least try.*

I chew my lip. Is that true? Do I owe it to myself? Do I owe it to that version of me that fell hard for him two years ago? Do I owe it to him? To 'us'? I take a deep breath and read the text message once more, my thumb hovering over the screen, searching for the right words. With a shaky sigh, I reply honestly, with the only words I can be sure of:

I need time, I type slowly. *Time to process everything. Time to figure out if trying again is what I want or need.*

Switching off the phone, I'm left in the quiet of my room, wondering how I'll find the answer. The laughter and light from downstairs seem a world away. The dark thought occurs to me that Halloween's most ghoulish specters have nothing on the haunting uncertainties of my own heart.

20

Quinn

I study the email from my younger brother Brad—an invitation to the second wedding of his daughter Jenny. The wedding's in two weeks, right here on Cape Cod. Brad writes that when he learned I'm here in Chatham, he realized there's "no reason in the world" I shouldn't come to the wedding. Maybe that's true from the standpoint of geographic proximity. But from the perspective of emotional ties or family bonds, it's nonsense. Now that both our parents are gone, what links me and Brad? The nostalgia of shared moments, an obligatory family allegiance, some inexplicable genetic connection? have no idea. I've as much in common with Brad as I do with the Emir of Kuwait! It makes no sense to go to the damn wedding.

Besides, Brad hadn't cared enough to invite me to the first of Jenny's weddings. Why should I go to the second? The apparent answer is, because I'm close by! That logic is as solid as a chocolate teapot. Still, what kind of asshole would I be not to drive 20 minutes to witness Jenny say her second "I do"?

The big event is to be at the Ocean Edge Resort and Golf Club over in Brewster. Good lord. What a pretentious affair that's going to be! Sounds like a page right out of 'Lifestyles of the Rich and Absurd.' Plus, haven't these people heard about that early-August wedding in Maine that turned into a super-spreading event? The pandemic's not retreating! So what if Brad's trying to sell this Cape wedding as a "small, COVID-conscious, all-outdoor" event? Doesn't convince me.

My brother Frank won't even be there. If he were going, maybe I'd attend. At least he'd make it fun. Who would I hang with at this thing? There's nothing worse than standing around at a social event you're already not keen to be at, feeling constantly on guard against people you'd like to avoid.

I could take Hallie with me. That's assuming she'd want to go. She may not. She's been in a strange mood since getting that call from Nick yesterday. That whole episode has me in a lather. She hasn't said anything to me about it, which only increases my concern. What's going on? Is she getting back together with him? What is she keeping from me? Anyway, yes, Hallie would be fun to have along at a wedding. Like Frank, she'd at least make me laugh.

But now an unwelcome memory comes to me. Less than a year after Mom's death, Dad appeared at a family graduation party with a woman he introduced as his "new friend." His arm around her was like a neon sign saying, 'We're much more than friends.' Most family members were appalled that Dad was already playing the field when Mom hadn't even been gone for ten months.

Frank, ever the family lawyer, stood up for Dad, arguing that nobody else had a right to set a timer on our father's period of grief. "What do you want him to do? Mope around in funeral garb, holding candlelight vigils for Mom? That's nonsense! Let the man find some sunshine. If this new woman makes him happy, eases his pain somehow, then who are we to criticize him?" Frank could sell ice to Inuits, but some folks weren't buying his pitch.

I mull the whole problem over for a while, then decide not to try to resolve it now. So, I dive back into Erik Larson's great book about Churchill during England's first year in WWII. An hour in, Megan calls. She's heard from Jenny that I've been invited to the wedding and is all bubbly about me potentially showing up. I'm not sure why she cares; she's not even going, because of some work commitment. I explain to her that I haven't decided if I'll go.

"Because of COVID?" Megan asks.

"Mostly," I reply, deciding not to add that I don't want to go alone. I know better than to say I've been thinking of taking Hallie along. "The whole COVID thing is too problematic. It wouldn't be fair to Paul and Lisa and their friends here to risk bringing the virus back to the house," I explain, and Megan sees the logic in that.

We shift gears, chatting about the virus, the presidential-election circus, and the generally gloomy state of life in America. After bumming each other out, we switch to personal updates. Megan buzzes about recent work projects and a new guy she's dating. I spill about my life here in Chatham, providing more detail than I have in past weeks. I bring up Hallie and say I enjoy her company, praising her humor and intelligence.

The pushback from Megan is immediate. And severe. "You know what, Dad? I talked to Jack yesterday, and he said you'd recently mentioned this woman to him, too. It ticked him off!

And now I'm pissed, too!" She accuses me of being 'unfaithful to Mom' as well as "inconsiderate, selfish, and opportunistic." She concludes her tirade with, "Be a better man!" then disconnects.

Tension clenches my shoulders. I try to release it, rolling my neck, breathing deeply. Perhaps Megan and Jack are right. Maybe I'm being too quick off the mark with Hallie. They're reacting just like I did about Dad and his new 'friend' before Frank talked some sense into me. But all I did was refer to her briefly. It's not like I announced our engagement. In any case, what a strategic error it was to mention her to the kids! They're obviously not ready to hear about a new woman emerging in my life, not prepared for Dad 2.0. But it annoys the hell out of me that they think they can dictate my behavior, decide the contours of my life. Jesus Christ! Seriously, what am I, a puppet on their strings?

I'm too keyed up to go back to the Churchill saga, so I flick through my emails again. Ah, there's another one from a colleague at the University of Wisconsin. Damn. I remember now— two voicemails from him late yesterday, still unanswered. I think this Nick business has me too distracted for my own good.

I call Stewart Gaines right away and end up on the phone with him for forty-five minutes. The Wisconsin English department is looking to hire in my field at the full-professor level. They want to know whether I'd consider a lateral move. Wow. I didn't see *that* coming! That's a huge opportunity, but even as we spoke about it, I felt deeply conflicted.

I need a walk to untangle the web of thoughts in my head— about the wedding, my kids' reaction to my mention of Hallie, the Wisconsin job. It's all a bit overwhelming, a lot to process. Aiming for the back door, I head through the kitchen. And there's Hallie, causing a great clatter as she empties the dishwasher. I've learned over the years to intuit the mood of someone performing this task by the volume of the clatter with which the flatware is being shoveled into the drawer. The current loudness doesn't bode well for a cheery conversation. "Hi. What's up?" I say, adopting a light tone that I hope Hallie will feel compelled to match.

"Certainly not me," she replies, acknowledging her mood for the past 24 hours.

"Yeah, I've noticed you're a bit off. Sorry. You want to talk about it?"

"Not really. It's a mess."

I pause, not sure it's wise to go there, but plunge ahead. "Is it about Nick?"

She nods.

"He wants to get back together?"

"Yeah. He does."

I don't know how to respond, so I stay quiet. There's a long pause. Her eyes search mine, as if she's calculating how much more bad news I can bear. But then she looks down, offering nothing more.

I finally ask, "How are you feeling about that?"

She groans. "Oohhhh, I don't know, Quinn. I'm in a real tangle over this."

Just as I feared. She's drawn to him. Unbelievable! "What do you mean, you 'don't know'? He abandoned you, Hallie. Cruelly. Disappeared like a sock from a dryer. Ignored you for months! And what, now he wants you to pretend none of that happened? Surely, you're not going to consider getting back together with him!"

"Honestly, I don't really know how I feel."

"You're kidding, right?"

She looks like a deer caught in the headlights. "Well, I, ah, no, I'm not kidding ... I mean ... I don't know. ... there's so much to think about."

"I suppose I'm out of bounds for asking this, but what in god's name is there to think about? How could you consider going back to someone who treated you that way?"

Now, her startled-deer look has been replaced by an an angry-bear look. "I think you may be right, Quinn: you may be overstepping your bounds here. Look, I was with him for more than a year and a half, and we really clicked. Emotions are complicated things. So, you may think this is a slam-dunk matter, but it's not that clear-cut for me. ... Now, if you don't mind, I don't want to talk about it any more. Let's change the subject. ... How are you doing?"

No time like the present. I might as well tell her my own news. "I have a couple things to tell you. But I'm really hungry. Could we have some wine and cheese while we talk?"

"Sure."

We silently prepare a plate of cheese and crackers and baby carrots, then take the food and some wine out to the patio, where we turn on the overhead gas heater.

I tell her first about Megan and Jack—and the reaction they each had when I mentioned her to them. She's quiet while she takes a moment to process what she's heard. Finally, she rakes her fingers through her hair and says, "Look, Quinn, I get it. I do. In their minds, you're inextricably woven with their mother. Naturally, they're going to be upset if they think you're attracted to another woman. I know I'm not a disinterested party here, but I think they're overreacting. It's been three years since Alison's death. I'm no expert on the etiquette of mourning, but that seems like a respectful—and respectable—amount of time.

I mean, come on. What do they expect you to do? You have a lot of years ahead of you."

I settle into a long pause, staring at the floor. Eventually, I speak. "I shouldn't have said anything to them about you. My mistake. But I ... I was hoping for a different reaction, something positive, encouraging. I guess I was looking for ... a form of permission."

"And now that you didn't get it?"

Good question. I lift my gaze to Hallie. I like her and have started to picture a future together. But how can I pursue her if Megan and Jack would be so opposed, so upset by that? "I don't know," I say. "I don't know."

"Really? You 'don't know'? They're not five-year-olds. They're adults, for chrissake! They can handle you moving on with your life at this point. Would you really let them block this? Us? Forgive me, but where's your backbone?"

"You do realize, don't you, that you're frustrated by my indecisiveness in precisely the same way I'm confused and exasperated by your namby-pamby approach to the whole Nick issue?"

She starts to sputter and then groans and fixes me with a glare. "I'm not sure it serves you well to characterize my indecision as 'namby-pamby.'"

"Nor does it serve you well to ask if I have a backbone. ... We're both doing some hand-wringing here. Maybe we need to cut each other some slack."

Her face softens very slightly at that, then we slip into a long, uneasy silence, each of us waiting for the other to speak. To break the tension, I decide to switch topics again, even though, for all I know, discussing the job opportunity in Wisconsin might be jumping from the frying pan into the fire. I straighten my posture. "There's something else I want to talk with you about."

Hallie's voice is cautious. "What is it?"

"A few days ago, I got a call from a colleague at the University of Wisconsin. Their English department is looking for a full professor in my field. They're interested in me for a lateral move."

Hallie's reaction is almost visceral, her eyes widening in surprise, a soft gasp escaping her lips. "Really? That's, uh ... big news! What are your thoughts?"

"I don't know—"

"Again with the indecision?" she shoots back, rapid fire.

I'm thrown off by her sharp tone. "Well, there's so much to consider. From a financial standpoint, it probably wouldn't be a wise move. State universities all around the country are financially hard-pressed, and all my friends who teach at state institutions are always complaining about their lousy salaries—which isn't an problem at Tufts. Moving to a new university also would mean navigating a whole new set of collegial relationships and institutional dynamics."

Hallie's nod signals her understanding.

"Plus, I don't know that it makes sense to consider such a big move at this point in my career. I'll probably only do this for another fifteen years, at most. What if I get out there and hate it? It'd be hard then to make another lateral move. I'd be stuck. I know what I have now at Tufts, which I like well enough. And, as I told you a while back, I'm not that invested any more in academic writing. It wouldn't be fair to Wisconsin to go there, not a fully engaged scholar."

I pause for some cheese and a sip of wine. "On the other hand, Wisconsin's department is prestigious, and it'd be fun to work with better grad students. Plus, I love Madison. It's an appealing little city."

Hallie's brow furrows, her eyes darken, the creases around them deepen.

I continue. "There's also the attraction of a fresh start—away from Boston, which carries all the memories of my life with Alison."

Hallie's been fidgeting in her chair. With an expression of exasperation, she slides to the edge of her seat. "That's all hard, Quinn. A lateral move in academia is ... well, as you say, there's so much to consider. You know, I'm sorry. I'm not feeling well ... I hope you'll excuse me." When she stands, she bumps the table with her leg, accidentally knocking our wine glasses to the flagstone, where they shatter. She looks at the mess, then up at me. Her eyes blaze and her tone is sharp when she says, "Do you realize that in your laborious weighing of pros and cons, not once did you mention me? Am I that invisible? That easy to overlook? That unimportant to you?" Her eyes are now clouded with tears.

I would normally be moved by her reaction, but right now I am like a wolf circling an injured deer. "And do you realize that in your dithering about Nick, you didn't mention me?"

We glare at each other, each of us hurt, each of us weighing the severity of the blows we've landed on the other. Hallie says, "Maybe we're both narcissists, thinking everything should be about us."

"Or maybe what's going on between us is all surface-level fizz."

Perhaps that punch was too hard. She literally twists like I landed a roundhouse to her jaw. Then she completes the turn and storms away, leaving me to deal with the shards of glass.

21

Hallie

The aftermath of crossing swords with Quinn several days ago has left me feeling so unsettled that I've mostly stayed in my room since then so that I don't have to talk with him. I feigned illness. In truth, it wasn't entirely a facade; I was genuinely nauseous over that whole conversation. His wimpy indecisiveness about his kids and the Wisconsin job drove me up the wall, made me want to shriek. I guess I *did* shriek, at least a bit. And I guess I gave him reason to complain, too. It's true that I didn't say how much Quinn is a part of my calculus about Nick. In that moment, I was responding to Quinn's comments about Nick. I suppose, if I'm to be fair, Quinn was similarly focused on the job, not me, when he told me about Wisconsin's interest.

Still, this is not good. What did he call this thing between us? "Surface-level fizz?" Maybe he's right. Maybe our feelings for each other aren't real. Maybe this is like an extra-marital affair—outside of real life, where it's easy to mistake the fun and thrill of it for genuine emotion. A case of holiday romance syndrome, where everything's rosy and we have no obligation other than pleasing each other. Here we are, out here in this incredible house, in a beautiful town on the ocean. Our days are as effortless as coasting downhill on a bicycle. Superficial fizz is about right.

I'm knee-deep in this emotional stew when there's a knock on my bedroom door. I open it to find Maria, looking as shocked as if she's just seen a zebra doing the salsa. "What's up, Mar?"

"You better brace yourself. Nick is here."

I shriek. "What? Here!"

Maria nods, all wide-eyed.

I hurry to my bathroom, run a brush through my hair, pinch my cheeks, check my clothing in the mirror, and follow Maria down the stairs to the main foyer, heart pounding like I'm heading into a surprise exam. Christ! What's he doing here? What am I going to say to him? I still have no clarity on any of this.

But there he is: honey-colored curls, a mask on his face, holding a bouquet of autumnal flowers. Good thing Quinn isn't standing here to see this!

"Hi, Hallie," he says, as casually as if I just saw him two days ago and he's now popping back for tea.

My heart hammers. "Nick, what in the world are you doing here?"

"I hadn't heard from you and I needed to see you," he says.

I groan and usher him to the sunroom, where we perch on the edges of facing armchairs, like we're about to negotiate a peace treaty. "Nick, what's the deal? You can't just show up like this with no notice."

"Well, I did. And I apologize if my arrival has upset you."

I stare at him with disbelief and growing anger; I'm not in the market for whatever nonsense he's here to peddle. "I don't know what fantasy world you're living in, Nick, but let me make something clear," I say, my tone razor-sharp. "I've moved on. I'm putting my emotional life back together after you tore it apart. I finally feel like I can breathe again."

Although his mask hides most of his face, I can see those sad-puppy-dog eyes. They have no potency with me. "I don't know what you thought you'd achieve by coming here. Did you think I'd just forgive you and we'd pick up right where we left off?" I let out a bitter laugh. "How delusional can you be?"

He tries to touch my arm, but I yank it away. "Don't!" I warn.

"Please, just hear me out," he pleads, his eyes searching mine. "I know I don't deserve it, but I'm asking for a chance to explain everything, try to make things right. We need to work this through. I ... We need time together."

"Meaning what?"

"My mother loaned me money for us to stay at an inn for a week."

I stare at him in stunned silence. A week together at an inn? On his mommy's dime? Is he serious? After everything he put me through, he thinks he can just show up unannounced and I'll agree to go away with him, just like that? Does he not understand the depth of the hurt I still feel? I take a deep breath, trying to calm the storm of emotions swirling inside me—confusion, hurt, anger. Part of me wants to slap him, unleash the full fury of my pain and heartbreak. Another part wants to collapse into his arms and pretend recent months never happened.

"Nick ..." I begin, but trail off, trying to gather thoughts scattered by this cyclone of feelings. "You think we can just run away together and work through everything. But it's not that simple."

He reaches for my hand. This time I let him take it. His palm is familiar against mine. "I know nothing can make up for how badly I hurt you," he says softly. "Believe me, I hate myself for what I did. But, please know these past few months without you have been torture for me."

He rises from his chair and kneels by mine. He pulls off his mask and brings his face close. Our eyes lock, and there's this zing, like an electric shock. Not fizz; pure high voltage. My heart thrums in my chest. His face is saturated with sincerity, with his raw need for another chance. My defenses weaken. When he brings his lips to mine, I let them stay. When I feel his warm hand on the back of my neck, his thumb tracing the whorl of my ear, I release an involuntary moan. "Oh, why are you doing this to me, Nick? ... I was doing fine without you!"

"Is that what you want? To 'do fine' without me?" he asks, standing and pulling me up into a bear hug. Oh, god. He smells so good—the woods after a rain. He kisses me again, deeper, and I'm a goner. His tongue slides along mine, sending bolts of warmth up my spine. My heart races as his fingers trace along my sides, his breath hot on my neck.

God almighty! "Nick, ... no! This isn't fair!"

"I don't care about 'fair.' I want you. I love you! To hell with fairness! I need you."

Thoughts of Quinn rush into my mind, and I force myself to break from the warmth of Nick's embrace. I have no chance at all against him if we keep kissing; my brain will turn to mush. If we're only talking, I have at least some hope of mental clarity.

I resettle in my chair and take a deep breath, trying to steady my racing heart. Then I make him talk to me.

An hour later, I hunt for Maria and Lisa, finding them in the living room, sitting cross-legged on the floor in front of the coffee table, their heads bent over a colorful jigsaw puzzle like they're defusing a bomb. They look up at me with curious expressions that scream, 'Spill the tea, girl.' My cheeks heat with embarrassment. I blurt out that I'm leaving for a while to sort things with Nick.

Maria pops up like she's on a spring, at my side in a second, all concern and furrowed brows. "Are you sure this is what you want to do?"

"I ... I don't know what I'm doing!" I say, and collapse into her open arms, unable to stop the tears that suddenly appear. "I'm in emotional quicksand, Mar!"

She lets me stay in her arms until I regain my composure. Then, she steps back, all wisdom and grace, and says, "Then you shouldn't do anything until you've figured it out. Nick's not going to help you with that. You've got to do it on your own. Until then, you should stay put."

I nod, knowing she's right. But part of me says I can't figure it out without knowing what it's like to be with him again. I don't think I'll gain any clarity by sitting around here, strumming my lips.

"You're probably right, Mar. But I've got to do this. It may be the stupidest thing I've ever done. And you know I've done plenty. But I need to know."

Maria shrugs and turns away. Lisa replaces her at my side. Gently placing her hand on my shoulder, she says, "Call us if you need backup, Hallie. ... And take care of yourself."

I nod, grab my hastily packed runaway bag, and head for the

door. "Please tell Quinn and the others I'm sorry for the Irish goodbye," I say, fleeing the disappointment in Maria's eyes.

22

Quinn

To say I've been having a hard time with Hallie's leaving would be like saying a hurricane is a bit breezy. I'm absolutely blown away by it. How could she leave without saying goodbye? This is exactly what she'd grumbled about Nick having done to her! Talk about irony with a capital I.

It's made me question my whole sense that she and I had been growing close, that we might actually have something. I guess I'm wrong. Apparently, it's been a one-sided thing. What an idiot I am. This is precisely why I've hesitated to jump in with both feet. I've obviously been out of the romance game too long. My antennae are rusty, warped. I should've known better.

Plus, I'm totally aware that my botching of our conversation last week probably figured into her decision to leave with him. My waffling about the kids and Wisconsin was a mistake, my failure to mention her inexcusable. But the worst thing was the "fizz" comment. Why wouldn't she go off with Nick when I've led her to believe I think there's nothing more between us than some ephemeral effervescence!

I squirm when I picture what might be going on between her and Nick at their cozy inn. She's now been gone five days. That's like five years in romantic-getaway time. That doesn't bode well for me. Then again, things looked bad for me the minute she went off with him. Still, each additional day she's with him makes it more certain that she's gone off with him for good.

Lisa sees me staring out a window. "You have the blank, forlorn look of the bereft, Quinn. This is the third time I've seen you moping around like a little boy who's lost his action figure. Let's get you out of this funk, spring you from this Heartbreak Hotel." She rounds up Maria. Soon, the three of us climb into Lisa's Mercedes SUV, and she says, "I thought we'd drive up to Sandwich and then meander along 6A all the way back to Orleans. We'll stop at whatever looks interesting."

Maria claps. Her eyes bright with anticipation, she says, "Brilliant. A spontaneous road trip! We should've done this one sooner!"

When we reach Sandwich, we stop at the picturesque Dexter Grist Mill. The mill itself isn't operating this far outside tourist season, but we're able to walk around the grounds and appreciate the view of the small, weathered mill nestled next to Shawme Pond.

I can't help but let out a wistful sigh. "What a gorgeous setting! Thanks for bringing us here." It would have been great to see this with Hallie, but there's no chance of that now.

In East Sandwich, tiny Titcomb's Book Shop beckons us. A sign by the front door warns of a four-customer limit because of the virus. A little flip-sign shows two people already inside. Lisa stays back, calling Maddie, while Maria and I venture in. Wanting to be fair to others who might show up, we dart through the aisles, our usual relaxed search converted into a speedy mission. We each find a few gems.

Our next stop is for take-out coffee at Nirvana in Barnstable before continuing on 6A. We hit the Brewster Book store, where we're greeted by a similar COVID-restriction sign. But this shop is larger, and the customer limit is higher. We're able to steal a precious twenty minutes among the stacks, each of us walking away with still more reads. For me, each new book feels like a promise of escape from the tangled mess inside me.

As we resume our drive, I recall a weekend about five years ago that Alison and I spent here in Brewster with a Tufts colleague of mine and her husband. It was a lovely little place on Sheep Pond his family had owned for years. Alison and I were hesitant to accept the invitation because we barely knew the husband. But we had a great time, and I remember Alison saying on our way home that it was good for us to spend time with new people. *Yeah,* I think now, with a twinge of bitterness. *Unless you fall in love with them and they break your heart.*

On the way to Orleans, Lisa and Maria talk idly about what they might cook for dinner tonight and where we could stop for groceries on the way back to Chatham. A Shaw's supermarket soon appears on our left, and Lisa decides to stop there. My mind drifts again to that weekend trip to Brewster with Alison. Somewhere near here on 6A, we'd visited a model-railroad museum. The "Ballad of Casey Jones" played on the sound system. A pang of anguish hits me now as I recall those lyrics: "Headaches and heartaches and all kinds of pain / Ain't no different from a railroad train." Talk about a metaphor for my life crashing off the rails.

When we get back to the house, I help carry in the groceries. Then, mustering a smile, I say to Lisa and Maria, "Thanks, you two, for distracting me and trying to lift my spirits—like attempting to inflate a punctured tire, I'm afraid, but I really appreciate your game effort." They each give me a reassuring hug. I say, "I think I could still use a few more hours away from here. I'm going for a bike ride."

"Want company?" Lisa offers.

"That's nice of you. But no, I think I'll go alone." I snag one of the three Treks from the garage, along with a helmet from the collection hanging above the bikes. I give the tires a quick squeeze, tweak the seat height, and head down the sloped driveway. I'm soon pedaling west out of Chatham on the Old Colony Rail Trail, slicing through the Harwich Wildlife Sanctuary's lush woods. At the bike rotary past Harwich Center, I hop onto the Cape Cod Rail Trail and head north.

An 8-foot-wide asphalt ribbon, the trail is a playground for runners, walkers, cyclists, and even horseback riders ambling along the dirt shoulder. On a summer day, it's a buzzing hive of activity, but today few are using it.

Soon, I weave past Brewster's glacial ponds. These ancient, crystal-clear pools, born from retreating glaciers, reveal striking sandy and granite bottoms. I can't shake the feeling that Hallie should be here, soaking in these sights with me.

A pit stop to use a restroom at Nickerson State Park has me sanitizing my hands like a surgeon prepping for operation, then munching on a granola bar at a picnic table. A rustling breeze dances through the trees. Flax Pond, its freshwater beach covered not with sand but with pine needles, offers a tranquil view. I can't help but wish that Hallie were there to enjoy it with me. But the reality is that she's not. I gamely put the helmet back on, hop on the bike, and continue north for another ten miles. Reaching Orleans Center, I decide to turn back.

Back at Lisa and Paul's place in Chatham, I grab a quick shower and settle in to read. Eventually, I nod off, only to be roused by a gentle tapping at my door. I open it to find Hallie there, effortlessly breathtaking in a burnt-orange cashmere sweater and black corduroys. The sunlight streaming through the window in the hallway backlights her hair with a lemony glow. Could she possibly be any more radiant?

"May I come in?" she asks, her voice tentative.

I manage a nod, feeling an instant cocktail of emotions—a mix of relief and anger. She steps in, tones of her perfume trailing as she comes closer. She's clearly uneasy. The corners of her mouth twitch occasionally, like she's trying to remember how smiling works. She shifts her weight from one foot to the other.

"How are you doing?" she asks.

"I've been better." I give her my best attempt at a life's-just-peachy smile.

She inches closer. "Yeah, no, about that ... Look, I apologize for leaving the other day without finding you to tell you I was going. That was wrong of me."

"You ... you were gone a long time."

A half smile. "I was. But I'm back."

"To pick up the rest of your things?"

"No. I told Nick he's not the person for me. It's over. Definitely over."

Inside, I'm thinking, *You spent most of a week with him in a cozy inn, and now he's Mr. Wrong?* But I say, "Are you sure you're not acting precipitously?"

"I'm sure."

I draw a deep breath, slowly release it, and give her a hesitant nod, determined not to make this easy for her. When I don't say anything, she backs away.

"Okay, then … I just wanted to say hello and see how you are," she says. "I'll let you go back to reading … or napping … or whatever."

After she goes, I'm left here, hands covering my face, trying to make sense of it all. What did she expect me to do, welcome her back with open arms? Tell her I hardly noticed she was gone? Let her know that I didn't lose any sleep thinking of her curled up next to that motherfucker? The whole thing is an impossible puzzle, like trying to solve a Rubik's Cube in complete darkness.

23

Hallie

Knowing I deserved Quinn's frosty reception doesn't make it any less painful. It's been almost twenty hours, and his reaction still gnaws at my insides. I'd naively hoped for a warmer reception, perhaps even an affectionate one. Fanciful thinking! His eyes were like a guarded fortress. Why didn't I just leap over that wall and tell him how much I'd missed him? I guess I was thrown off by his icy demeanor. No use hitting replay over and over. There's no changing the fact that I really botched both my exit and my return.

I'm into full-scale self-chastisement mode when, out of the blue, my phone pings with a text from Quinn, asking me to join him for a walk. I quickly agree, and twenty minutes later we meet by the back door off the kitchen. He suggests we go out to Morris Island again—just us this time, without Charlie.

The ten-minute drive is as quiet as a gathering of mimes. So, when we get there, the sound of chickadees chirping away in the scrub woods seems loud, like a clock's ticking in an empty house. The landscape has changed since our last visit. The previously vivid purples of the sea flowers have softened to a muted lilac, and the sunlight now slants through the pitch pine at a lazier angle.

We walk, the crunch of needles and twigs under our feet laying a base line for the sharp and insistent birdsong. Finally, Quinn breaks our silence. "I've got to be honest, Hallie, I was pretty upset you went off with Nick. And angry you left without saying goodbye. Even though I missed you, I felt really let down."

His words hit me like a bucket of ice water. Soaked in regret, I say, "Quinn ... I'm *so* sorry. I acted without thinking. I was inconsiderate. Definitely not my best moment."

"No, it wasn't," he says, his voice carrying no trace of the forgiveness or understanding I hope to hear. After a while he continues. "Forgive me for asking: why did it take you five days with Nick to discover ... how did you say it? ... 'he's not the person' for you? Did you really need four nights in the same bed to figure that out?"

His words knock the breath from me, so I have to draw deep to continue. I run my fingers through my hair. "Right. ... Well, I can't look you in the eye and tell you we didn't have sex. We—"

"I don't want to know!" He looks away, his lips pursed in a thin crease.

I hurry on. "But there was nothing about it that felt right. Believe me. I no longer felt an emotional connection to him. At all."

"And that took five days—what, ten fucks?—to discover?" His eyes blaze with hurt and anger.

"Quinn, I understand that I hurt you. And I really am sorry about that. But you and I don't have any hold on each other, no claim. I know we like each other a lot. But this reaction seems ... over the top, unfair."

"Oh, really?" He snorts a derisive laugh that's so sarcastic it could curdle milk. "Well, it felt pretty unfair that you silently snuck off with him after we'd been ... I almost said 'making love,' but apparently that's not what it was." He looks away, his gaze fixed on the distant horizon, his face contorted with anguish, like a tragic hero in a Greek play. "You really hurt me, Hallie."

My stomach twists with guilt. "I messed up. Badly. And I am truly, deeply sorry. I didn't mean to hurt you." I reach for him, hoping to bridge this awful chasm between us. But he's not ready for a peace sign. He leaves my hand hanging there, awkward, until I let it sink to my side. "Look, I know there's no excuse for the way I behaved, so I offer this as a partial explanation, not an excuse. When I left, I was still in a bad mental space from that combative conversation you and I had last week. Your last words were that maybe our relationship is just 'surface-level fizz.' On top of everything you said about your reluctance to buck your kids and about the Wisconsin job, that superficial fizz comment left me reeling. And so I wasn't in a very positive frame of mind about our relationship when Nick showed up unexpectedly." I look over at him. He remains unmoved. "I know I made my own missteps during that conversation, and I apologize for those as well."

He offers the slightest nod. We walk on in silence, unspoken words heavy between us. I ache to tell him the rest, but I want to honor his emotions, not hurry past them or run roughshod over them. After an eternity of quiet, I ask, "I don't want to monopolize the conversation, but may I say one more thing?"

He nods, finally.

"I had sex with him just once, right when we got there. After the first night—a totally sleepless one for me—I knew it was over. I knew I couldn't, wouldn't get back together with him. My feelings for him just weren't there anymore. I knew, deep down, that there wasn't going to be any reviving of them. So, that next morning, I sat him down and told him all that."

Quinn's eyes flicker.

"He left about an hour after that. I don't know where he went. Back to Maryland, I presume. Anyway, he left. I stayed on at the inn that night, then moved over to a cheap motel for the remaining time. It's not that I wanted to be away from you, away from the others, but I knew that I had to think things through on my own. I wanted to call and tell you what was going on, but I knew if I did, I'd probably come running back here and ... I needed time to figure out ... what I want, sure, but more than that, I had to figure out who I am, what I'm all about. To do that I had to be alone, have time to think."

Now Quinn's eyes are wide with a mix of surprise and what looks like hope. "What did you come up with?"

My hands find refuge in my pockets. "Well, two things, really." As soon as the words are out of my mouth, I want to take them back. I'm not ready to tell him about the second thing, the job possibility. I try to cover myself, saying, "The first is you, Quinn. The second is us." I kick aside a few twigs and nudge his shoe with mine. I draw a deep breath, trying to figure out how much to reveal.

"I'm not sure if I'm falling in love with you or just grasping for something stable. But I really like you, Quinn. Very, very much." I glance up and catch his expression softening. "I know you might not be up for something serious, but I keep imagining what it could be like, you and me, after Chatham. I'm just being honest here."

184

The air around Quinn lightens, tension and anger visibly melting away from him like wax from a flame. Yet, I can tell he's grappling with a whole new set of emotions now. His face is a complex crossword puzzle I can't quite solve. "Hallie, I ..." He trails off, his eyes scanning the horizon as if helpful words might be written there in the clouds. "I don't—"

I cut in, sparing us both agony. "It's fine, Quinn. You don't have to respond right now. I know I just dropped a lot on you. And I've been a bit of a human wildfire lately, not exactly something you'd want to get close to without hesitation."

Quinn's got plot twists of his own he's dealing with. I decide to address them. I say, "Plus, you've got things on your plate that may complicate your feelings about us. Like the whole Megan-and-Jack situation." He gives me a small nod. "And the Wisconsin job? Any new developments?"

Quinn's a deer caught in headlights, probably recalling my peevish reaction earlier to both topics. I'm prepared now to force myself to accept whatever he says with more composure.

He runs a hand through his hair. "Well, Wisconsin has made me a formal offer. That surprised me, because I figured they'd want me to give some sort of talk or seminar. But because of the pandemic—and because so many of their faculty already could vouch for me—they dispensed with that. Anyway, it's a generous, attractive offer. I told them I'd think about it."

This news—that he might be leaving Boston—hits me like a gut punch, but I try to keep my cool, remain upbeat. "That's great news, Quinn! Congratulations. Very exciting for you. Maybe a big change of that sort is just what you need!"

"Thanks, but I'm not at all sure that's what I need."

I'm about to dive into the deep waters of his kids' disapproval when I stop myself. It would be presumptuous of me to bring it up—their feelings only matter if Quinn sees a future for us, and that's still a big 'if.'

But before I can shift the topic away, he adds, "I haven't spoken to Megan or Jack, so I don't know of any change there." He takes my hand, and my heart skips a beat. "As for us ..." He leans in, gently resting his forehead against mine. "I care deeply about you, Hallie. You're incredible, and I keep thinking about us—about our having more, much more."

My heart does a gymnastics routine, leaping and flipping, while Quinn continues, "When we talked early last week about the Wisconsin offer, I made an unforgivable omission. I should have told you upfront that you're the main reason I wouldn't want the job. If I don't take it, it will be because I want to be in Boston with you, to see what we could become. But I was wary of rushing into anything. And these last several days have not exactly given me a warm fuzzy about our prospects for anything ongoing."

I take a deep breath, trying to calm my heartbeat. "I can't begin to tell you how happy I am that you want to see what we ... this ... could become. And I understand that you have reservations. How could you not—especially in light of how I trampled your feelings last week? I'm sorry again for being so insensitive."

A smile pulls at the corners of his lips. "Let's take things slow and see what happens."

We resume our walk through the scrub oak. Soon enough, we come across the little clearing where I'd flipped the flat rock on our previous visit here. Quinn, adopting a humorously pompous tone, says, "Life's unpredictable: you never know where it's going to take you or what's going to happen next." Pointing to the rock, he says, "That rock certainly didn't know last spring what wild upheaval was in its future."

His tone is light, and I appreciate that he's subtly nudging us back toward the comfortable, easy sort of talk we're used to. And it's working: the tension from earlier has dissipated. As if nature has formed a pact with Quinn to brighten things, the clouds part and sunlight hits our shoulders. The air fills with the sweet scent of pine needles, intermingling with the earthy aroma of damp soil. "Stupid rock," I say, poking it with the toe of my shoe. "It shoulda known."

As we stroll, he recounts his outing with Lisa and Maria, telling me places they stopped along 6A. When he mentions the bookshops, I say, "Oh, I wish I'd been with you!"

He shoots me a playfully snarky glance and says, "Coulda, shoulda, Hallie."

"Yeah, yeah, my bad! Sorry." Our footsteps crunch softly on the forest floor, accompanied by the occasional rustle of leaves and chirping of birds—nature's own soundtrack playing around us. "It would be fun to hit those spots on 6A, just the two of us."

Quinn drops a mini-bombshell. "Not much time left, I'm afraid. Lisa and Paul are thinking of heading back to Chestnut Hill soon—a day or two after Thanksgiving. Looks like our idyllic retreat will be drawing to a close soon."

This news hits me harder than I expect. Our interlude here has been so damn good. And I'm afraid of what might happen when the reality of ordinary life comes crashing back. I can't help but groan. "Oh, I don't want to leave. I love it here. With you."

He pulls me into a hug, and it's like stepping into the warmth of a summer sunbeam. He cups my cheek, his thumb drawing gentle circles. He brushes my lips with his. Omigod, this reconnection feels so good. It's like I'm a patch of parched earth and he's a long-awaited, quenching rain. I lean into him, enjoying the closeness, the smell of his skin. So damn good. He kisses me again, a kiss that starts sweetly but quickly deepens. I part my lips, allowing his tongue to find mine. A growl escapes from low in his throat and I can feel him hardening against me. He gasps a little as I breathe into his ear and press my hips against him. He breaks away, laughing. "Uncle! I cry uncle! Christ Jesus, can we go back to the house? Fast?"

I reel him back in and reach down to palm his hardness. He groans again, a mix of frustration and ecstasy. "House?" I tease, giggling at his plight. "You think you'll even make it back to the car?"

24

Hallie

Maria's nestled into a corner of the deep-cushioned couch in the sunroom, engrossed in that Ibram Kendi volume she snagged at the bookstore on Nantucket. "Looking pretty cozy there," I say, entering the room and breaking her quietude. "Mind if I crash your reading party for a chat?"

"Be my guest." She gestures to the chair next to her.

"Thanks. We haven't talked in a while."

Her eyebrows knit together in a tight frown. Her lips press into a thin line, holding back what she's thinking. She doesn't have to say it out loud, I know that it was inconsiderate of me to stay away without letting anyone know what I was doing.

"Yeah, yeah. I know. But, look, it all worked out okay. I completely got Nick out of my system. I really did. And now I don't have to think about him anymore. That's good, right?"

"It is."

"You never approved of him, did you?"

She pauses, choosing her words. "I ... I just wanted you to be with someone who appreciated you fully, every dimension of you. And Nick wasn't that person."

I jigger the stuffing of a couch pillow. "You were wiser than I."

She gives me a half smile. "A good friend of mine reminded me not long ago that we all make mistakes."

I chuckle. "Smart cookie! ... How *are* things with you and Mike?"

"Still frosty. But I think we're thawing."

"Good. And with Joli?"

She sends out a lungful of air. "I have to say, Hal, it still blows my mind." Her gaze becomes distant and unfocused as she gets lost in thoughts of Joli having that abortion. Finally re-engaging, she says, "That's another piece of damaged trust that's going to need some serious repair work."

"But you and Joli are tight," I say. "You two will bounce back sooner than you think."

"I hope you're right." A long pause. "You know, our first or second day here, I had this heart-to-heart with Lisa. She told me that she felt emotionally disconnected from Maddie and Paul. And I felt so judgmental toward her—so superior, so smug about my close relationships with Joli and Mike." Maria looks down at her hands for a moment. "Turns out, I had nothing to be smug about: my family relationships are as screwed up as hers."

I reach over and give her foot a reassuring squeeze. We lock eyes, and I hope she sees the empathy in mine. Finally, she breaks eye contact, and smiles. "So, what's up? I know you well enough to know you didn't seek me out to hear about my existential well-being."

I chuckle again. "That's not true. I did want to know how you're doing. But, you're right: there's something I want to talk with you about, get your feedback on."

She sits up straighter, alert. "Shoot."

I draw a dramatic breath. "I did a Zoom interview today for a job in Los Angeles."

Her jaw drops. "As in, land of movie stars and traffic jams?"

I nod. "That's the one."

"Tell me, tell me!"

"Disney owns this production company called 20th Television. With so many of their shows being shot differently now because of COVID, they're looking for a slew of theater- stage-set designers. The pay is great—much above what I'm used to earning in Boston for my work."

"How did you hear about this?"

I feel my cheeks redden. "Nick tipped me off to it."

Her expression sours like she's just eaten a lemon. "Nick? Is he applying for work there, too?"

"Said he might."

"So ... your decision to apply ... it's not because of him, is it?"

"No way. The thought of him being there almost stopped me from applying. But that would've been silly." She nods in agreement. "I'm actually excited about this job, Mar!"

"Where would you live?"

"Carter's offered me a room at his house. It's plenty big enough to accommodate me. So I wouldn't have to pay for housing or commit to an apartment lease."

She mulls all this over. "When would this happen?"

"Well, they asked me how soon I could start, and I said I was ready to hit the road yesterday."

"Have you told Quinn about this?"

I shake my head, feeling like a kid caught concealing brussels sprouts in his napkin. "I ... don't want to worry him if it's not a done deal." I pause, realizing I'm considering two deals that are not quite done, one of them being what lies ahead for Quinn and me. "But I'll tell him right away if I get it. Promise."

Again, she takes a while before she responds. Then she simply nods. "Please tell me if I'm being too nosy," she says. "Where do you see things going with Quinn? It's clear you two like each other, and there's real magic in the way you relate."

I light up, "We do have something special, don't we? We'll continue to see each other. We've agreed to take it slow and see what develops. But it's not simple."

"What's complicating it?"

"For one thing, Quinn's been offered a good job on the faculty at the University of Wisconsin, in Madison. There are reasons he might not accept, but he finds the offer appealing, so there's that. Even if—and this is getting way ahead of myself— even if he were to ask me to go there with him, I don't see how I could find work there. The stage-theater world there is small— mostly, university theaters, where students do the stage designs."

"Okay. What else?"

"Quinn casually mentioned me to his kids, and their reaction to the idea of a new woman in his life was ... well, not pretty. They're not exactly rolling out a welcome mat for me."

"They ... what? Think three years is too soon for him to move on?"

I nod.

She snorts. "What? Are they five years old? That's ridiculous."

"Tell me about it. But feelings aren't always rational."

We fall into a thoughtful silence. Then she asks, "Is this L.A. gig a backup plan, a hedge against you and Quinn not working out?"

"I suppose that entered my mind, but no, it's really about the job itself."

Maria leans forward, scrutinizing me. "Hallie, are you even happy any more doing stage-design work?"

Her question brings me up short. "Well, I ... what do you mean?"

"I mean, you haven't really seemed happy the past couple of years. Yes, I know you might point to the turmoil in your personal life as an explanation for that, but—and I'm saying this as someone who has known you and loved you for a very long time, *chérie*—I've wondered if all that relationship mess was partly a result of your no longer being happy at what you do for work."

I'm taken aback, her insight hitting me like she's grabbed my face and forced me to smell a bowl of rancid food. Yes, my personal life was a mess, but linking that to my job dissatisfaction is a revelation. That had never occurred to me. As for no longer finding the design work fulfilling—well, there are lots of reasons for that: the artistic compromises forced by budget cuts, know-it-all directors and producers ... I could go on. But the real reason is that I'd much rather be working with words, language —my true loves.

As if she's been tapping my thoughts, Maria continues, "And seeing you interact with Quinn is like watching very smart puppies frolic, Hal. You're so animated when you two are engaging in your crazy wordplay. You're a different Hallie, one who's truly in her element."

My heart races as I listen to my best friend say aloud what

I've silently thought many times. She's hit the nail on the head. Yet, all I manage to muster in response is, "Yeah, but that's just having fun!"

"Exactly my point! You're as happy as a clam at high tide when you're lost in words!"

"But, Maria, I can't earn a living by selling tickets to a patio pun-off with Quinn!"

She rolls her eyes. "No, of course you can't. But now you're just being obstinate! You know damn well you could earn a living by, say, being a translator or adaptor, finding just the perfect words and phrases to capture the meaning of a text. ... You're like a walking-talking Rosetta Stone with all your languages. You'd have no problem getting plenty of work."

"You can't be sure of that."

"And you can't be sure you wouldn't be the next big thing in the translation world!"

"It would involve taking a huge risk, a leap in the dark."

"It would be a leap, yes. But when's a better time to jump? You're not tied down with work, you have the time to look for opportunities that might fit you, and you have a safety net with me and Mike."

We're quiet as I allow my thoughts to steep in this brain *buzio* she's stirred up. Finally, she breaks the silence. "One last thing: I know you, Hallie. You're not meant for the shallow end of the pool. You've always been a deep-end diver. Playing it safe isn't your style. And this Disney thing? It's like changing lanes on the same highway. It would mean keeping yourself comfortably within the design world. Maybe it's time to take the exit ramp to something new, something you're passionate about."

Listening to Maria is like eavesdropping on my own heart.

25

Hallie

Everyone's up early on Thanksgiving morning. The house buzzes with activity. Maria and Lisa have planned a full day of cooking—their idea of fun. Paul and Mike each have a couple hours of work they want to get out of the way. Quinn has Zoom calls scheduled with Meg and Jack. I wonder if the subject of our relationship will come up in those conversations and what Quinn would say about it. I'm guessing he'll avoid talking about me at this point. He's emotionally bruised by my callous behavior—and that's on top of his other reservations about us! So, I doubt there'll be any movement of the Jack-and-Megan rock today.

When I ramble into the kitchen, Maria's already there, having started her culinary marathon. She's busy preparing Cape Verdean *cuscuz*—little yellow cakes made out of flour, cinnamon, honey, and sugar. They look like the love child of corn bread and lemon cake. "We can snack on these throughout the morning," Maria says. "They're best warm, with a bit of salted butter."

She sets me up at the big round table in the kitchen alcove and gives me coffee and a plate of these cakey delights. We dive into a chat about *cuscuz*—its spelling, its origins, the times it graces Cape Verdeans' tables. Then Maria shifts back to the counter and starts chopping fresh cranberries and oranges for a chutney that the Barros family has been preparing for generations.

Quinn saunters in, catching sight of me in my jade-green kimono. He smiles and quips, "Good morning, *Cio-Cio-san.*"

I smile at his reference and flip my locks with dramatic flair. "Yep, a dark blonde makes the best Madame Butterfly. It confuses the hell out of the audience, keeps 'em on their toes!" I turn to Maria. "Just make sure I'm far away from big knives today, will you, Mar?"

She gives the two of us a bewildered look. "Will do—even though your esoteric jokes are flying straight over my head, as usual."

Quinn plops in the chair next to me, having served himself a plate of *cuscuz* and a mug of coffee.

I grin at him. "The conflict-avoider in you must feel a real kinship with Pinkerton."

"True, I do. Perhaps because I find my own flaws more palatable in others."

"How magnanimous of you!" I nudge him and point to his plate with my chin. "Know what that is you're eating?"

He inspects the yellow mound on his plate. "Cake."

I roll my eyes theatrically. "Ha! 'Cake!' Did you hear that,

Mar?" I lean forward to instruct him. "That, my dear man, is not cake, it's *cuscuz.*"

"Couscous?"

"Try to pay attention, It's kooze-kweeze. Not kooze-kooze. Kweeze! ... I guess your ear has trouble with that fine distinction," I tease.

He grabs hold of my ear and twists it playfully. "Your little Japanese scoop might need some tuning when I'm done with it, *Cio-Cio.*"

"Ouch! Watch it, buster! Now you're in trouble!" I pull him into an arm-wrestling match, and soon we're in fits of laughter. The bittersweet variety in my case. I can't help thinking that this sort of spontaneity may soon end.

Lisa comes into the kitchen, mid-contest. Nodding toward us, she asks Maria, "What in the world's going on there?"

Maria shakes her head. "Just their usual antics. Trying to out-do each other. They're incorrigible. They're like fourth-graders! I swear if we left them alone, they'd make prank phone calls, smear Vaseline on doorknobs, fill salt shakers with sugar."

Lisa chuckles. "Yeah, fourth-graders with the vocabularies of Oxford dons." She gives Maria a hug, less in greeting than in commiseration over their having to put up with us. "God help us. It's going to be a long day with these two clowns."

I'm giggling with Quinn as our locked forearms sway, first tipping one way, then the other. "Good thing you're not a professor of weight lifting," I mutter through gritted teeth, straining with the effort of battle. "You'd never have gotten tenure." When I start giggling harder at my own joke, Quinn slams the back of my hand down to the table with a loud thwap.

My jaw flies open with surprise. "You were *toying* with me?!"

"Did you really think you were holding me to a draw? I may not be Arnold Schwarzenegger, but I'm not a pussy."

"Too bad," I joke, licking the back of his hand. "I like pussy."

"Eeeeeww!" Lisa's shriek of disgust just adds fuel to the chorus of laughter.

By 11 AM, Mike and Paul have glued themselves to the TV, ready for a football marathon. Quinn is peripatetic, drifting back and forth between the living room and the kitchen.

Charlie trots in, curious about the smells. When the dog swerves his nose too close to the turkey—now in repose on the counter, awaiting its ingress to the oven—Lisa shoos him away. "Not for you, mister!"

I call to Charlie to console him. "Come here, Charlie. Is mommy being mean to you? She's a bad mommy. Poor, poor Charlie," I murmur, ruffling the top of Charlie's head and the furry scruff of his neck.

Lisa smiles at me and Quinn. "Why don't you two trouble-makers do something useful, like take Charlie for a walk?"

Maria says, "Oh, what a good idea! Get these obnoxious lovebirds out of here for a while!"

"Quisling!" I jeer, snapping Maria's rear as I leave the kitchen to get dressed for the walk.

Outside, the wind's howling like a banshee with a mega-phone. I dart back in for a heavier jacket, then we head down the drive, Charlie leading our little pack. When we hit Old Queen Anne Road, I say, "Let's do Maria's route. Takes about 45 minutes. You cool with that?" Quinn nods his assent. We walk in companionable silence, stopping regularly for Charlie's inves-tigative sniffs.

Quinn says aloud what I've been thinking every day. "I don't want this Chatham venture to end. The prospect of returning to normal life seems so daunting."

"Are you worried that what we have here won't survive outside this paradise?"

He nods and releases a heavy sigh. "I admit it's crossed my mind."

We walk on, each of us lost in our own fears and hopes. I don't believe for a moment that this has just been some infatuation. But for us to make it out there, Quinn will have to open himself fully to all we could become. Will he? Or is he too worried he can't count on me for the long haul?

When the clock ticks toward dinner, Quinn and I finally join the others in the living room. Maria greets us. "Well, hi there! Dinner's almost ready. We're watching ... uh, what game is this now?" she asks, turning to Mike.

"Washington and Dallas," he replies, eyes glued to the TV.

"That one. We're watching that and drinking wine. Want a glass?"

"We're good. Don't get up. We'll grab our own, thanks," I say, pulling Quinn toward the kitchen like he's a rolling suitcase and I'm late for my plane. I pour us wine, then wrap my arms around him, ready for a Hollywood-style smooch, when Maria comes in to give the turkey one last basting.

"You two doing okay?" she asks.

"Better than okay," Quinn confirms with a grin.

Maria lays a hand on each of our shoulders, like she's about to cast a spell or confer a blessing. "*Rei de sabi*," she says. "In Cape Verdean Creole, that literally means 'the king is good.' But what it means in this context is, 'You're the best.' You two ... you're the best." The three of us huddle into a hug, and I can't help but exchange a giddy smile with Quinn over Maria's head.

Before long, Lisa shuffles in, followed by Paul and Mike, who somehow have managed to detach themselves from the TV's gravitational pull. The turkey makes its grand exit from the oven, the potatoes get a mashing, and the sauerkraut gets its warm-up.

"Sauerkraut?" Mike says.

Lisa launches into a culinary history lesson. "It's an Alsace-Lorraine thing. My mom's family was from there. Thanksgiving dinner always had sauerkraut at the table. It goes well with turkey. You'll like it, I promise."

We gather around the dining table, clinking glasses and sharing a chorus of gratitude. The mood is bittersweet, all of us aware we're soon Boston-bound. Quinn stands up like he's just won an Oscar and gives a heartfelt thanks to Paul and Lisa for their generous hospitality. His glance takes us all in. "You're all special people. Here's to our friendship," he toasts, then we all dive into the feast.

Mike moans like he's being filmed for a food commercial. "So good! I need to pace myself!"

Paul says, "Every Thanksgiving, my dad would give my mom the 'you've outdone yourself' speech. Tonight, I can say, Lisa and Maria really have outdone themselves!" We all cheer, then pass serving dishes around again like we're in a food relay race. The room buzzes with laughter, the clinking of cutlery, and the warmth of shared company.

As the conversation hits a pause, Maria scans our faces like she's a talk-show host, hoping to fill some dead air space. "Any Thanksgiving tales to share?"

We all do a deep dive into our memory archives. Since nobody else speaks, I seize the spotlight. "Okay, so I was a teen. We had this Thanksgiving bash at our place, full of my parents' artsy friends. Picture this: my parents, ready to unveil the turkey, like it's the Crown Jewels. But as they lifted it from the roasting pan to the carving plate, the big forks they were using bisected the damn thing, thrusting it up and showering turkey carnage all over the kitchen. It was like a scene from a poultry horror movie!"

"Omigod!" Quinn chuckles. "Did they end up serving floor turkey?"

"No, some of the meat managed to avoid the floor. They salvaged that. And, of course, there were still various side dishes. My mom, a culinary MacGyver, plunged into rescue mode. She turned the asparagus into a main dish by serving each portion of it with a fried egg on top, along with little curls of prosciutto, drizzled with oil and vinegar. She was a genius in emergencies. It turned out to be our most delicious and memorable Thanksgiving meal ever."

After the feast winds down, I hop up to clear dishes, and everyone else joins the cleanup crew. Lisa brews coffee, and we reconvene at the table. Maria appears, brandishing a tray of what look like gourmet donut holes drizzled in honey. When I spot those, my taste buds leap like they're tiny treasure hunters who've just spied gold. I've had those before at Maria's table, and they're fabulous—a sweet, starchy root's love affair with honey.

"Behold," she proclaims. "*Bolinhos de mandioca com mel*. These are made with eggs, molasses, *aguardente*—a strong alcoholic spirit—and manioc flour. Manioc's like a potato. You might know it as cassava, what tapioca comes from."

Paul bites into one and moans like he's Mike's understudy. "These are absolutely amazing, Maria. Thanks for the treat."

Maria beams. "Glad you like them." She regales us with stories of past Thanksgivings in New Bedford or Dorchester, teeming with Cape Verdean people and food. "Not unusual to have 30 to 40 folks at one home for Thanksgiving, everybody bringing dishes they've prepared. One set of cousins is even doing a big bash this year, in the middle of a pandemic! Talk about crazy!"

Lisa says, "That reminds me. I wonder what the girls are doing for Thanksgiving dinner. Did you talk with Joli today?"

Maria checks the time. "I was waiting until later this evening. It's only 6:20 there."

Paul says, "Let's Zoom with them. Lisa, would you text Maddie and see if they're free to do that?"

"I'm on it," Lisa says, grabbing her phone.

Mike jumps in with a tech solution so all of us can see easily. "I've got a Roku mirroring app on my laptop. Let's Zoom in the living room and beam it onto the big screen."

Lisa returns with a thumbs-up from the girls, and soon Mike and Paul are orchestrating the technical setup. The rest of us finish clearing up, all of us buzzing with the anticipation of connecting with the girls, a perfect end to our Thanksgiving extravaganza.

At 9 PM sharp, the living room turns into our own personal theater, with the big screen taking center stage. Mike gets the Zoom show on the road, and soon enough, Maddie and Joli's larger-than-life faces beam down at us. "Happy Turkey Day!" they yell, their smiles alive with enthusiasm.

We all wave back like we're on a Macy's parade float. The girls called Lisa last week to apologize for the way they each took her to task in the wake of the abortion revelation. So, apart from the long-term work that Joli and I have to do on our relationship, feelings are pretty much back to normal. Lisa says, "Looking fabulous, girls! Did you guys do the whole turkey shebang?"

Joli laughs. "Nah, we ditched the bird for a boneless lamb roast. Way easier, and nobody missed all that turkey-prep drama.

And, *Manman*, I made those manioc balls with honey for dessert!"

Lisa chimes in. "Your mom made those for us, too! They're like little drops of heaven!" When the conversation meanders from food to future plans, Lisa gets down to business. "What's the verdict on next semester? You all staying there?"

Maddie says, "We took a vote by secret ballot yesterday. It was 5-to-1 for a change of scenery. Time to do something different in the spring, although campus is still a no-go zone, for everybody but seniors."

Relieved to hear the outcome of the vote, Maria says, "Glad you'll be coming home, Jo. We'll figure the rest out." I realize with a start that Joli's planned return means I'll have to vacate her bedroom. What will I do? Where will I go?

After the call ends, we all stay on in the living room for a while, some of us having another glass of wine. My newest anxiety keeps me on the outer edge of the conversations swirling around me. Just as I've working myself into a right tizzy over this quandary, it occurs to me that a job offer from Disney might come any day now, ending any housing worries: my head would be hitting the pillow at Carter's house in California, not searching for a place to rest in Massachusetts.

My attention snaps to Quinn, who's laughing at something Mike has said. Guilt gnaws at my gut over keeping him in the dark about my possible relocation. But I don't know what else to do at this point. Soon, events will force my hand, and I'll have to play the cards I'm dealt.

26

Maria

I don't see how much longer I can put this off. I've been dodging this moment since we returned to Boston three days ago. But it's time to rip off the band-aid and tell José I can't keep giving him regular cash donations. As I make my way into Dorchester to see him, my nerves are as jittery as a caffeinated cat's. The thought of letting José down twists my stomach into knots.

He greets me with his usual warmth. "*Modi bu sta, chérie?*" he asks. His hug feels like a lifeline.

"*Muiti ben,*" I reply, but I'm sure my voice must betray unease.

"You've been gone for ages."

"Yeah, longer than expected. How are things here?"

José's face darkens. "It's a nightmare. The need is skyrocketing, Maria. I feel like I'm ... trying to plug a dam with a toothpick." He shares stories of families we both know, their struggles hitting me like a punch in the gut.

Trembling a bit, I hand him an envelope. "José, there's a check in here."

His gratitude is a warm blanket. "You're an angel in disguise, Maria."

Now comes the hard part. "But, José, this is the last donation I can make. I'm sorry."

His smile doesn't falter. "You've done so much. You've been a godsend. Please don't worry."

Tears blur my vision as I tell him the truth. "My husband didn't know about the money. He found out, and ... well, he wasn't thrilled about my secrecy."

José's face softens, a blend of understanding and appreciation. "Your heart is as big as the ocean, Maria .... I'm sorry this caused you trouble."

I try to explain. "He's a good man. He's not mad about the giving, just the hiding. This last check from us is for $5,000. We both hope it helps."

José's chest rises and falls as he takes the envelope, his face full of unchecked emotion. He places a hand over his heart. "How can I thank you enough? This is huge for us."

I reassure him. "I might not be giving more money, but I've got hands and time. I'll be back to help soon." Remembering that Lisa told me she wants to volunteer here with me, I add, "And I'll be bringing a friend to help, too."

He blesses me with a smile and wraps me in a hug, his gratitude evident in the way he holds on tight. "*Obrigadu,* dear Maria. Your spirit is our treasure."

As I leave, I feel lighter. I've faced the music, and the tune wasn't as harsh as I'd feared.

Hallie's still not home when I get there. She's been out all afternoon with Quinn. He's joining us for dinner tonight, so they'll be here before long. After freshening up, I make my way through our small, tidy house to the kitchen, where Mike's in the midst of prepping mango salsa for our baked-tilapia dinner. The counter is a rainbow of ingredients—bright yellow mango, vivid red bell peppers, a medley of green from cilantro, jalapeño, and lime. A lone red onion sits untouched, like the last guest at a party. "Leaving the best for last?" I tease.

Mike grumbles. "Yep. I'm no fan of onion tears."

"Allow me," I offer, taking the knife and chopping the onion into smaller and smaller pieces with the precision of a surgeon. I gather the diced pieces into a pile. Then, inspired, I arrange all the colorful bits into a cheerful little Christmas tree.

Mike leans in, admiring the culinary artwork. "Festive salsa!"

"Just adding a bit of pre-holiday spirit," I reply, proud of my impromptu decoration. Pointing to the bottle of *vinho verde* on the other side of Mike, I playfully say, "Now that I've bravely tackled Onion Mountain here, how about rewarding a humble kitchen expeditioner with some wine?"

Mike raises an eyebrow. "What's in it for me?"

"My undying devotion and eternal gratitude?"

He makes a show of weighing his options. "Hmmm, not sure that's quite enough. Got anything else?"

I snatch the dish towel, twirling it into a makeshift whip. With a flick of my wrist, I send some onion bits flying, a demonstration of my towel-wielding prowess. "How about I agree not to snap your ass with this?"

Mike jumps back, mock horror on his face. "You wouldn't dare! There'll be dire consequences!"

Ignoring his threat, I snap at his legs. "Better pour that wine, or else!"

"Okay, that's it!" Mike exclaims, adopting a wrestler's stance. Before I know it, he's hoisted me over his shoulder like a sack of potatoes. "Time for you to learn a lesson!"

I'm in fits of laughter, pounding on his back. "Put me down, you scoundrel!"

He laughs. "Scoundrel? What is this, a pirate movie?"

"Okay, put me down, *fiju di puta*!"

"Son of a bitch, eh? Well, how about I drop you out in that big slushy puddle on the back lawn?"

He feigns heading for the door, and I shriek, laughing and walloping his back even harder.

Finally, he gently sets me down. We're both red-faced and breathless from laughter and exertion. The air feels lighter, the past weeks' tension between us now resolved. I learned an invaluable lesson from all that—I'm not saying it was worth the pain I caused both Mike and me—but it was indispensable in that it got me to take a good hard look at myself, and my particular kind of self-righteous arrogance that glosses over sins committed in the name of charity.

Catching his breath, and pouring me some wine, Mike asks, "Did you talk with Joli about the plans for Christmas?"

I nod. "She was bummed about skipping the family bash, but she understood." During our FaceTime chat this morning, I told Joli we'd decided against attending the Barros family's huge annual Christmas-night celebration in New Bedford. Still too much risk with the virus, too much uncertainty. "She perked up when I mentioned the Campbells' invitation."

"That's a relief," Mike admits. "I wasn't sure how she'd take all that."

I place my hand on his chest, meeting his eyes. "Mike, I need to thank you again for this last food-bank donation—and for your understanding about the previous ones."

He tries to shush me. "There's no need to keep talking about it, Mar. We've been over it enough."

"No, I know. What I want to say is that, thanks to all your hard work over the years, we really are in very good financial shape. We're not even feeling a pinch by my giving away that large amount. ... I think all this time, I've been embarrassed by how well off we are, had a hard time admitting it to myself. And that led me to be ... well, unnecessarily tight-fisted around the house. I've stood in the way of you and Joli enjoying the benefits of our abundance. I want to change that."

He gently cups my chin. "Maria, your frugality and your charitableness are things I love about you. You don't have to change anything."

I smile, determined. "You're sweet. Still, it's time we enjoy our blessings. I'm thinking a new car for you. And for Joli's Christmas gift, I'm thinking we should—"

The front door opens and there's a shuffling of feet in the front hall, heralding the arrival of Hallie and Quinn. After a brief commotion involving coats and winter gear, the four of us settle around the kitchen table with wine in hand.

"*Txin-txin,*" I say to them, raising my glass.

Mike echoes, "Yes, cheers!" We clink glasses and pass around some *pastel com diabo dentro*, the same spicy appetizer I made early in our time in Chatham.

Something's off between Hallie and Quinn. They seem like two actors who've forgotten their lines. Quinn's smile doesn't quite reach his eyes. The tension between the two of them is as thick and strong as these empanadas.

Quinn says, "Hallie has big news."

I, of course, know that this must be news about the Disney job. But I didn't tell Mike about that, so his eyes dart to Hallie;

he's clearly thinking *baby news!* I almost burst into a laugh at his expression, but manage to hold it together.

Hallie says, "I accepted a job offer today. It's in California."

I'm disappointed by this news—fearing what it might mean for Hallie and Quinn and believing that Hallie should be pursuing work she'd find more fulfilling. But right now, she obviously needs me to pretend I knew nothing about this Disney thing and just play along. So, I do my best to provide 'oohs' and 'aahs' at the right moments as Hallie talks about the work, the salary, the plan to live at Carter's. All of it.

"How did you hear about this?" Mike asks, obviously curious how a California television job had come to her attention—and oblivious to the mine field he's just steered the conversation into.

Hallie's cheeks redden. "Nick told me about it when he came to the Cape last month."

I sneak a glance at Quinn, who looks like he'd rather be anywhere but here.

Hallie goes on. "I did a Zoom interview with them before Thanksgiving. They called me this afternoon and offered me the job. I accepted."

Mike says, "That's fabulous, Hallie! Congratulations." I see Quinn's back stiffen, the thin set of his lips harden.

"When will you go?" I ask.

"Sunday," she replies, as if it's only a casual trip to the grocery store.

I can't help but blurt, "This Sunday? That's super soon!" Quinn's sigh is so heavy it could sink a ship.

"I know. But they need me to start right away. And I can do it, so ..."

Quinn catches my eye. "It's a lot to take in, right?" His tone is hard and I totally sympathize,

I nod, imagining how difficult this must be for him. "How long will this be for?" I ask. "Do you see this as a permanent job?"

"Oh, no, no, not at all. When COVID is under control and theatre work in Boston starts coming back, I'll return. This is just short term. And, hey, I'll come back having new experiences under my belt, new arrows in my professional quiver."

Sounding thoroughly beaten down, Quinn says to her, "You can't be certain you won't be there long! The pandemic may go on for many months, Hal. Or you may get out there and love everything about your life there."

Hallie touches his hand. "Oh, Quinn, I know this is hard for you. This is not the time to go into all that again."

He retracts his hand and crosses his arms. He looks at me and Mike, his expression flinty. With all the subtlety of a sledge-hammer, he says, "The other delightful news is that Nick's there, too!" The room goes as quiet as a cloistered convent. Mike's jaw almost drops to the ground.

Hallie squirms, her face now a shade of deep crimson, as she avoids eye contact. She fidgets, shifting in her chair. "Yes, he's been there since before Thanksgiving. Apparently, he went out there soon after I saw him."

Mike and I exchange glances. I say, "Have you talked with him? How do you know he's there?"

"No, I haven't talked with him. The person who called me with the offer knew that Nick and I had once worked together and told me that Nick had recently started work there."

Now, really exasperated, Quinn slaps the table. "What do you expect me to make of all this, Hallie?"

"Don't make anything of it! My going there has nothing to do with Nick! Absolutely nothing! I'm going because I want interesting work! That's all there is to it!"

I believe Hallie when she says Nick has nothing to do with this, but she's being less than fully honest when she says she wants this "interesting work." More interesting than food services, sure, but far less interesting than working with words or language, which is the path she should be pursuing.

Quinn's tone drips with annoyance. "If that's 'all there is to it,' why weren't you forthcoming about Nick when you first told me about taking the job?"

"I did tell you!" The anger's building in Hallie's voice, too.

"Three hours later, yes. But only because I asked! If I hadn't asked, you wouldn't have told me!"

"I knew it would upset you!"

"Of course it upsets me!"

"Quinn, please don't do this. There's absolutely nothing to worry about. I have no feelings at all for Nick anymore." A long silence descends. The tension could cut diamonds as the two of them lock eyes.

"I don't want you to do this, Hallie. Please stay."

"I'm sorry. I want this work. I'm going."

Quinn abruptly pushes back his chair and bolts from the room. The front door opens, then slams shut. But no car engine roars to life, so I figure he's just stepping out for some air and space. True to my hunch, about twenty minutes later, he returns, fairly composed and calm, like a coastal village after a storm has passed.

Approaching Hallie, he gently takes her hands, a gesture of peace. "You're right, Hallie. You should go. It's not my place to hold you back."

To me, it seems clear that Quinn is trying to convince himself of what he's saying.

But Hallie doesn't seem to notice that. Like all of us, she hears what she wants to hear. And right now, she wants to hear this indulgence from Quinn. Relief floods Hallie's face at the generous gift he's giving her—setting aside his own interest in favor of hers, pushing back his uncertainty and jealousy.

"What made you change—"

"My mind? I realized I shouldn't try to dictate your life when I don't like Meg and Jack trying to dictate mine."

She palms his cheek and says, "You're a dear man, Quinn. Thank you."

He kisses her, and I'm just about to signal Mike that he and I should leave the room, when Quinn speaks again, this time in a lighter tone. "Besides, staying here and redeeming customer coupons or picking groceries would underutilize your talents and intellect, 'waste your sweetness on the desert air.'"

Hallie tilts her head and squints, thinking. Then her eyes light up. "Thomas Gray's *Elegy*, right?"

The smile he gives her radiates warmth and appreciation. "Yep, only you would get that."

She plays bashful. "Aw, shucks. Easy-peasy."

Mike, ever the practical one, breaks the spell. "Alright, enough drama. Who's hungry?"

He jumps into action, shuffling the tilapia from the fridge into the oven. He then sets the rice cooking, while I place the salad bowl on the table and pour more wine for all of us.

The atmosphere lightens, and soon we're all laughing. Quinn takes the salad bowl and turns to Hallie. "Want me to toss your salad?"

A mischievous look crosses her face. She flicks her tongue at him and says, "I think I'd like that *very* much."

Her reply almost gets past us unnoticed. Then the bawdy idiom hits all three of us at once. Mike and Quinn groan. I squawk. "Ick, Hallie! You're *so* disgusting!"

She laughs and—now frisky—sings, "Watcha gonna do when a feller gets flirty / And starts to talk purty ...?"

Giggling, I join in, the two of us swaying and singing, "... Whatcha gonna do? / I'm just a girl who cain't say no ..."

Mike and Quinn roll their eyes. Quinn says, "Slutty little Okies!" We all dissolve in laughter.

Later, as the sounds of clinking dishes and running water fill the kitchen, Hallie tugs me into the quiet of the living room, her face a canvas of worry and urgency. In hushed tones, she confesses, "Mar, I'm so sorry for dropping my news on you like that. My afternoon was so busy dealing with Quinn's reaction that I didn't have a chance to alert you. Please, don't be upset. I hope you're not let down by my decision to take this job."

I offer her a reassuring smile. "I'm not upset with you, Hal." But inside, my disappointed heart is reading her the riot act: *TV set design? Sounds soul-sucking! You could be a world-class translator!*

Her eyes light up as she explains. "The salary is double what I made at Emerson. They've seen my work, Mar. They said they knew right away I was the perfect fit."

Her enthusiasm is infectious, yet I can't shake the feeling she's stepping into a gilded cage. I hold back from voicing my concerns.

"They told me, 'You're exactly what we want and need.'"

Ah, the sweet allure of being desired and valued. It's hard to resist that! I muster the most supportive tone I can. "How terrific for you, Hallie! It does sound amazing!" The words scrape against my conscience, and I can't help but wish she'd pay more attention to what truly fulfills her, not just what flatters her.

27

Hallie

What should be an easy drive to Logan airport on a Sunday morning proves a challenge. Gale-force winds howl while rain furiously tap-dances on Quinn's windshield, rendering the wipers comically inadequate to their task. Just as we're about to reach Terminal B's drop-off zone, my phone buzzes with a text from United: my flight to L.A. is delayed. Quinn insists that we spend the extra hour together. So, we head to the cell-phone waiting lot, push back our seats, and turn to face each other in our makeshift storm shelter.

Quinn's thumb traces soothing circles on the backs of my hands. "Excited? Daydreaming about California?" he inquires, commenting subtly on my silence during the drive here.

Am I excited? Honestly, my excitement has been performative the last day or two. Sure, the job's a great opportunity, but if feels now like I'm dragging myself toward it, not marching to it all cock-a-hoop. But now's not the time or place to say that. Instead, I offer an apologetic grin. "Sorry. I didn't mean to be silent all the way here. I guess I'm just a bit overwhelmed—new job, new city, leaving you ..."

He ponders a moment, then offers a lifeline in the form of a familiar Latin phrase: '*Ad astra per aspera.*'"

I smile and squeeze his hand. 'A rough road leads to the stars.' Quinn's trying to tell me that the turmoil I'm wrestling with will lead me to what I want. "That's sweet of you, Quinn. But I suppose that assumes I know what I want!"

"You seem to! And you seem determined to go get it."

Why wouldn't he believe the Disney job is what I want above all else? I've given him no reason to believe otherwise. There's no point in confessing the truth now, as I'm on the brink of leaving Boston to design doll houses for TV. So, I evade the topic, turn it back on him. "How about you? I haven't wanted to press you on the Wisconsin job. Any developments in your thoughts about it?"

His expression is sheepish, his face flushes. "Well, actually, I called them a few days ago and turned down the job. It was the same morning you accepted the Disney job. I was going to tell you when I picked you up for lunch, but you shared your news first, and after that, there didn't seem much urgency—much point, even—to sharing mine."

"Oh, Quinn! How awful. I'm sorry. Well, I'm surprised you didn't strangle me on the spot when I told you my news. You must have been livid. ... What made you decide to turn it down?"

"How much irony can you tolerate?" he says, his smile wry. "I decided I wanted to be in Boston with you, not in Madison, Wisconsin."

I stroke his cheek, and through teary eyes, try to look into his. The truth I've been suppressing for several weeks becomes crystal clear: I love him. My heart starts to race as I struggle with whether to say the words, express my truest feelings. "Quinn, it's so wonderful of you to have declined the job for me—for us." I pause for a long beat, trying to hold back. But a dam inside finally bursts and the words cascade from me. "I love you, Quinn O'Neill. I love you deeply and genuinely. So, so much."

I hold onto his hands and gaze into his eyes, waiting for his response. None comes. His gaze drops from my eyes to our hands. The silence stretches on between us, thick and unbearable. It finally hits me that perhaps I've dropped too potent a burden on him. "Maybe I shouldn't have said all that, Quinn," I groan.

"No, no, it's okay. I'm glad you told me." His words are sparse, containing not a hint of what I hoped to hear in return.

Each half-minute that ticks by is heavier than the last. Finally, unable to stand it any longer, I manage to whisper, "Don't you have anything to say? ... What feelings made you want to stay in Boston?"

His reply is slow in coming, his face a blank canvas. "I ... I don't know ... what to say."

Now, a different dam inside me breaks, allowing one sob to escape, then a spate of them. In a desperate move to flee Quinn's awful, heart-breaking muteness, I fling open my door and pitch myself into the rain.

Thank heavens for a six-hour flight; this one is a lifesaver. It's like a forced timeout—a long, solitary stretch to mull over what just happened with Quinn. There's something about soaring above the clouds that makes you think, or overthink, as the case may be. I've been pretty sure that Quinn and I are on the same wavelength. That zing in the air when we're together isn't just static cling!

But what just happened back at the airport has me replaying reels of our moments together the past few weeks. Have I been reading things incorrectly? Did I miss some blinking sign: 'Warning: Affections Might Be One-sided'? I'm half tempted to ask the flight attendant if she's got a crystal ball along with those tiny bags of peanuts she's handing out.

I groan in my confusion and fall into another round of weeping—a mound of wet, crumpled tissues growing in my lap. The guy next to me is getting a front-row seat to an in-flight soap opera. Poor dude, probably wishes he'd sprung for first-class and avoided my mini-meltdown.

By the time the Uber has whisked me from the airport to Brentwood, I've managed to morph back into something resembling a composed adult, prepared to greet my brother—which means bracing myself for Carter's usual whirlwind of a welcome. Sure enough, he throws open the front door and yanks me in from the porch like he's saving me from the path of a speeding bus. "Welcome to La La Land—the land of dreams!" he bellows.

Grinning despite myself and trying to match his high energy, I play along: "Land of dreams? Try: land of eternal gridlock, juice bars, and beach bimbos."

Now, his grin is as wide as the Hollywood sign. "That, and every smoothie comes sprinkled with a dash of movie magic!" He leads me into his living room, which is a cluttered mess—a far cry from the Campbells' pristine Chatham home. This place has character and chaos in equal measure. Stacks of books and esoteric journals everywhere. It feels familiar, filled with the haphazard, bookish charm of our childhood home.

While he goes to get us some icy refreshments, I grab the chance to survey the room in more detail. I inspect a mini-museum along one wall, the shelves cluttered with a hodge-podge of books, quirky knick-knacks, and trinkets, each a memento from some corner of the globe. Returning, he hands me a tall glass of seltzer with lemon slices bobbing amidst the ice cubes. "Thanks. ... So, Carter, I know you travel a lot, but I had no idea you've been to all these places! Got any favorites?"

He ponders, then nods thoughtfully. "I'd have to put Japan at the top of my list. Thailand is also amazing. I'm a sucker for places that turn language on its head."

Intrigued, I say, "Both must be paradise for your brand of linguist."

A professor in relaxation mode, he sips his water. "Japan's fascinating. The language is like a delicate dance of nuance and context. It's all about what's between the lines, where the unsaid often is more important than the spoken." He barely pauses before moving on to Thailand. "What intrigues me there is how social hierarchies and respect are linguistically encoded. They've baked their whole social order straight into the language."

"No wonder those places are among your favorites."

He grins. His mind already has relocated again, and he's ready to launch into another mini-monologue. "And India! Let me tell—"

I cut him off, checking my watch with feigned urgency. "No time for a lecture, Dr. Bancroft."

He mock-pouts. "Hey, you asked!"

"I asked what countries you liked visiting. I didn't sign up for "Carter Bancroft's Linguistic Experience." I'm sure it's a great course, but I can get by with just the highlights reel." I let the jest hang in the air, then, with a chuckle, add, "Just kidding. You know I eat this stuff up."

With a hint of relief in his smile, he says, "Good to see the pandemic hasn't tamped down your snarkiness."

"Not a chance," I say, brandishing my signature smirk. "Still an acerbic little smartass. ... Now, how about pointing me to my room? If I'm to dive into the whole L.A. body experience, I'd better freshen up this sack of bones."

Carter shows me to the doorway of a charming guest room, my new sanctuary of sorts. "You must be beat after that flight. Shannon's cutting her workday short. We'll have an early dinner so you can crash."

"That's considerate of you guys. Thanks. The time-zone tango's not my favorite dance."

"Feel free to sprawl out and relax. I'll be gone for a while, scavenging some dinner essentials."

We share a quick, grateful-sibling hug, then I'm left alone with the room. I take a minute to explore, my fingers brushing against the smooth surfaces and soft fabrics, before I start to unpack. There's always a certain thrill in setting up camp in a new place, but as I methodically move my belongings to drawers and closets, that initial spark of excitement fizzles.

I flop onto the bed and scroll through photos of Quinn on my phone. Each image stirs a cocktail of emotions—an ounce of anxiety, a dash of longing, a twist of dejection. I shift my gaze out the window, watching palm trees swaying gently, as if they're nodding in sympathy at my inner turmoil.

Carter's passionate descriptions of Japan and Thailand echo in my mind, highlighting the stark contrast between his fervor and my own lukewarm feelings about the job awaiting me tomorrow morning. I toss the phone aside. The anvil of uncertainty and regret in my stomach makes me wonder if I've made the right choice.

C arter and Shannon burst through the door like a sitcom duo—Shannon balancing two pizzas in one hand, Carter brandishing a six-pack of beer and two wine bottles like they're trophies. We hastily assemble a salad, the kind that's more lettuce than substance, and gather around the kitchen counter. "This is perfect," I say, and mean it. The simplicity of this meal feels like a blessed relief from the complicated dishes produced in Chatham—or even the other night at Maria's house. Raising my glass, I give a heartfelt salute, "To good food and great company. It's so good to be with you two. Thanks for having me."

We clink glasses, and Shannon, with eager eyes, prompts me. "So, Hallie, are you excited? Tell us about this new job!"

I launch into a description of the position, injecting as much enthusiasm as I can muster. By the time I wrap up, Carter's giving me a look that says he's not entirely buying my Oscar-worthy performance.

Cocking his head, he says, "You know, Hal, you're about as convincing as a cat in a dog show."

I blurt, "I'm thrilled, really!" But as I say it, my eyes betray me, welling up with tears. I fumble for a napkin, muttering something about overly spicy sausage. Shannon and Carter exchange a glance that's a mix of concern and confusion. Her hand finds my arm, and her simple "What's up, kiddo?" is the emotional equivalent of cranking open my floodgates. I dissolve into a sobbing mess.

Eventually, the blubbering subsides, and I start to unravel the tangled yarn of my emotions. I speak of Quinn, but in my frazzled state I apparently do a poor job of conveying my love for him. They're not grasping the depth of my feelings. It's as if they think he's just another bookmark in the novel of my love life.

So, I pivot to the territory of work; they're suddenly as attentive as fresh lifeguards. I pour out my heart about wanting an occupation I can love with every tendril of my being, like Carter loves linguistics. My brother, bless him, doesn't feed me pablum about nobody loving their job as much as I think. Instead, he does what I wish he'd done years ago, when I was young enough to set myself on the right course. He suggests, "Ever think of making a living writing, or working as a translator or interpreter? Maybe an editor? You're a wizard with words, Hallie."

Shannon's face lights up like a Christmas tree. "Great idea! Or, ... oh! Those people who do subtitles and dubbing for foreign movies or TV shows!" She squeezes the arm she's been petting. "There are so many things you could do with your amazing skills." Their enthusiasm is infectious, and I can't help but think of Maria's similar suggestions. It's like they've all tapped into the same brainwave.

Carter's now reminiscing about my teenage years. "Remember how you used to make up dictionaries of fake definitions? Or when you were in high school and spent months translating that French rom-com novel you adored? You were never happier than when you were playing with words, Hal."

He's right. And now here I am, sitting in the kitchen of a linguist, with a slice of pizza in one hand and a revelation in the other, wondering whether and when I'll find the mettle to start working with words again.

28

Quinn

The damn pandemic has meant that in the past nine months, lots of people around the world have had to have difficult conversations over video calls. But this is us! Hallie and I have limited experience with thorny discussions, much less with handling them remotely over little screens. Some Zooms this past week have been really damn hard. Our first, the next night following her departure, was the worst.

"I need to talk with you," I said, feeling the weight of our horrible goodbye.

Hallie's face was a mix of wariness and hurt. "You had that opportunity yesterday, remember? You stiff-armed me," she said, her voice laced with a guarded edge.

"No! ... Well, yes, I guess I did. And ... I apologize." I watched her expression defrost ever so slightly with my acknowledgment. She seemed to sense that my remorse was genuine. I plowed on. "I'm very sorry about yesterday, Hal. I get why you're upset—my lack of response, my inability to communicate, ..."

"Oh, your lack of response communicated plenty! It said everything: you don't feel the same way I do. And you left me just sitting there, open-mouthed and adrift, like I'd just stepped into thin air."

"I'm sorry! I wanted ... needed ... time to think about what I wanted to say. To find the right words."

"Feelings are either there or they're not, Quinn. They're not about finding the right words."

"No. That's not true. You can have strong feelings without knowing exactly how to express them. ..." And on it went, the delicate conversation taxing us for an hour. I tried to convey the depth of my feelings, even though I couldn't utter the three words she longed to hear. I still don't feel I can do that until I've settled this whole matter with Jack and Megan. So, the conversation was rough for both of us, but in some ways it was like the first application of salve on a cut, and I think it helped.

That's not the only call that was difficult. Some others also were like steel wool across a sunburn. There's the time I casually asked how she was doing. I expected a breezy 'fine' or 'great' in response—what people usually give you back when you ask how they are. Instead, she launched into a rhapsody about California: "I love it here, Quinn! The job is great. It's so fun to be with Carter and Shannon! And, the weather is spectacular! You guys in Boston just had a foot of snow!" Here, she threw in a gratuitous laugh. "In February, when you all are facing the worst New England's winter can throw at you, I'll be strolling a beach in my bikini!"

She was practically singing her delight. Listening to her gush over her new circumstances made my stomach churn. I pictured her on that beach, sun-kissed and carefree, with me here in Boston, where the most exciting thing in February is watching snow turn to slush. My mood plummeted faster than an ice-coated balloon.

My mood that day wasn't the best to begin with. December's never my best time of year. The whole Christmas season depresses me. Always has, and it's been worse since Alison died. In any case, when Hallie's FaceTime call comes in just now, I'm again not in a tip-top frame of mind.

"Are you lonely?" she asks at one point.

The shout back from my inner Scrooge could scare off Jacob Marley. *Damn right, I'm lonely! And it's all because you've self-ishly moved to a smog-choked shithole of a city so you can work for a disgusting, money-grubbing company that perpetuates sexism and harmful stereotypes! But, hey, you do you!* What I actually say is, "Yep, pretty lonely! It's like a mausoleum around here, which is great fun, of course!" I grimace at my own foul mood, and my mind rebukes me by replaying Megan's admonishment: "Be a better man!"

I vow to be, starting right now. So, I say, "Does it sound too pathetic to admit I miss you terribly?"

"Aw, I miss you too, sweet cheeks. ... You know, I was think-ing: if you're lonely, maybe you should get a dog! You loved being with Charlie on the Cape."

"True." Then, dragging my voice into a cheery tone, I describe Charlie's behavior when I'd seen him a few days earlier at the Campbells. "He bounded through deep snow from the front door out to the stone wall, which he'd dart back from, then he'd leap toward again, all the while barking at a couple walking by with a golden retriever. It reminded me of the day you and I took him to Morris Island, and he chased the tidal swash in and out, lowering his front and barking as the rushing water approached him."

She releases a giggle. "Oh, I remember that. It was so funny."

This reminiscence of our time on the Cape draws me into a better mood. I say, "That was the day you dazzled me with the breadth of your intellect. I think it's when I fell off the edge, head-over-heels for you."

"What?" She teases. "That didn't happen the very first morning in the kitchen when I hummed 'Oh, What a Beautiful Morning' for you?"

With the most lascivious expression I can muster, I say, "Well, that was when I started desiring you, lusting for your kimono-clad body. But no, it was that first trip to Morris Island when I realized you could talk intelligently about almost anything—and thoroughly charm me no matter the topic." Her smile now beams as bright as a star on the Hollywood Walk of Fame. "Wait," I say, reconsidering. "Maybe I'm wrong. Maybe it was the day we went to Nauset Beach, and you let me smear sunscreen on your back. Good thing you were on your stomach with your head turned away, so you couldn't see how much that turned me on."

She laughs. "Oh, I knew, tiger!" There's a long pause, then she says, "You know, I became certain of my feelings for you the day we went to Provincetown. But I think our conversations on the Nantucket ferry were when you first opened the door to my heart and walked right in, making yourself at home. You were so vulnerable and trusting with me."

The conversation is a balm, the memories of our time together soothing the rough edges of my loneliness. I venture, "Really? Am I still there? Sealed in your heart?"

"Of course you are, sweets."

"You're sealed in mine, too." For a moment, the distance between us doesn't feel quite so vast.

29

Quinn

I pull into the Campbells' semi-circular driveway. As I step out of my car, Charlie—AKA, The Furry Whirlwind—greets me with the enthusiasm of a long-lost friend. He leaps up, smudging my overcoat with muddy paws and showering me with affectionate licks. Lisa emerges on the porch, apologizing for Charlie's overzealous welcome. We watch him dash off on his next adventure, leaving snowy paw prints in his wake. Brushing off the mud, I play it cool, saying to Lisa, "No need to apologize. This coat was due for a dry-clean anyway."

Lisa ushers me inside, where the living room has morphed into a festive wonderland. Pure Lisa—anything worth doing must be worth over-doing. A towering Christmas tree—majestic and lavishly adorned with a couple thousand little white lights—

dominates the room, stretching up to kiss the high, vaulted ceiling. My eyes widen. "My god, what an amazing tree!"

Lisa radiates pride. "We went all out this year, needing extra light and joy. But except for choosing the ornaments over the years, we can't take credit for this stunner. The crew that does our outdoor holiday lights put this up for us. But, you're right: it's amazing! And we love the vibe in here this year—like having Rockefeller Center in our living room!" She offers me a glass of wine.

"Red, please, if you have some already open. ... Is Maddie home from Colorado yet?"

Lisa's face lights with maternal joy. "Got back two days ago. She's out with friends tonight. Safely distancing, I hope. She asked us to wish you a happy birthday, Quinn. You know she adores you."

"The feeling's mutual." As I admire the tree, a cluster of COVID-themed ornaments catches my eye—a miniature of Dr. Anthony Fauci, a six-pack of toilet paper, and a jug of hand sanitizer. I point them out and chuckle to Paul. "These are a cheeky nod to 2020!"

"As if any of us will need reminders of this year!"

Soon, Mike and Maria arrive, looking particularly sharp in clothes more stylish and polished than any I saw them wear out in Chatham. The evening quickly escalates into a lively *soirée*, with wine and laughter flowing freely. Before long, Lisa shepherds us into the dining room, where, enveloped in the glow of candlelight, we feast on her culinary creation—a small salad of field greens with a delicate balsamic vinaigrette, followed by petite filet mignons, roasted brussels sprouts, and small hasselback potatoes.

Unable to resist my usual urge to start an 'event meal' with a toast, I raise my glass. "To our gracious hosts: thank you for saving me from my recent diet of frozen meals and takeout, which has been quite a comedown after all that high cuisine on the Cape. This is a much-needed upgrade. Thanks for this sumptuous repast!"

Lisa smiles. "You're always welcome to join us for dinner, Quinn. You know we don't always eat like this. Still, if I know you're coming, I promise not to serve you frozen pizza. ... Happy birthday to you, and here's wishing you a year filled with joy and good health." She salutes me with her raised glass. The others join in with their birthday wishes, then we tuck into the food. As we savor the exquisite meal, conversation meanders from one topic to another.

Paul asks me, "Have you settled your Christmas plans yet? You know you're welcome here."

"Thanks. Things have sort of fizzled out on my end. Jack has to work and will be with his girlfriend when he has any time off. And, as you know, Megan was going to come home, but she called yesterday to say that a Christmas trip she and some friends had planned to Turks and Caicos is back on. Apparently, the islands have decided the virus is sufficiently under control that they're letting people in there again. So, anyway, that's where she'll be."

"Well then, you have to come here," Paul insists.

"Absolutely! Please do, Quinn," Lisa says. She gestures toward the others. "Maria, Mike, and Joli are coming, too. It'll be merry, merry!"

Setting aside my inner Grinch, I beam at the prospect of a festive celebration among friends. "I'll look forward to it."

Driving home along my usual path back from the Camp-bells'—my own personal 'Tinkers-to-Evers-to-Chance' route—I replay the conversation Hallie and I had in the airport's cell-phone lot. She spoke of what she wants in life—fulfilling work that uses her talents, and a fulfilling love relationship. That's what it boiled down to. Every time I think about that, my heart stirs, pushing me to confront my own wants and needs. At the core of it, I crave emotional security and the love of a partner. I've spent too much of my life feeling the sting of abandonment, my losses leaving me wounded, vulnerable. And Hallie's move to LA has only exacerbated my sensitivities.

At home, silence surrounds me. This is a big house, meant for a family. Yet here I am, its sole occupant. The advice many people gave me upon Alison's death—that I avoid major life decisions for at least a year—has led to a sort of inertia that three years on keeps me rooted in this oversized space. On nights like this, when the quiet is deafening and the darkness seems to press in from all sides, the house really does feel like a tomb—an echo chamber that amplifies my solitude.

Fortunately, I don't have to wallow in my loneliness for long because Hallie made me promise that when I got home from the Campbells, she and I could have a birthday call. I reach her via FaceTime. The awkwardness that afflicted us last week has dissipated, replaced by a renewed sense of comfort and possibility, the idea of "us" feeling natural and right again. After we've done our initial catch-up, I say, "I miss you. A lot. I think of you all the time." We're each peering into our tablets like voyeurs, the intimacy of the moment as good as it gets with little screens between us.

Finally, she breaks the eye hug. "Did you get my package?"

I grin and point at the parcel on my table. "You mean this one screaming 'DO NOT OPEN UNTIL OUR BIRTHDAY PHONE CALL!!!' in all caps on the front? ... Exciting! May I open it?"

"Please do."

"Alright, here goes." I angle the iPad so she can play spectator to my unboxing. The package is a Russian nesting doll of protective boxes, the final one being a classy foam-board box with my name in calligraphy. Sliding the top off, I unearth something cuddled in tissue paper. As I strip away the layers, the object reveals itself: a miniaturized Race Point Lighthouse, so detailed it could've been plucked right from a Provincetown museum. "Omigod, Hallie, it's beautiful!"

She beams. "Remember when you said you wanted a drawing of it, and I said I might do one for you, if you played your cards right? Well, you've played your cards well enough." I understand that last comment as a sassy nod to my botched reaction to her profession of love. "I figured you deserved something better than a drawing. So, I thought, why not go big?"

"Wait, you mean ... you *made* this? How? When?" I ask in amazement.

"I'd taken multiple photos that day, and I planned it out in my head while we were still in Chatham. But I needed my supplies and tools, which were at Maria's house. I built it here, last week."

"It's incredible. How do you know how to do this?"

She gives me a perplexed look. "It's the most fun part of my work. I always make a scale model of a set I've designed. Some people prefer to use 3D-design software, but I find it useful to create a physical scale mock-up, like architects do. For me, it's the best way to get a strong visual sense of how my stage designs will work in real life."

I say, "I get that. But I'm referring to the craftsmanship, which is incredible!"

She blushes. "Thank you! I guess I've gotten good at working with all the tools of the trade: X-Acto knives, T-squares, foam board, Styrofoam, sculpting tools, cardstock, glues, epoxies, paints ..." She trails off, laughs, and covers her face with her hands. "Sorry, got a bit carried away there. More than you need to know! But crafting this was a blast."

I'm genuinely touched. My eyes tear up. "This is such a lovely gift, Hallie. I'm really moved that you made this for me. It's a genuine piece of art."

"Aw, sweets. Just the first of many gifts we'll give each other, I'm sure." She pulls her tablet closer to her face. "I love you," she says, determined to keep those words in our spoken vocabulary, even if she hasn't heard them from me.

Later, as I'm cleaning up the crumpled wrapping paper, I lift the lighthouse, admiring its artistry. I notice something etched underneath. Squinting in the dim light doesn't help, so I bring it under a lamp. It reads, "I love you, Mindy Minx." A jolt of realization hits me—it's been really unfair of me to hold back from her.

30

Hallie

I'm savoring the final pages of *Middlemarch* like they're the last pieces of chocolate fudge in the universe. This is my third rendezvous with the masterpiece, but this reading of it has had a greater impact on me than the first two. It's like the book's whispering secrets about life choices directly into my ear. Thanks to George Eliot, I'm elbow-deep in thoughts of marriage, compatibility, and the potential disasters awaiting romances, when I'm startled by a knock on my door. Opening it reveals an excited Shannon, shaking her hands like she's ridding them of water drops. "Hallie, you won't believe this. Quinn's downstairs!"

I emit a squeal that could shatter glass. "Quinn! Here?" I'm already halfway to the mirror, attacking my serpent's nest of hair with a brush. I race downstairs, Shannon trailing behind. There, in the foyer, stands Quinn, masked like a bandit, clutching a flower bouquet that screams 'I'm sorry' or 'I love you' or maybe both. I launch myself at him, a human cannonball. Smothering him in kisses, I cry, "Quinn, what in the world are you doing here?"

He's got that this-is-something-important look. "I came to talk with you. I have things to say that I didn't want you to hear over the phone." Wondering—and fearing—what this is all about, I grab his hand and whisk him up to my room.

Any apprehension vanishes when I see that, although his eyes are earnest and serious, they're also brimming with affection. He says, "Look, there's a lot I want to say, but the main thing is this: I love you, Hallie. I love you with all my heart."

Blood rushes to my head and my heart does a gymnastics routine, complete with a double backflip. "Quinn, I—"

He looks down at his hands. "And now I need to explain why I've been as emotionally articulate as a rock until now."

I'm dying to shut him up with a kiss, but my curiosity is piqued. And he flew 3,000 miles to talk, so I figure this is his time. I hold his hands like they're precious artifacts, and listen as well as my thrilled heart allows.

"Back in my college days, I'd been going with a girl I was pretty sure was "the one." We were great together. But I had a campus job that put me in the company of this other girl twenty hours a week." I give a nod, clueless about where this time-travel trip is headed. He continues. "'Work girl' and I grew fairly close. One evening, we went back to her dorm room after work, drank too much gin, and ended up having sex, something I hadn't even done with 'the one.' During ... it, she said, 'I love you, Quinn.' And without thinking, I blurted, 'I love you, too.'"

I interrupt him, gesturing for a time-out. "Quinn, I'm sorry, but I don't think I want a front-row seat to this—"

"Please, bear with me, Hallie, I'm trying to explain. You can imagine how all that changed things between me and 'work girl.' I distanced myself from 'the one,' eventually breaking it off with her, to our mutual pain and my regret. I then entered a long, emotionally wrought period, having hurt someone I truly cared about, and feeling trapped in a relationship with a girl who'd declared her love and to whom I'd recklessly proclaimed my own in return. It was awful."

Now I'm totally exasperated. He started this by telling me he loves me. Is he now saying he's afraid he'll feel "trapped" in a relationship with me? "Quinn—"

"So, that day at the airport, when you said you have feelings for me, that you love me, my first thought was that—"

"You didn't want to make the same mistake again?"

"Well, yes, but not in the way you think."

"How, then?"

"I wanted to be sure I wouldn't hurt you or myself, so I needed time to talk with Jack and Megan again. If they were going to have screaming fits and condemn me, I wanted to be certain I could withstand their opprobrium. I didn't want to commit to you and then find myself back-pedaling in a week or two—or regretting having said it to you—if I found their disapproval unbearable. So, anyway, I've finally had the chance to talk at length with each of them."

Now, understanding better where all this was headed, I ask, "How did it go, speaking with them?"

"Surprisingly okay. I told them more about us, how we grew close over those months on the Cape, what drew us together, why I know this isn't just some evanescent infatuation. I told them you're here in L.A. right now, but that we're going to continue seeing each other."

I kiss him on the cheek. "And their reactions?"

"Jack took it well, seemed genuinely pleased for me, said I deserved happiness. Megan was more hesitant, but she warmed up to the idea. She just asked me not to rush into marriage. Then she asked if you'd be moving in with me when you return to Boston."

I raise an eyebrow. "What did you tell her?"

"I assured her that a wedding is not on the horizon and said I hope and expect you will move in with me—if not at the Arlington house, then somewhere else.. She didn't freak out. I promised we wouldn't, and she seemed content with that. Of course, that assumes you're coming back. Are you?"

I'm caught off guard. "Of course, I am. Exactly when, I can't say ... I do like it here, and the job is much more interesting and challenging than I expected. But right now, all I can think about is you, here, saying you love me."

He pulls me to my feet and hugs me, whispering, "I never imagined when I agreed to go to Chatham with Paul and Lisa that it would lead to me falling in love."

"You're pretty sure that's what you've done?" I run a few fingers through his hair.

"Yep. Absolutely certain." He pauses, then adds, "I've fallen down the rabbit hole."

I think for a moment. "What was Lewis Carroll's line? That Alice had followed White Rabbit down there 'never once considering how in the world she was going to get out again'?" I pause, then say, "I find it fascinating down here in this hole you and I are in. I don't ever want out." I pull back to look in his eyes. "You know, in every previous relationship, I always felt I had to downplay my love of literature and language, clamp a lid on my vocabulary, curtail my wordplay. Most people are put off by all that—or, at best, they're uninterested. But not you. You're the first person I've ever known outside my family who cherishes words and loves playing with them the same way I do. And it may seem like a small thing, a weird hook to hang a relationship on. But it's a good hook, a solid hook. A humor-filled, mind-stimulating hook. Lots of relationships have no hook at all, other than sex, which is one reason they don't last."

He starts, "But—"

I gently press my finger to his lips, silencing him. "Let me finish, sweets. You know I've always struggled with a damaged sense of self-worth. I didn't feel good enough to deserve another's true love. But you've turned all that around. And here's the paradox: you're absolutely the most amazing person I've ever encountered, yet I feel confident with you. And that's *because* of you. ... I love you, Quinn O'Neill."

He wraps his arms still tighter. I bury my face in his neck, feeling his pulse race along with my own. Then he starts listing things he loves about me. "Your sense of humor, the joy you take in bawdy jokes, your affection for literary allusions, the incredible breadth of your knowledge ..." I've never had someone speak this way to me, about me, and his words set off an emotional depth charge. My eyes well up with tears, blurring my vision, while my heart beats faster and harder against my chest, as if it's trying to break free from its confines. I stretch my neck to kiss him, then kiss him again and again.

He runs his hands along my sides, teases my breasts, kisses the hollow of my throat. Our breaths quicken, bodies shift. Each second becomes a blur of heat and desire as we struggle to shed ourselves and the other of clothes. His hot breath in my ear, on my neck, sends shivers down my spine, drawing more heat and wet where I'm already quivering. He drops wet kisses, tender nips, and long licks from my throat to the backs of my knees and everywhere in between.

Deep moans escape me as his tongue circles my nipples, then

slides down between my legs. My body squirms and writhes and arches with an intense craving. He's whispering that he loves me, that I'm beautiful, that he wants me with him forever. My breaths come heavy and fast, my moans become hungry cries, as his licks and touches bring me to a cliff. With several last swirls of his tongue, he sends me over the edge. ... My body shakes, a wild shudder that goes on and on and on.

31

Quinn

Standing in the doorway of the Campbells' living room, I survey this scene of Christmas cheer. Half-empty coffee cups and picked-over plates of delectable pastries bespeckle the room. The once-grand pile of gifts under the towering tree has dwindled, while a colorful sea of torn wrapping paper has stretched across the floor like a tidal wave. Laughter now rings throughout the room, a soundtrack to the joy and warmth enveloping us all.

They're down to the last gifts for the girls. Lisa enters the room, carrying a large, square gift box. She deposits the box in Maddie's lap, then steps back to watch as Maddie removes its top and cries out with delight, lifting a tiny kitten from the box and cradling it in her arms.

Lisa says, "We thought he might keep you company, Mads, wherever you are next semester."

Maddie's face turns from surprise and wonder to gratitude as the true significance of the little feline's presence sinks in—it's a gift of love from her cat-loathing parents. Maddie fawns over the purring tabby for a moment, then entrusts it to Joli's lap so she can hug Lisa and Paul.

Maria, the embodiment of today's festive spirit in a stunning new dress, turns to Joli and says, "And for you, Jo." She presents Jolivia with an envelope. "*Boas festas, chérie!*"

The gift—two round-trip tickets to Cape Verde and a generous check for vacation expenses—sparks a shriek of delight from Joli that cuts through the room's chatter. "Omigod, *Manman*! Dad! This is much too extravagant. I can't do this!"

Maria says, "Of course you can. We want you to! Probably by summer, vaccines will be available, and you'll be able to go for a couple weeks."

"But I would want to go with you, *Manman*!"

Maria laughs. "There'll be time for that. This trip, you should go with someone your age. Maybe your cousin Marcelina. Or a friend. Your dad and I want you to have fun." Crying with joy, Joli stands to hug Mike and Maria, momentarily leaving the kitten, only to have it pee on her chair.

As the flurry of gift-giving subsides, Maddie and Joli regale us with tales from their Colorado adventures, their parents' reactions alternating between amused shock and fits of hearty laughter. Recognizing this as their families' moment, I quietly slip out the front door, stepping into the biting chill.

A cold rain lashes my face with icy droplets. I think of Hallie today, warm in sunny Los Angeles, comfortable in the embrace of her brother's family. I imagine her on other days, charming her new work colleagues, making new friends, enjoying her new life there. I envision her in a couple months, strolling a beach on a warm February weekend.

My phone pings, drawing me out of my reverie. Sheltering under the porch, I check the message. It's a text from Megan, wishing me a merry Christmas. I scroll through other messages until I find the one Hallie sent three nights ago and I reread it for what must be the thousandth time:

"... my God he said after that long kiss I near lost my breath yes he said I was a flower of the mountain yes so we are flowers all a woman's body yes ... then I asked him with my eyes to ask again yes and then he asked me would I yes to say yes my mountain flower and first I put my arms around him yes and drew him down to me so he could feel my breasts all perfume yes and his heart was going like mad and yes I said yes I will yes."

I know the source of this magical language. These are the last lines of Joyce's *Ulysses*—Molly Bloom's interior monologue as she lies in bed, waiting for Leopold to return to her. I love the passage both for its passion and for its fulfillment of Joyce's stated intention to end *Ulysses* with "the most positive word in the English language."

What I don't understand is why Hallie sent this. Is she telling me that she finally finished her latest re-reading of the novel? Reminding me of our sublime lovemaking in L.A. a week ago? Is she invoking that shared passion, or is there something more in her choice of Joyce's words ... some other message she's trying to convey?

32

Hallie

The Uber drops me at the Campbells' grand front entrance around 4 PM. The house is alive with the hum of Christmas festivities. Standing on the doorstep, all my luggage in tow, I ring the bell and peer through the sidelights. I overhear Lisa muse to someone inside, "It's probably one of Maddie's friends, popping by to say hello."

The door swings open, and Lisa's face is a picture of shock and delight as she spots me. "Hallie! My god! What a wonderful surprise!" She steps outside. "What are you doing here?"

My tears, unbidden, come in an instant. "I couldn't ... I just couldn't stay away ... I need to be here. With Quinn."

Lisa smiles and pulls me into a tight, welcoming hug. "You'd better come in." I trail her into the house, the rich aroma of roasting meat whispering to my appetite. We enter the living room, and all conversation halts as heads turn in unison toward us. Maria and Joli whoop. Quinn's face is a canvas of incredulity and joy as he stares, speechless.

I can't contain my excitement. "Merry Christmas, everyone!" Quinn seems momentarily transfixed, his mouth agape in surprise. Gradually, a smile begins to curve his lips. His eyes sparkle, holding back tears, as he moves toward me. In a soft whisper, he asks, "Why?"

I gently pull him into the hallway, not wanting our reunion to be a spectacle. We slip into a nearby sitting room, effectively shutting out the rest of the world. My tears now escape without restraint. "Staying away wasn't an option. I need to be here, with you."

He searches for the right words, then says, "But just the other evening, you told me again how much you're enjoying your work, the camaraderie with your new colleagues, the climate, the joy of being with your brother and his family—"

"And it was all true. ... Yet, after we got off that call, I took a long walk, and before I knew it, I was crying uncontrollably—far worse than this mess I am right now." I pause and wipe my eyes. "It hit me that, despite the things I like about LA, they couldn't tip the scales against how much I missed you, how much I wanted to be back here. By the time I returned to Carter's, my decision was clear: I was coming home to you."

Quinn's eyes light up. He lets out a soft laugh. "So, that text you sent me, quoting the closing lines from *Ulysses*—that was your way of telling me you were returning."

I nod, my laughter mingling with tears, "Yes, though it seems it was a bit too enigmatic. Hard to say which of us missed the mark on that one." I playfully tap my head, then his, with my knuckles. He clasps my hands, his thumbs gently caressing my fingers. I continue, "Look, I know you and I aren't a sure thing. This is new, and we could still screw it up. But I don't think we will. What I do know is I love you and want to be here, with you. Is that alright? May I stay?"

"Yes," he replies, holding me tight. "My god, yes."

EPILOGUE

Hallie

He's glued to my back like a cheeky shadow, his hands resting lightly on my hips, his chin on my shoulder, a lascivious grin stretching his face. I'm all dolled up in a new little black dress that could give Audrey Hepburn's a run for its money. Quinn's making the most of this moment as he checks out my reflection in our bedroom mirror, his eyes tracing the curves of the black sheath. He presses his hips against me, kisses the nape of my neck, nibbles at my earlobe, then whispers, "You couldn't look more stunning or elegant for your big night, Hal."

I tip my head back against his shoulder and kiss his jawline. "Thank you, sweets. ... You must be able to see I'm jumpy as a cat. It's been a long time since anything's made me this apprehensive."

He pats my bottom, then turns to get his tie. "You have nothing to be nervous about. Your words are going to take flight on that stage tonight. It'll be fabulous. We both know that."

Easy for him to say. I take a deep breath as I smooth my dress and check myself in the mirror one last time. I tell myself he's right: tonight is going to be fabulous. I'm proud of my work; I believe it's good. But I can't stop the butterflies in my stomach. Critics can be harsh, audiences fickle. What if they hate it? What if I've failed?

As I poke at my earlobes with the sapphires Quinn gave me for my birthday, I reflect on my path to this moment, which has been slow, but certainly not tortuous. In fact, I enjoyed almost every moment of it. I'd plunged headfirst into a one-year Masters program in Literary Translation at Boston University. It was the perfect program for my interests.

I developed a passion for translating songs and musicals. My faculty advisor warned me this is among the most challenging of all translation or adaptation tasks. Her word to the wise only made me more intent. For my capstone project, I translated the songs from a 1967 French musical-comedy film, *The Young Girls of Rochefort*. Think *La La Land* with baguettes.

Then came my big break. Speakeasy Stage in Boston wanted to present a theatrical version of a 2008 French film, *Les Chansons d'Amour*. They needed someone to do the adaptation of the songs. They hired me, on the basis of my capstone work, along with my advisor's strong recommendation and my stab at new versions of two of the fourteen love songs.

The project nearly brought me to my knees several times. The original songs belonged to a strain of contemplative, literate French pop that, for music fans not from France, is something of an acquired taste. Awkward translation of some of the original love songs' delicate erotic metaphors had led to English subtitles for the film that included lines like: "Keep your saliva as an antidote, Let it trickle like sweet venom down my throat."

So, my task went well beyond translation; the need was for a far-reaching adaptation that would still preserve the meaning, mood, and style of the original work. The challenge came in creating new song versions within the restrictions of rhythm and rhyme, aligning music notes with lyrics, and dealing with any loss of atmosphere in the translation process. To say the whole thing almost broke me apart is an understatement.

Now, as Quinn and I make our way from our comfy little house in Newton's Waban neighborhood to the theater in the South End, the songs run in my head, and I'm in a tizzy. An involuntary groan escapes me at the thought of the theatre filling with people, hundreds of critical eyes and ears. What if they don't respond to the songs? What if they don't understand the subtleties of the lyrics? What if ... what if ...

Quinn, the patron saint of calming jittery nerves, does his best, reaching across the gear shift and giving my hand a comforting clasp. "Aw, my love, I'm sorry this has you so over-wrought. Really, it's going to be great." Quinn and I have been married for a year and a half now, and he's become the Sherlock Holmes of deciphering my stress signals, especially when it comes to this translation project. He knows how much it means to me. He's been my rock, witnessing me pour my heart and soul into these adaptations, agonizing over every word and phrase. And yet, despite his unwavering belief in my talents and his warm reassurances, my anxieties cling to me like a koala to a tree.

I take a deep breath and try to calm myself as we reach the theater and Quinn pioneers the way inside. We settle into our seats smack-dab in the middle—prime real estate for my evening's undercover work: Operation Audience Reaction. The lights dim, the overture kicks off, and my heart starts doing the cha-cha in anticipation.

The cast, bless their talented hearts, breathes life into my words, making each note and lyric pirouette and leap across the stage, a vivid reminder of my countless hours of adapting and fine-tuning these songs. The audience is hooked, eyes glued to the unfolding drama. When the curtain falls on Act One, the theater fills with thunderous applause, the kind that rings in your ears and sends shivers down your spine. When it finally subsides, Quinn laughs and says to me, "I hope you can calm down now. That roar was so earth-shattering, it probably registered on the Richter scale."

In the lobby, Quinn and I plunge into the buzzing throng of theatergoers. The air crackles with energy and laughter. From the surrounding chatter, my eavesdropping ears happily vacuum up lots of snippets of praise for the songs. Maria, Mike, Lisa and Paul are all here, radiating excitement like human sparklers. Maria clasps my hands. Her eyes are practically stars in the night sky as she says, "Hallie, these songs ... they're incredible! How on earth did you pull this off? You're a wizard!"

Paul, usually as expressive as a statue, is all animated, nodding like one of those dashboard bobbleheads. "It's like these songs were always meant to be sung in English, Hallie. You really nailed it! Hats off to you!"

I'm on cloud nine, blushing and basking in their praise, feeling absolutely buoyant. "Thank you, really. Having you all here, soaking it in, means more to me than you know." By the time the final curtain drops and the last echoes of *Les Chansons d'Amour* dissolve into the standing ovation's roar, I'm convinced all the insomnia and self-doubt were small prices to pay. Pride swells in me like a balloon ready for takeoff, and I'm thrilled at having gifted the music of these songs a new voice in another tongue for an entirely different audience to enjoy.

I can't help but feel this is a whole new beginning for me. My past may be written in indelible ink, but the future? It's a fresh, blank page. And, baby, I've got the pen.

AFTERWORD

Thank you for reading *Love, Literally*.

Reviews are absolutely crucial for indie authors. If you enjoyed the book and have a few moments to spare, please post a brief, honest review on Amazon, That would be enormously helpful in connecting this novel with more readers.

If you enjoyed this book, you might like to know about another new book by J.T. Tierney—*The Butcher on Colfax*, about four Irish immigrants to Denver at the turn of the Twentieth Century. It's available for pre-order or order on Amazon.

Made in the USA
Coppell, TX
29 May 2024